AT THE END OF EVERY DAY

a novel

ARIANNA REICHE

ATRIA PAPERBACK

NEW YORK   LONDON   TORONTO   SYDNEY   NEW DELHI

ATRIA
PAPERBACK

An Imprint of Simon & Schuster, LLC
1230 Avenue of the Americas
New York, NY 10020

First Atria Paperback edition April 2024

Simon & Schuster: Celebrating 100 Years of Publishing in 2024

ATRIA PAPERBACK and colophon are trademarks of Simon & Schuster, LLC

For information about special discounts for bulk purchases, please contact Simon & Schuster Special Sales at 1-866-506-1949 or business@simonandschuster.com.

The Simon & Schuster Speakers Bureau can bring authors to your live event. For more information or to book an event, contact the Simon & Schuster Speakers Bureau at 1-866-248-3049 or visit our website at www.simonspeakers.com.

Interior design by Erika R. Genova

Manufactured in the United States of America

1 3 5 7 9 10 8 6 4 2

Library of Congress Cataloging-in-Publication Data is available.

ISBN 978-1-6680-0794-5
ISBN 978-1-6680-0795-2 (pbk)
ISBN 978-1-6680-0796-9 (ebook)

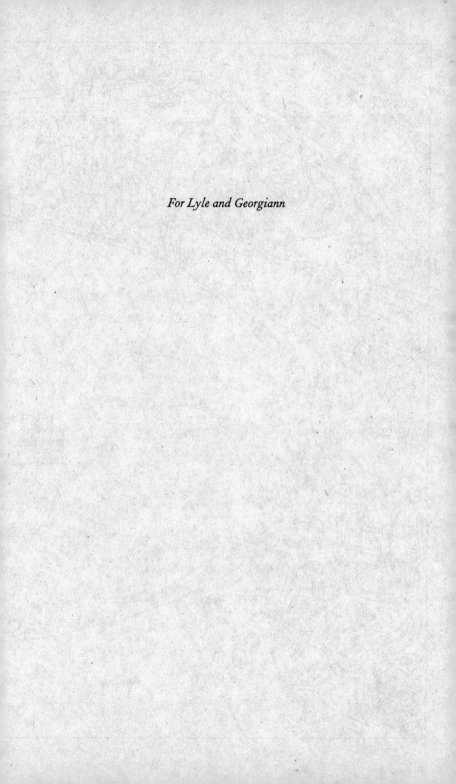

For Lyle and Georgiann

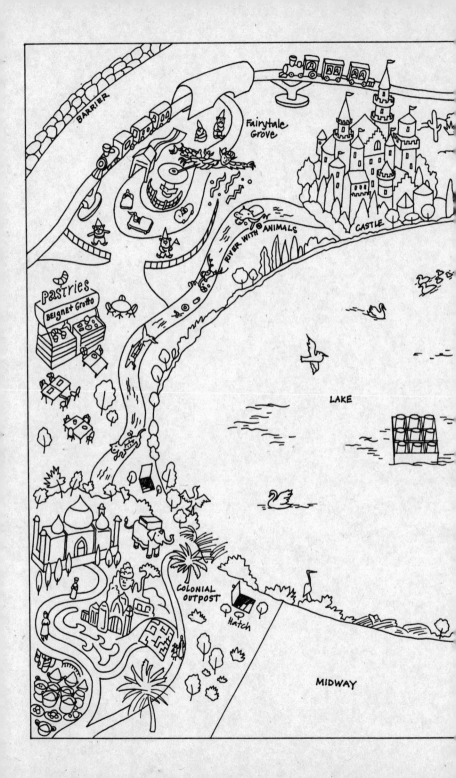

AT THE END OF EVERY DAY

CHAPTER ONE

During those years when I was spending so much time in the shed, I would sleep at night and dream of a theme park. The park, when dreamed, was an island, even a planet all its own. There was nothing else in my dream geography; no bordering territories. There was no gravity or cartography or linearity of time, but night after night, it would in fact be the same place, the park, waiting to be explored.

Forgive me. I'm trying to untangle this all now. How the park first called out, I guess. What it was about my earliest years that made me so fixated on starting a life there. I need to do this because things are starting to feel strange here. Something isn't right. And it seems important that I keep my feet on the ground, that I remember what's real and what's not. The park really tries to confuse all that. It's sort of the selling point. Come here to fall into a fantasy. I don't know how much longer I can do that, though. I'm seeing things. People who don't belong here. Doors that I never noticed before. And something else that I don't quite have words for.

I could be imagining it. I have been standing here, staring, for a long time.

There's the turret. Underneath it, behemoth, plaster castle. Beyond it, the faint fingerprint of a daylight moon. My body is strong today. I feel ready for anything. But I'll stay here a moment longer, trying to pinpoint what isn't quite right. It's a little itch, but nothing too bad. An off note in a beloved song. Maybe there's nothing wrong with the park at all. Maybe I should try to keep on truckin', even though it's all ending. Maybe I should turn that frown upside down.

What I know: The park has never been the same since the actress crumpled in that boat. They rolled out the new land anyway, despite the crumpling in the boat, but no one could get it out of their heads. That was the beginning of the end.

There's footage of it everywhere. Each time lawyers manage to get it taken down from one platform, it just pops up elsewhere, re-downloaded and redistributed by people who enjoy—is *enjoy* the right word?—that kind of thing. I've seen it plenty of times. It doesn't get less sad, the way things can sometimes become less disturbing on repeat. Every time I watch it, I wonder why her boyfriend didn't take her in his arms, or why the children seated behind her didn't react like she did, or react *to* her, or react at all. They looked bored. Of course, the video only caught the last moments of the whole ordeal, just a few seconds before the lights came on. Then it showed about a minute of Callie still bent, but staring up at the electronic version of herself suspended above her, before she—the real flesh-and-blood Callie Petrisko—curled into herself once more, wailed, and heaved over the side of her little lagoon boat. The video stops there, and on the whole, it might not have been so disturbing if we didn't all know what happened to her, later.

I'm wrong, I suppose. About the boyfriend. It's no mystery why he didn't leap into action. He was probably shocked, too. Shocked at her, and at the lights coming on in the middle of a dark ride. No one likes when the lights come on. I know I don't.

Maybe that's why the shed was my first real sanctuary. It was a place where I controlled the light. I was a child and a teen in Nebraska, south Omaha, in one of those regions that doesn't feel like a city or a town at all, but a spill of boxes and roads without connective tissue. Iowa was across the river. I can't remember when Whit appeared. One day, the crankiest man in the Midwest, with the most Santa Claus beard you've ever seen, was coming over for dinner at 10:30p.m., after my mother woke. She hadn't told me about him coming over. She didn't tell me anything because she didn't like to look me in the eye after my short stint in foster care. The next day he was making breakfast for both of us, army rations he'd ordered in bulk online. Chicken chunks in a tomato sauce. Something a little bit like ravioli. Loose oats, no sweetener. Before long Whit was there every morning, and those bag-meals would greet us, fresh from the microwave, steaming, and if Mom was on a shift, it'd be just Whit pouring me orange juice and explaining what the Fed was, the shortcomings of the Cato Institute, how to buy antibiotics online, how his sons weren't smart in the kind of way that made them right for college but that they'd do all right anyway. And I'd smile into my gruel, surprised, and say "It's good!" and he'd say "Bitchin'." He built his studio, the shed, later.

Before the shed, my life was those breakfasts, school, the library. Later, it was school and the shed, staring into molten light for hours on end, alongside Whit. Neon, his neon, his craft, for hours and hours. By that time his medication made him a little less sturdy, prone to stuttering, and therefore, prone to long periods of silence, which was fine by me, because by then he'd run out of things to say about his days waiting out The Bomb in Montana in the seventies with a couple buddies, and we could simply enjoy the harmony of working side by side. I was always sleepy, because it was all so trance-like, the crafting we did, and that constant half-dreaming meant I could never sleep deeply at night.

It was worth it, though, if all that time in the shed left me with skills that the park valued. It was worth it, if all those dreams made me more at ease among the real geography of the place, the curving bow of always-warm concrete footpath that wove between towers and rainforest vines and trolley cars; the secret alleyways; the shadows that might conceal a hidden door, even if it was just a maintenance cupboard. It took some time, but here I am. I have been here, happily, ever since I left home. I'm thriving. Just look at me.

There came a day shortly after training was finished when my feet ached from standing and my nerves were shot from rude guests—the ones who demanded to know why Caves of Chirakan was so scary, or not scary enough, why they couldn't find the kiosk to buy a photo of their child on the ride, and had anyone even thought to take a photo of their child on the ride? My face hurt from the strain of the smile we'd been carefully trained to deliver, which was not a toothy pageant smile, as some might guess, but an impassive and content one where immobility of the brows was key. Maintaining it was exhausting in its own way; you felt it in the molars.

After I'd been working at the park for a few weeks, I accepted an invitation to a party after work, at these two baristas' apartment "just north." I'd never met them before, but they found me in the Tech Crew changing rooms and loaded me into their minivan like we were old friends. Half an hour on the freeway and I came to understand that "just a little bit" could mean any distance, expanse of space, in this part of the world. Already I was imagining how I'd fail to get home again, how I'd have to sleep in this mystery home, but I had faith that I'd be able to stake out a section of carpet. I can fall asleep anywhere.

When we turned off the 5, one of them asked what my training was like, but didn't let me answer. She told me about her video, which had been straight out of the early nineties, an actual warbly VHS tape, and most of their day had been spent discussing *cultural sensitivity*, but she heard that now the park had begun calling it *cultural neutrality*. I didn't know about either of those terms—we practiced giving directions without pointing, because of how much of the globe finds pointing to be lewd, and how to explain that there are no prayer rooms in the park, but that many locations in Marine Kingdom, especially the spacious and often-empty Orcas-In-Fedoras Millinery n' More, were suitable. That was the extent of it.

One of them asked if I'd heard any information about The Founders, and what I made of it. The way they explained it, there were two schools of thought. They said the first school was, essentially, that there's so little information about the brothers, The Founders, because they did some fucked-up stuff during the war, or before the war, or maybe after. World War II, you know—*that* war. The other barista chimed in to say she thought it was definitely before the war. They'd toured parts of Europe where "all the gnarly Surrealist stuff" was happening, and they stole a bunch of the more dazzling, more cinematic fever-dream designs that things they came across. All that splendor and tricks of the eye, ridiculous costumes, big sets made of wire and satin. And later The Founders got tied up with some artists who sort of went fascist-ish maybe (at this point the barista who was talking and driving reached behind her seat, waggling fingers at a near-empty tub of Pringles, which I nudged toward her hand while I paid sudden, close attention to the road's meridian), but they made a few animated shorts that became hugely popular. Plans for the park, with all that enchanting, entrancing stolen art, were already set in motion.

The second school of thought was that it was all boring. Just violently boring. And that there never even were any brothers. They were just two anonymous old men whose vision for the park was nothing more than a group venture at an opportune moment with the same type of partnerships you'd need for any type of conglomerate.

This theory seemed most likely. Why else would they have kept The Founders so mysterious? Why else would it be that the world knows them as The Founders, rather than their real names, which were so dull and long that neither barista could recall them, even now? There must be no *there* there, no real story at all.

The backs of my hands had begun to itch. When I was about to weigh in, one of them cut me off.

"You forgot the third theory."

"There's no third theory."

"There is!"

"I've never heard of a third theory. You're literally making this up right now."

"Jesus Christ, let me explain it first, then you can decide if I made it up"—the barista pulled her passenger side seat down to a luxurious recline—"like *damn*."

The third theory was that the park built itself. One day there were simply swollen masses of earth and slim trenches marking out the perimeter, and an inexplicable arrangement of soil dunes where the castle would go, little markings where the main pathways threaded themselves between the park's many kingdoms, and tunnels running deep into the earth. All of this was tied into the Los Angeles Satanists, of course: Aleister Crowley and the Brit spiritualists who came over, at some point, and maybe a burial ground. Scientologists were tied into all that, right? And stuff in the desert? There was some physicist who was like also a magician and accidentally blew himself up. Forgot his name, but it was like . . . like you know Oppenheimer—

"It's not Oppenheimer. He was the atomic bomb. You're thinking of that one guy. What's his name. He was making other bombs and got all involved with L. Rod Hubbard."

"Did you say *Rod* Hubbard?!"

"Whatever, but it's not Oppenheimer."

"Okay fine, but it's like I said, all that stuff *is* tied up together, all those things in those early decades last century and LA, right?"

I sat in the silence before I realized I was supposed to respond.

"Right. Sure," I said. And then, when it seemed like they wanted me to keep talking, "Um, they just gave us a list of names and said these guys designed the first rides. And the castle. I'm not sure if they were, like, *The Founders*, capital T capital F, I guess. And the rest of it was like, Theory 2."

"Boring," said one.

"Of course they'd say that," said the other. "But what do you believe?"

I wanted to say that I believed that spending my teen years in a dark shed, building little useless totems of glass and fire with a feeble man, made my eyes more sensitive to magic, to spotting things that don't appear in daylight. I wanted to tell them that that man had helped raise me and I left him to rot, wearing grip socks, medicated within a microgram of his life, in a facility that looked more like a prison than a hospital. I wanted to tell them that I didn't need to believe anything at all; I could be brain-dead and wheeled into the park, and something about entering its territory would allow an invisible hand to reach within my ribs and pull me across its length. And whether the park was intentionally designed to be like that—a place that fostered devotion, coded into minds subliminally, beautifully, with treasure cove geometries and magic mountain magnitudes— couldn't matter less. It was all those things, regardless of its architect.

"I like Theory 3," I said. "Didn't Aleister Crowley look like a wizard?"

For the rest of the drive they talked about their cousin's wedding in Tecate, and whether nuts are vegetables. When we got to their house, I found that I was surprised at how nice it was. It was thoughtfully furnished. The things that were meant to look new looked new; the things that were meant to look old looked old. There was something made of real wool on the couch, and a panel of blue and green stained glass leaning against a wall.

People were already there when we arrived. Maybe ten. Someone was bent over a sink, doing something complicated to a pineapple. I felt comfortable offering him help because I recognized him as one of the princes. Very handsome, obviously. Speaking to him made me feel as nervous as speaking to a diorama of colonial Jamestown, or a small airplane. But when he said thanks and admitted, more painfully than I'd expected, that he wasn't very good at it, at accomplishing with the pineapple whatever he was trying to accomplish, I started to see small flaws in his countenance and in his skin that gave me something to hold on to. I became so light-headed that I almost dropped the bottle of vodka that was, in some way I didn't quite understand, meant for the pineapples, and he noticed the scars on my hands and I tried to excuse myself, but he touched my elbow and said, "You can't leave me here like this. Seriously, I'll fall apart."

I didn't stop smiling after that, even when the pineapple

concoctions made us wince. Eventually I did leave him, to go through the motions of talking to other people. The living room was so packed it was impossible to tell where the line for the bathroom began. Other people, other girls, spoke to the prince, made bright eye contact and lightly touched his chest when they laughed. But I noticed that he never drifted more than a few feet from me. Once or twice when I looked over my shoulder to check the distance between us, I found him looking at me, and he would look away with genuine embarrassment. One of those times, in a shaky motion, he went to bite the rind of his mangled pineapple and met something sharp, and he jerked the fruit in such a way that he almost smacked a gondola girl in the back of the head.

By midnight I found that being near him made my chest hurt, and that it felt better than the morphine they gave me in the hospital, after what happened in the shed.

"Who are you friends with here?" he asked, later, and I struggled to give an answer, because I convinced myself that this was him asking about other people, other people he might want to be talking with more than me. So I slipped away from him, and spent some time in the bathroom alone staring into a mixture of vodka and sparkling wine that someone handed me, and the line had grown longer when I returned to the living room. I found it hard to see a line of people and not ask questions about group size, and to start guiding them to loading sections for their ride vehicle.

It's foggy, what happened between those hours and the moment on the couch when my lids became heavy, but when I woke, he was at my feet. The prince. Brendan. His hand was on my bare ankle. His head was lolled back, but when I looked closely I saw that he was awake. He seemed to be watching the weak, watery sunrise leaking through a skylight I hadn't noticed over the course of the night. A section of dawn grew on the floor by a radiator, and it made everything behind him start to glow.

"Have you been up this whole time?" I croaked.

"Yeah," he said. "Just making sure you're good."

Is there a name for the thing where time distends? When a week or a year becomes longer than another week or another year. Everyone experiences it, but it doesn't have a name. It doesn't matter. After that party, time changed. It took two years after my arrival at the park, just a bit more, for everything in my life to become symphonic. My feet no longer ached inside my shoes, and I learned to soothe fussy families before they could voice their complaints. Managers learned about my mechanical skills, skills absorbed from Whit, and I officially became Load-Mat—managing the loading of guests into the cars of the ride and able to oversee basic maintenance tasks. I decided to move out of my shared room in a halfway house that had called itself an intern dorm online, and I found Brooke, who knew how to work an air fryer and how to keep someone company without demanding chitchat. She came to after-work drinks, sometimes, after I'd made a handful of solid friends at the park, and occasionally I went to drink with her teacher friends. They, like Brooke, did their self-tapes in the teachers' lounge or an empty locker room, and took pride in the fact that they weren't waiting tables while they auditioned and tried to attract agents. But only Brooke seemed to care about both—being a good teacher, being a good actor, even when that acting was, by and large, looking delighted by a CGI reflux pill that had come to life and begun listing its own side effects.

After that party, I could count the nights that Brendan and I spent apart on one hand. If he stayed at my place, he'd hide upstairs to let me and Brooke watch TV and share stories about shitty children. If I stayed at his, he'd show me his little projects: A terrarium he'd found intact next to a dumpster in Sunset Park. Two squares of timber that he was sanding down to assemble into a lazy Susan. Nondescript putty that he'd molded for the inside of his running shoes to improve his gait. He bought a book on palm-reading from a flea market, and the fact that it was clearly geared toward preteen girls didn't dampen his enthusiasm.

I became awkward when I saw that last one; he hadn't asked

about my hands by that point. By then I had my gloves. I wore them almost constantly. Sometimes I slept with them on. Someone else might read this as an aversion to touch, to physicality. But Brendan never stopped picking me up, not as a flirty stunt, but almost as a nervous tic, gazing off into the distance, trying to work out some problem while bending at the waist, wrapping an arm around the front of my torso, gripping me with his elbow, and quietly trying to flip me upside down. If I leaned on him, he would demand that I do it harder, with more weight than I was able to give, so he could push back against something and create an equilibrium. He would mash the tip of his nose on my scalp until I could hear cartilage click.

"This seems like a dog thing," I'd say.

"Mmh . . ." He'd think. "Pig thing."

I rarely saw him at work. His was a moving circuit among the guests. The guests came to me, where I was stationed. But it worked, perfectly. All of it did.

But time flies. For so long, the park had seemed invincible. It was some vital spinal fluid of America. Then came the video of that actress, Callie Petrisko, crumpling in the boat. It had seemed bad when it happened, when the video leaked, but after what she did a few days later, there was no going back. The damage was irreversible. Now the park doesn't have long to live.

It's been a long process, the ending. From the official internal announcement of the park's "transition" to an overseas presence, we were given a year, and each team received a specific Action Plan for *mindful disassembly* and ongoing reduced capacity maintenance. And once each team had an Action Plan, individual team members got a directive. One day, I opened my locker, with its digital display built in, to show a message sent to me and me alone. *Baxter, Delphi— c3230912—Private and Confidential.* It was my own Action Plan, with separate points laid out for day-to-day disaggregation and clo- sure tasks that were to be done alongside my normal work. There were also milestone closure projects within the land containing Caves of Chirakan, group tasks that would be completed either after hours or remotely, in the mechanical bays, the ones just beside the main tunnel where we arrived and changed and had lunch.

It took a long time for us to understand what "transition" meant, although it was all anyone talked about for a long stretch of time. This park was closing. This, the first, the only one on this coast, the only one of this size and scope. It's probably for the best that we didn't really understand. It would have been too much to bear.

There were problems even before Callie: an outstanding lawsuit involving a cheese by-product found in one of the dining locations; something to do with the passholders, the adult park die-hards, antagonizing "casual" guests; harassment mishandled by park security. Settlements over whiplash were made almost every year. I suppose all those, plus Callie, might have made management rethink how the park operated, but I know in my bones that they wouldn't have forced the gates to shut permanently. No, there was something else. The big dream of the future. There was something big planned for Hong Kong. A new park. We didn't know much more than that, much more than the rest of the world knew in little press releases—breathtaking sketches that might get "leaked" from the studio, depicting palaces (plural) overlooking a vast stretch of lush terrain, coasters, hang gliders and hot-air balloons, all on the backdrop of a prismatic star system that certainly was not our own. It seemed this park wouldn't have themed lands but would be a staggeringly complex harmony of every fantasy that the park, the studio, the guests, could muster.

Of course management confirmed nothing, and we were left with our Action Plans.

Over those first months countless friends were let go, the little notes slipped into their lockers in the underground corridors, and some unnamed, omniscient manager asking them to pop into the corporate campus just a "hop, skip, and a jump" across the freeway. At consolation drinks in February, Amber, who operated the steamboat, and Kenji, who worked in makeup, realized they'd experienced something identical when they got to the offices beyond the park. The first HR rep opened with "Let's start at the very beginning" and the second one chimed in with "A very good place to start!" and both reps laughed and laughed.

We continued to watch individual C&C—cast and crew—get their letters. Mascara dripped onto the itchy lace collars of Arthurian princesses, and a man in lederhosen punched a wall.

Then people disappeared in small groups. First, the entire team at the Beignet Grotto, then all the ladies from the unnamed Edwardian section, and Springtime Canyon, and the Colonial Outpost. They even got rid of Beth, who was famous among C&C for her ability to remember details about the hundreds of children who took photos with her every day. She could recall the story of how a boy got the scar on his knee if he approached her a year after his first visit. It baffled parents. They always tried to have a quick whisper with her, to guess how she managed it ("Is it cameras? Face recognition software or something?"), and Beth, in her lilting soprano, would answer, "Oh no, Madame Lily could simply never forget such a special child!"

They fired the live actors embedded within the mummy thrill ride, even Eric, who'd paid for facial filler and laser hair removal to achieve the Pharaoh's famous straight brows. The guests' favorite thing about that ride was the fake-out breakdown, where the wooden carts in which riders were seated jerked to a halt that felt, convincingly, like a mechanical problem. Then, after ten full seconds, Eric would appear at a rocky ledge toward the ceiling, slide down a greased pole made to look like a dangling rope, land, howl, and charge toward the cars, only to have them sputter to life and shoot away right in the nick of time.

Thinking about it now, after the footage of Callie Petrisko was released, it might have been in poor taste. The ride pretending to be broken like that.

But they didn't fire me, and they didn't fire Brendan. Somehow I knew they wouldn't, even though there are more popular rides than mine, and there aren't enough guests to require a full-time prince. We felt guilty, in a way, especially when the lederhosen guy got escorted out by security. But we can't help it if management has a soft spot for us. Most people do. The unlikely love story: the prince and the cave dweller.

In the moments when I'm not panicked about the future, I try to fill myself with a kind of wisdom, like when I read the contents of a self-help book from the library back home, or the sage-like yak from *Himalaya Hootenanny 2* who greets guests in Springtime Canyon at 11:20 a.m. and 4:15 p.m., and I think: It's all right that things end.

But how do you end a place like this? A park the size and scope of a small city? Not too long ago I asked Brendan that question, while he tinkered with tweezers inside that terrarium he found. We were about to go to this market where he'd heard you could get hermit crabs. (This did not turn out to be true.) He asked what I was looking at, and only then did I realize I'd been staring out the window above his kitchen sink, which smelled like moss. "I guess I'm trying to fig-ure out which section of sky belongs to the park."

"No section of sky belongs to anywhere. It's sky."

I didn't tell him that I thought he was very wrong. "The park is bigger than some incorporated towns. Did you know that?"

"No," he said. "You're the tiny town authority."

"My town wasn't that tiny. It was bigger than the park. But the park is bigger than some towns, is what I'm saying." I heard little pebbles clinking on glass.

"How do you know that?"

I shrugged, even though he wasn't looking. I let my hipbone push into the sink and wrapped my gloved hands around my waist. I leaned forward until my forehead was touching the glass. It felt nice.

"We got a CD-ROM in the mail once, when I was like twelve. You could click through different areas of the park and play grainy videos about each ride. There were all these facts you could uncover, if you clicked on enough of them. And one was about the size of the park. But that's even before Nebuland."

"How much time did you spend on that CD-ROM?"

"Two years, I think."

He didn't say anything, and I didn't turn around.

"I mean," I continued, "I knew most of the audio by heart."

Later, before we went out, I pressed Brendan into the couch, where he'd taken a break from his miniature arrangement, and rested on top of him, like his gently expanding torso was a raft, and he pressed his fingers into the back of my skull. I almost fell asleep, but he whispered, "*Hermit crabs*," and we knew that if we stayed there any longer we'd get naked, or fall asleep, or both.

I felt a little unsatisfied that he didn't understand what I was saying about the sky. If you found yourself somewhere like, I don't know, the Scottish Highlands, or the Louisiana bayou, and the sky was doing something particularly beautiful, you'd say to yourself, *This Highland sky is sure somethin'. Only on the bayou would you get this kind of sunset.* The park, too, has its own sky, and that makes the disassembly seem impossible. It kept me in disbelief about the closure, even though my workload became heavier than most.

There are tasks in my personalized Action Plan that the others don't have. From the shed, with Whit, I know a little bit about engineering. Only the basics. I qualified to pass an online safety test that was designed for work-experience machinists, day laborers, that kind of thing. And so I can do some mechanical work inside the rides. They don't have to pay me any different, unless I go into overtime. I'm happy to help. I want them to remember me, if I ever find myself in Hong Kong, or if something in management comes up here, remote. I'm resourceful, I think. I'm up for any task. Except for one.

I made the Nebuland lagoon ride, Callie's ride, part of my deal with management. That I would never, under any circumstances, set foot in there. I'd rather be fired.

I'm standing, still, feeling strong, underneath that faint lunar stamp above the clouds. Staring.

"Delphi, right?"

I jump a little at the sound, and my eyes water. I must have also been staring into the sun.

"Yes?" I offer.

I can't see who it is. No, it wasn't the sun I was staring at. It was the turret, so high, and so huge. I can't stop blinking.

The voice again: "I recognize you from those . . . all those . . ." It's gravelly and familiar. Black spots wiggle across my line of sight. I rub my eyes.

". . . those *all-hands* meetings. You always ask good questions."

"Oh!" I try to laugh in the direction of the voice, but now the black is morphing to yellow, then red, bruising across my vision.

"What you looking at there?" he asks.

I finally make him out: thick brows. He's carrying a mop and bucket on wheels, but he doesn't have the sad posture of most janitors. They carefully costume the custodians in tans and reds, cowboy colors, and though I can't see much, I can see that he's pulling it off. His pass is dangling out of his pocket. I almost want to say something about how he needs to be careful; it shouldn't get into the wrong hands—but now I see his gentle expression. He's old. I wonder how long he's been here.

"Oh, just this ol' beaut!" I say and sweep an arm out toward the castle. The turret I'd been staring at is my favorite—the one where the violet base fades to coral at the tip, a regal tie-dye, a trick to keep its contours visible even during sunset. "I could watch her all day. I think I accidentally looked straight into the sun, though!"

I try to laugh more. I'm conscious that my shift hasn't started yet. I'm not in costume. I'm not really supposed to do that—be aboveground before I'm changed, enter through the gates rather than the C&C tunnels—but I woke up spacey today. I couldn't see the harm in taking my time, aboveground.

"I was wondering if you knew who we had today," he asks. "In the park."

"Oh, I'm not quite sure, to be honest. If it's anything like the last two weeks, it'll be more German package guests and"—I take a quick look around to make sure that there's no one within earshot—"the HQ kids."

He shakes his head and pulls up on the belt of his pants. They look like they could slip down his skinny hips. "Shucks. That's bad news for me!"

"Yeah, they can be . . ." A shrug and a grin. We've been running at reduced entry for how long now? Some weeks. No more pass holders. No more casual guests. Only those who made group bookings a year ago or more, and the children of execs, who've never treated the park as anything more than an additional property of theirs, another place to be disaffected or messy or moody or high.

"Silver lining is there's only a few more weeks of this!" I say to fill the silence.

I can't quite read his face, but his lips, sunken into the lines of his mouth, keep their friendly shape. I wonder if he's heard me. I start to repeat myself, but he interrupts: "That's right! And heck, maybe we'll make it to Hong Kong someday!"

"Maybe. I'd love to see it!"

I find myself reaching out and patting his sleeve. It feels antiquated, condescending, but I can't stop myself. It's something I've seen women in old movies do to friendly old men, but his eyes catch on my gloves. I forget that there are people who don't know that I don't take them off. I don't judge them for staring. It was management who encouraged me, in the first place, to keep my hands covered whenever interacting with guests.

"What's your name?" I ask.

"Sam. Old Sam Ybarra."

"That's right!" I lie. "How could I have forgotten?"

I check my watch: just after seven. I pass the station where Peter, character Peter, a waif twenty-year-old in Peter's trademark costume of nylon and fluffy white feathers dangling down his back like an angel wing that had become dislocated, would stand and sign autographs. He'd need to stand still because of the wires, which would lift him up and away when his shift was done. The other actors were always jealous of Peter; it's hard to get away from the throng. Getting flung into the air is the ideal exit. I was never close to the Peters, though. It was because his story is my favorite, and so I suppose I kept a respectful distance. Somewhere on the border between Nebraska and Iowa, there's a page torn from a magazine, an antique *LIFE,* I think, that's been ironed and attached to a wall with a gold thumbtack. It's a still from *Peter and Wendy,* the scene where Peter has just caught his own shadow, which had been running rampant across the Darling children's walls. Wendy (played by a twelve-year-old Renata Revere, gamine and toothy and wonderful) in her iconic yellow sleep set, is sewing the shadow-foot to Peter's flesh-foot. Peter looks sheepish. Wendy looks proud.

I don't know if it's still hanging in my bedroom. I don't know what's become of that house. I didn't pack much when I left. Maybe my mother burned my things, or maybe she abandoned the house altogether, like she'd so often threatened to. Maybe all my wrinkled magazine pages and plastic figurines, my doodles of Pinocchio's whale and Baba Yaga and Cosmonaut Calvin, all my favorites from the park and the studio's cartoons, have been reabsorbed into moss.

Brendan says he would have liked to see it. Where I'm from. I can't imagine anything worse. It's sweet of him to say, though.

I thought I might meet him on my way to start my shift. He hadn't stayed over last night. He said he hadn't been sleeping well, and the thought struck me as funny. Since we'd gotten serious, he'd never, not once, slept solidly through the night. In his rare moments of deep sleep, he would often bicycle his legs, like a dog, but slower, warm thighs jostling against mine. I'd let him do this for as long as he needed to, but he'd usually wake himself up and worry he'd kicked me. Or he'd wake with a sharp pain in his limbs. He said it was something to do with some bodily acid being misplaced when he lies down for too long. He talked about it like his internal workings were unique to him or belonged to some prehistoric understanding of how bodies work. Acids and vapors and whispers.

We'd needed to move my bed to the other wall because of the morning light and the ineffectiveness of my blinds. He'd drape my arm over his face, elbow crook covering the bridge of his nose, and when I suggested he get an eye mask, he said it would make him panic.

"Every morning I'd wake up and think I'd gone blind."

"Yeah, but just for a second."

"I like your arm better."

"But your face is big and my arm is small."

"It's big enough."

"Just what every girl wants to hear," I said. "Arm just big enough to get the job done."

"Some girls *would* want to hear that."

"I guess. Wait, what are we talking about?"

"I don't even know."

On nights he kicked a lot I'd wake exhausted, imagining falling asleep at my control post, letting two cave Jeeps crash into each other. This was impossible, of course—there hadn't been a crash in the park since the seventies, and that was only the Miss Muffet Cruise Boats, yet another friendly bit of whiplash and a settlement out of court. It was worth it, though. Enduring Brendan's kicks. Knowing this thing about what his body did at night. It was yet another glimpse that I got, a glimpse at how different he was from the prince. He was faulty and a little neurotic and his enthusiasm for things out-weighed his skill. On those mornings when he'd drape my arm over his eyes, I'd let his heat accumulate in my skin, watch his jaw clench and unclench, and listen to his fretful pattern of little throaty snores. What a world, that would allow me to have him.

I notice that when people ask to hear the story of Brendan and me, they choose their words very carefully. I can see them laboring.

"How did *you* . . . you know . . ." and "Did you swoon over him while you were buckling those kids into the Jeeps?"

"Sure," I tell them. "You know how you've got to keep your mind occupied with something!"

But they look like I didn't quite get it, what they were getting at.

Brooke was pouring me wine the first time I told her about it, a few months after we'd found each other online and agreed to find a place together, about how they interrogate me. All those barbed questions and heads tilted. The implication that he's far out of my league.

"Oh what the fuck?" she barked while using both hands to pour. "That's a bit fucking rude!"

"Oh I don't know about that . . ."

"Stop doing that."

"What?"

"*Oh I don't know about that.* That weird fucking fifties cadence thing they have you do. No one talks like that. It's not welcome in our home."

"You're right," I said. "Sorry."

"The whole *league* thing is so fucked."

"I mean, they didn't literally talk about leagues—"

"It's such a fucking California thing. If I was at home and told a girl her boyfriend was out of her league, she'd batter me and she'd be right to do it!"

I remember the wine we had that night was the kind she liked best, almost green, and gentle. I took three of the largest gulps I could manage.

"Yeah, it is pretty fucking rude," I said.

Brooke rubbed her thumb on a yellow stain on our cheap countertop. Turmeric from Indian takeout. Without shifting her gaze, she reached a long arm into the open fridge and put a Kraft Single, still wrapped in plastic, between her teeth. Then she corralled me toward the couch.

"Sorry if I sound cranky."

"Cranky," I said back, mimicking her accent, quietly. I only did that rarely, because I knew she hated it. She always said it was the

one accent no one on the planet could stand. Whichever new class-
room she ended up in, the children always made her say "no," and
hollered it back at her, "*norr*." They'd pout and whine until she either
did it or slammed a chair onto the linoleum. The last school she
subbed at was "Montessori-adjacent," with a brush swirl of blue and
white printed on the uniforms. Brooke managed to get a sweatshirt
that I stole often, and she joked it was like living with a Ruta Valley
Elementary student. An elementary student who occasionally drinks
cheap wine with her, in the evenings. She often said that the drive
to the school was the saddest route she'd ever had, past the cluster of
nuclear power facilities down toward Long Beach, Alamitos, locked
away by endless concrete fortifications, but still very much in the
shadow of this idyllic, hippie compound where the school lived, the
school that gave the kids beeswax to play with during lessons, something about motor engagement and cognitive focus. Brooke said
that no one acknowledged it, the nuclear spread, which surprised
her. They didn't comment on its ugliness, or link her to some kind
of petition addressing it, or even speak a word about it. She said it
was like they'd trained themselves not to see it, that vast facility on
the water.

"What, so the joke is like, Brendan is an actor and you're a ride
operator?"

"No, it's the cave," I said. "The joke is they send uglies to work
down there."

"What?"

"I mean it's not really a joke, it's a fact."

"It's one of the most popular rides! People probably look at your
face more than Brendan's, on the whole." She tore the plastic off
the cheese with her teeth and sucked the tile into her mouth the
way Venus flytraps eat prey in sped-up documentary footage. "Your
ride's even more popular than the Sci-Fi Princess Swamp Adventure
or whatever it's called, right?"

I wished she hadn't said it. There was the footage again, clear in
my mind: Callie bent over herself, the surgical lights switching into

life. When the incident, or the footage, comes up unexpected like that, I know I won't sleep well. I'll lose a few hours on the internet, looking up theories and dissections of each frame of the video. I'll go through her filmography; only eight credits in all, two of the studio's kids shows, two made-for-TV movies, three films she made after her contract with the studio was up (which were more adult, for sure, I think she was even a prostitute in one, but none of which were well reviewed), and then of course *Nebuland*. Mention of what happened on the ride is a parasite, a worm, waiting to bore into me. I wish I knew how to cure myself of it.

"I know," I said. "But it's like . . . just a long-running joke. Uglies and kids with sunstroke. That's what you'll find in the Caves of Chirakan."

"Brendan's not even that good-looking," she said through the cheese.

I snorted. Wine burned the space between my throat and nose. "That is objectively untrue."

"Nah." She spaced out while looking at the wall. "He's so symmetrical. I don't trust it."

"Aren't there studies that show people inherently love and trust symmetry?"

"Most serial killers are extremely symmetrical. Think about that." A sweat patch had formed at the center of her bony chest. "Well fuck 'em," she said. "You're gorgeous and Brendan's a prince, so it makes sense. Princes love gorgeous cave women."

Sometimes if Brooke and I have fallen into the quiet before bed, me on the couch and her at the other end of the room behind the kitchen counter, I'll watch her shoulder blades as she does some repetitive task. Drying dishes, or grading papers on one of the stools at the counter that marks the start of the kitchen, even though it's all just one room. Whenever she stops whatever it is that she's doing, however banal, and announces that she's going to bed, a sort of cold will come over me. Just a small sadness. She's so good at . . . I'm not quite sure what. She's good at simply being, in a world I could never quite feel at ease in. The world outside the park.

Brendan must still be in makeup, something he has to do himself now. I look at my feet and wonder if he's right below me. It's unlikely. I'm walking along the river between Nebuland and the castle, one of several little pathway extensions from the lake at the center of the park, where pyrotechnic shows used to blast off, up until a week ago. We'd encourage parents to take note of certain markers on the wall of the lake as meeting points if their kids got lost.

This section of river is walled off from guest view with hand-painted signs that say *PLEASE PARDON OUR TRANSFORMA-TION!*, but two kids are trying to peek through. I never understand why they do that. Willfully destroy the illusion. Who wants to see the dug-out canal pit, the tract for the steamboat, the debris, the bottom half of a hippopotamus, bisected, made of gears and rotors? Who wants to be disturbed in that way?

"Howdy!" I call out. The guests don't turn.

I thought it was two children, but I see now that it is one very old woman wearing baggy clothes, clothes that have billowed in a breeze and taken on the impression of several dimensions, whose back is curved like a comma and whose legs are twigs hovering beneath some kind of board shorts designed for teen boys, slivers of reflective silver running down their sides. She couldn't possibly have chosen to dress that way.

"That spot's just under construction." I'm careful not to say demolition. "But I can help you get to whichever attraction strikes your fancy!"

She turns her gaze back to the peephole, as if I was only an apparition. There's no more I can do—if guests don't violate rules, I can't make demands of them. I just can't imagine why you'd look at all that, in that stagnant river. There's a specific phobia of machinery under water. It has a long name. I don't understand why it would be any more frightening than machinery on land, but I suppose it wouldn't be a phobia if everyone understood it.

The way guests see the park—what happens in their adrenal system and in their supine hearts—always seems to be in such delicate balance. Throwing off any one thing can throw off a deeper, more tectonic equilibrium inside each of them. If the lovely fantasy shifts, it makes room for something grotesque to suddenly appear. The park can mess with psyches in unique ways. Sometimes I want to write about that in those forums about Callie Petrisko, but I don't know that I could explain it well. But sometimes I think it's a wonder that so many of us give ourselves over to the park at all. Being in its guts, in its inner workings, fixing small mechanical problems, from time to time, when they need me, has made me less vulnerable to surrendering to the park, but still. I understand that guests have their limit. The illusion of this place can only glitch so badly before they, the humans within it, fall apart.

"What if I fast-tracked you onto the apprenticeship program?" a woman in HR had said, underground, a few months after I started. "To be honest you've demonstrated some real skill beyond the scope of those casual maintenance fixes we've got you doing. You don't need to be a ride operator forever." She winked. She smelled like stale coffee.

"Would I have to see the lights on?" I asked.

She hesitated. "Sure, yes, I do think that occasionally our teams need to work in full light, but I don't know the ins and outs of process there, hon."

I reiterated my rules. The lights can never come on. Not all the way. And never the lagoon ride. Never. There was more chat, over a couple of days. I think the woman liked speaking to me, I don't quite know why. But it was clear that my rules meant that I could never be a real machinist, a real maintenance gal.

The last time we met, the woman gave me a gentle touch on the elbow. "How did you learn to do these fixes anyway? That emergency with the chassis and the Saudi family . . . that was impressive. We noticed."

"My stepdad," I said, trying not to look at my gloves. "And the answer is still no."

They hardly ever come on at full blast anyway. The lights. Only for an injury or hazmat, really. I've only been on a ride when it broke down—really broke down—once. It was the coaster in the Kingdom of the Future, a section of the park devoted entirely to the idea of innovation. ("A monument to the great American, amphetamine-fueled Cold War aerospace machine," Brendan likes to remind me. I'm not sure why.) The coaster normally took place in total darkness. Riders tipped downward from a very high ramp, and whipped past a few sharp turns, and then there'd be smeared nova lights and a few stomach-drop jumps in the track.

But at this point, when I'd gone on the ride, there was a shrill scraping sound, and we came to an abrupt halt. We were there for five minutes total. A friendly voice came through our in-seat speaker to tell us that we'd be on the move again shortly. Then the music stopped. That was the ghoulish thing, the thing that gave an instant metal-on-teeth feeling. Maintenance lights bloomed dimly below us; just a night-light, not enough to let us see the whole architecture of the ride, or even the dimensions of the room, but enough to see how the track almost caressed itself, how tightly wound it was, how pregnant the whole thing was with pneumatic nodes, the kind which prompted the ride to stop if one ruptured, but would otherwise whisper in your wake as you flew through the dark. I felt sick, being stuck there. I shut my eyes very tight and tried to count. I began to see colors. I began to see the whirling of a blue light into a white one into something warm. It might have been different if I had been called in to help, on the ground, but I was locked into my position in midair, helpless, and trapped in the claustrophobic hinterland between fantasy and reality. We were on the move again shortly—I couldn't tell you how long it took.

Now that section of the park, the one once called the Kingdom of the Future, is called Nebuland, as in *Nebuland*, the movie, the CGI franchise, the one that starred Callie Petrisko, whose film world was replicated in the lagoon ride. It's about a beautiful and ferocious princess, Fiusha, who would stop at nothing to protect her ice kingdom, with its sexy and tropical subterranean under-stratum where much of the second act is set, from human invaders. After crash landing on one of Nebuland's tundra areas, a young lieutenant engages in hand-to-hand combat with Fiusha, and at some point they fall in love and there's a PG-13 moment in a hot spring and then a lot of war, martial arts from the quick-limbed Tsunami, Fiusha's army a tangle of visual details borrowed from Inuit, Chuvash, and Comanche cultures (facial scarring, headdresses, animal bones, copper masks, that kind of thing), and the twist is that Nebuland is Earth. The war-men are the *real* aliens. It's hopeful and sad at the same time. Get it?

The arrival of Nebuland had all been so strangely timed. It washed over the Kingdom of the Future, the one so beloved since its opening, only a year and a bit before the mutterings about the park's closure became impossible to ignore. "IP fever," people called it. Clunky branding took over the oldest attractions.

I pass some of the worst of it on my walk along the walled-off river: the Aqua Lounge, that room with its bossa nova animatronic revue of fish-themed song and dance. Some time ago it became the Tsunami Martial Arts Encounter (as in Tsunami, the hero's asskicking sensei-type man-shark friend from *Nebuland*), a live-action fighting show where a huge slab of a man kicks and spins under a kaleidoscope of green and blue light. The animatronic animals that had made the Aqua Lounge so iconic are now hidden in shadow, ghosts watching from the walls.

The opening of Nebuland also ushered in the new generation of robotic character features. The bots on the rides. The park was famous for these, for the kindly moving figures—like marionettes, almost—of all the studio's most beloved characters. It almost didn't matter what the characters looked like in their films, or how modern those characters were; these older models had always been recrafted into animatronics of the same style: apple cheeks, visible joins, movements as clunky as an electronic reindeer attached to a neighbor's roof at Christmas. The bots were an expression of the park's innocence, and their designers' sweetness, their sentimentality, their nostalgia for a bygone time. Guests could take comfort in these friendly renderings.

No one needed to be reminded of how robotics were integrating into the actual world—everyone had seen those videos of men in labs kicking at a metal dog thing in order to prove a point about its stability. No, even the villains of the park, the witches and fire-demons and evil step-siblings, were made of glossy wood and plastic, and nothing more menacing than an arched brow painted on their faces.

There was also something wholesome about the lore—the way the models and molds of the park, the small prototypes, the animatronics, were created. The place. Everyone knew about the designers' desert oasis outside Palm Springs or Mojave. One of those. It was officially called the Imagination Ranch, a retreat where the park's creatives went to brainstorm and manufacture their new rides and décor and inventions. In books and videos about how the studio works, they always describe it as a sacred haven "away from the noise of the city, where minds are free to wrangle and roam!"

The Imagination Ranch wasn't open to the public; no one could be altogether sure it wasn't a PR myth. Die-hard adult fans of the park made excursions into the blazing heat to try to locate it. They might arrive at some anonymous steel gates and get turned away by a huge mute guard, or they'd find nothing at all.

But then the bots changed. *Nebuland* made them change. With the implementation of the new land within the park, it was decided that the friendly doll-bots of antiquity needed to be retired. It happened little by little, but it might as well have happened overnight, the way the guests reacted to the sudden appearance of a hyper-real Scheherazade, Miss Muffet with pores, an alien princess whose lungs rose and fell underneath the faint impression of ribs, under luminous skin.

By the time half of the robots in the haunted house were swapped out, management had gotten cold feet: Guests complained that the new bots made the haunted house too scary. Genuinely scary. Those scenes of dinnertime exorcisms and bodies dragging themselves out of tombs were much darker when the participants seemed to be flesh-and-blood people rather than oversized figurines, with no discernible expressions of anguish.

I'm grateful they never got around to Peter and Wendy. I don't know if I could have handled it.

They slowed the rollout. And then Callie Petrisko happened.

And so the bots remain a mix of old and new; charmingly clunky and hyperreal.

I take a moment at the juncture point beyond the north-facing extension of the castle. I see Nebuland's gates, a flowing arch of built bioluminescence, spilling foliage that moves, a little bit, a little breathy writhing with the help of two pneumatic bladders buried underneath the vines, on either side of the walkway, every twenty minutes. Beside me there's a small footbridge and a shrub and an angled rock that functions as a bench, but of course there are no benches in this part of the park, where foot traffic gets—*got*—so dense. The rocks would offer a brief place to lean, engineered to a very specific angle, just the same way there are no concave surfaces in the park, not where guests can reach. Nothing for litter to get mashed into. All these countless details, details that no one would ever notice, all of that is the result of extensive, enduring testing, though who was doing the testing was never clear to us: designers, psychologists, hypnotists. It's all a delicious fog of forced-perspective tricks, clever angles of glass, music that inspires *galloping* but not *jogging*. They've thought of everything: how at night, in the absence of light, dark surfaces become reflective, and guests should never be able to see too much of their own faces while they're here. And so, in the walkable spaces, there's a well-placed torchlight that flashes its glow onto any dark surface, a surface pretending to be onyx or slate. Instead of your own face looking back at you, you find yourself replaced by a ball of light.

There's the rest of the castle, some meters behind me now, those turrets, parapets, this impression of a bastion that casts long shadows to where the road widens and then forks. When I stand here, right here, I'm shrouded in those sunset colors and the Cro-Magnon hum of something powerful behind my back. Sometimes I think I can hear it breathe. The castle. The battlements warm the body. It's wonderful as long as you follow the one rule of the park: Don't look too closely. If you can avoid it, don't look up.

There's a thump from under my feet that I feel all through my spine, and particles of lavender paint sift through the air. The breeze makes them hover like a stray ghost and then settle on the ground. A few flecks settle near my boots. How weird. Must be the demolition guys in the empty river, taking apart some animal half-made of gears.

Something beckons me to look behind my shoulder, a feeling like I'm being watched. But it's just Sam, in the distance, standing where I just was, looking straight up into the sun. He's watching the castle, just as I was watching it a moment ago. He looks so light, frail, like he's made entirely of dead skin, like the only thing holding him to the earth is the jacket of heavy canvas with his name embroidered across his heart. He looks lost, though, like he might not return from staring at the parapets. He seems to have become a static figure, harmonious alongside the other statues of unreal creatures and imagined sidekicks within the park, which are each rendered stately and almost austere in stone.

I wonder if I look like that, sometimes. Lost, and very content.

———

I find the tree with the door in back. I feel guest eyes on me; I suppose there's no avoiding them. It's not against park rules for them to see me go down below, through a hatch, but of course ideally you'd want to do it without anyone around. I think it adds to the whimsy: a door in a tree! But I can see how it might be unnerving. So I give them a wave, get no response, only slack-jawed curiosity, as I press my finger to my keycard, and the keycard to one of the stumps. I slot in the needle, companion item to each standard keycard, required of almost every lock in the park. I wait for the click, and pull open a panel of textured bark. I shut the door behind me and wait for the light.

Nothing. Just a damp darkness. I wait another few seconds, then

I wave a hand. Nothing. When did it go out? I feel for the walls and take the steps slowly, waiting for my eyes to adjust. One foot after the other. I stroke one glove with the fingers of the other.

"Keep walking!" I hear a voice call out from below. I know it.

"What's with the lights?" I shout.

"Just come here!"

I reach out to the wall on my right and feel the texture of the mural, a pastiche of different characters and stories, led by a flying Peter, spine-feathers fluttering, who's holding Wendy—Wendy with Renata Revere's face—by the hand. His claws aren't out in the mural. It's mostly pastels. In places, the paint had dried in thick glops.

"Almost there," he says. I see his teeth before anything else. Then the rest of him: Brendan's illuminated by something small in his hand. A lighter? No, a glow stick.

"Where'd you get that?" I ask.

"I found a stash of them in catering." There's the outline of his eyes, and for a moment it looks like his head is floating on its own, like something in the haunted house, and I don't like it. I adjust myself so that my weight is against his chest. He lets out a puff.

"You found me," he says.

I breathe in his shirt smell. "Where is everyone?"

"I think they must be under the castle, looking at the big breaker."

"Why would they do that? That's not where they're gonna fix the lights."

"You know how to fix the lights?"

I pull back and try to make out anything, a fire escape, a distant LED. "Are there more glow sticks?"

He kicks something, and there's the sandy sound of a cardboard box moving across the floor. I grab a handful and crack them, and they light up green and blue, but they don't help me see shit.

"What, so there was no cast down here?" How many were left? Who was doing their circuit? I should have checked. I should have come down here sooner.

"Yeah. A couple of Beignet girls and, you know."

"I don't know."

"You know." He pauses. "The rooster."

"Chanticleer?"

"Yeah."

He sounds stiff.

"Oh . . . okay, well, were the lights all fucked when they were down here?"

"Just when they were leaving. Don't worry about them, they're fine."

"I can fix them."

"Yeah?"

"Sure," I say, and approach a forking of corridors. One path leads to a makeshift soundstage, close to the control room for the fireworks and the fountain shows. The other path seems to lead into a new depth of darkness, a thin passage where machines built into the walls let off heat. I feel my feet stop, and Brendan feels my hesitation.

"Let's not worry about it. I'll help you feel around for your locker. My eyes are pretty adjusted."

"No, I . . ." I try to listen to something from that corridor. The hum of the machines has slipped into a harmony, I think. Can Brendan hear it, too? For a sickening flash, I feel certain that he can't. That it's something maybe only I can hear.

I shake my head. I rub my face.

"No," I say. "I can fix it."

Sent from:
PO Box 5538
43824 20th St W
Newberry Springs, CA 92365

Don't call. Don't email. Write + that's all. Letters, like this. Nothing typed, no saved files. One of the machinists who was here with us emailed his wife + now the machinist is gone.

I don't think you should go to the opening. I know you're going to want an explanation + I can't really give you one. It's a long story. So please, just do this as a favor to me. Get your husband, his people, whoever, to come up with an excuse. Do anything else that weekend. Don't go to the park.

I'm in the desert. I have to drive an hour into a town called Newberry Springs + be back before five to mail this letter, so this probably sounds manic. I'm not manic.

This PO box is the best way to reach me. I'll check it every other day as long as I can.

Again, don't go to the opening. I know I'm not always taken seriously in this family, but trust me now. I have a terrible feeling about the park + I hope I'm wrong.

-Bro

CHAPTER TWO

B rendan grew up watching music videos on afternoons when he was on his own in the house. What happened in them, what splashed across the screen, confused him. They rarely had any-thing to do with the actual song itself, with the lyrics, and he was hypnotized by the idea that the theme of each scene, the story the music video told, the palette and the characters and all of that, had been assembled through a dice roll. Random chance. And yet, it was still a music video.

This song about—*dice roll*—kisses had a video about—*dice roll*—drag racing in—*dice roll*—black-and-white.

This song about—*dice roll*—loneliness takes place in a—*dice roll*—ballroom, where all the people are clad in—*dice roll*—clown masks.

This idea, that the components themselves were inconsequen-tial and that they always constituted a watchable whole, remained Brendan's working definition of art for a long time, but he stopped thinking about art at all after age ten, when a spate of kidnappings in

California meant that he was no longer allowed to take the bus home from school, and so he had less time alone in his house to watch music videos. Every day Frankie Deeb's mother drove Brendan five miles down the endless shopping centers of McBean Parkway to the one containing his dad's office, where he spent the hours of 3 to 5:30 p.m. doing homework, or eavesdropping.

It was stale there, a series of box rooms carpeted in itchy gray, and the only large window in the whole place looked out front, toward the other single-story businesses and a mostly empty parking lot. There was a Costco across the road, in the retail park that was the mirror image of where he stood, but sometimes if there was dust or if the smog was bad, it would become lavender and faint, like a far-off mountain in a watercolor painting.

The office had the lighting of a dentist's office, blue-bright. Every room smelled like printer ink. But something also overtook young Brendan while he was there. When someone would knock on his father's door, Brendan got an awake feeling, a tingle of cleanliness, a little jolt. He got it when he saw someone smooth out the wrinkles on their shirt, or use a bulldog clip to contain a stack of fresh papers, or when the receptionist would use her calm voice on the phone, even if she'd been hissing curses at the pigeons in the parking lot just a minute earlier.

At first, he passed the time sitting among the row of chairs where clients would wait, with their jackets, if they had them, stacked on their laps. But over several weeks he migrated closer and closer to his dad's closed door, the name carved on a gold strip in the center of it: *Hank Boteros, Sr. Manager.*

Every day Brendan knocked on the door. Every day he got the same response.

"Do your homework outside."

If a receptionist happened to be within earshot, she might open the door a crack and croon "How can you say no to a face like that?" but his father was never up for banter. If anything, Brendan wondered if his dad minded her talking to him like that. If he minded Brendan watching her talk to him like that.

But being there, among the antiseptic fugue of a place of corporate hemming and hawing, gave Brendan an urgent new hunger, but the hunger didn't have a name. Not at first. It was simply a wish to be there more and more: Brendan would rush to the spot on the curb where Mrs. Deeb's car always appeared, sometimes getting there so early he gave himself a headache willing her car to arrive with what he hoped were vestigial demigod powers, so that he could sit among his father's employees, find a way to huff printer ink, and feel the velocity, the inner-ear rush, of sanitary, depressurized corporate air. And when he was older, he'd study hard, do whatever he needed to do in high school to become like his dad, whatever exactly that was.

His teachers stopped talking about how multitalented he was, how he would really have a go at any activity, how he applied himself with as much enthusiasm to long division as the crazy chicken dance they did as a reward when his class had been particularly well behaved. Being good at lots of things was for chumps. He was going to become good, very good, better than anyone else, at one thing, and that thing was being an important professional guy like his dad.

As he got older, he found his friends holding him accountable to this goal by accident, pruning away his polymath tendencies not because they shared his dream of focused talent, but because they'd decided that college was for chodes, lacrosse was for chodes, bio sucked so they should all go for chem. By the middle of high school, he'd stopped picking up side interests and sudden hobbies, but he couldn't crack a 3.5 GPA either.

His mother was ambivalent about the idea of college, seeing as she'd done fine without it, so she sat down with him in front of their ancient cube of a computer, all beige, and searched "pre law" on Alta Vista.com, intent on giving Brendan a cold splash of reality.

"This is what you have to do if you get into college." She said it half in Spanish, which he understood but couldn't speak very well, and which she only spoke to him, in a voice a lot like the receptionist's phone voice, something close to a whisper, which made him feel special. Then the weight of what she was showing him set in. The

Ivies would never be an option. No bother—to a boy from suburban California, they were always an old wives' tale anyway, as distant from Santa Clarita as Narnia. They looked at other private schools, then out-of-states more broadly, then the state schools that were mostly within a two-hour drive of them. His mother tried to explain that his family was not poor enough to qualify for most financial aid and not rich enough for the decent schools—even the state schools—to be an easy option.

At dinner, Brendan ate in silence, building up the courage to finally say, "You guys seem like you never really thought about this."

His father raised his eyes, but kept on eating. His mother considered her words.

"We never thought you'd have this problem."

"What problem?"

"Wanting . . . ," and she waved her hand.

"Wanting what?"

She put down her knife and fork. "Wanting to study hard."

He didn't know what she meant yet. But after that, Brendan started to notice things about the way he moved through the world, the way things in the world moved around him. Like what started happening at the mall just after his sixteenth birthday.

They would find him in the food court, or sometimes follow him into Foot Locker, asking if he'd modeled, if he wanted to be an actor, if he'd been in school plays, if he had done catalog work. Frankie told him it was just a radius thing.

"We're exactly fifty-five minutes outside downtown LA. You ever think about that?"

"I mean it depends on traffic," Brendan said.

"Nah man, it's fifty-five. Trust me. My cousin interned for one of those agencies. Fifty-five minutes is like perfect," he said, watching some girls watch Brendan through a pane of glass. "Those interns or scouts or whatever get told to look around the suburbs, but none of them actually wanna go that far. Even though they're supposed to. It's because they don't get paid anything, or not overtime at least. They don't wanna go more than an hour in any direction. But if they go out somewhere like here or inland and they get their shit done nice and quick, they have time to stop at In-N-Out on the way back. That's what my cousin says."

"Then why are they here? Why wouldn't they just go to LA malls?"

Frankie shrugged. "Every agent wants their agency to think they're James Bond. That's what my cousin says."

Brendan started going to different malls—even the shitty ones farther inland toward Agua Dulce—but the same thing would happen every few weeks. A too-leathery guy or a too-dimpled woman would appear before him, loud and overdressed in a blazer, and ask that he take their card. They weren't used to hearing no. They weren't used to anything less than flattered laughter and *Wait, really?* Brendan didn't always act like he heard them, even when they were standing right in front of him, and sometimes it got him into trouble. A forty-something guy with coke nostrils got in his face and told him to take a compliment, have some respect, most kids would die to be in his shoes. Frankie told him to fuck off. The guy said Brendan should get a leash for his fat fuck boyfriend, then the manager of the Panda Express told all three of them he was going to call security. That's the worst it ever got.

Top-tier college might not be an option, fate and his own face might be pulling him toward the least remarkable profession he could imagine, but he could still strive for that printer-ink smell, the cool rush of the dream office. He read *Bonfire of the Vanities* and asked his dad to teach him QuickBooks. He asked his dad to teach him Process Explorer. He asked his dad for anything that could give him a leg up. He asked and asked his dad. When he told his dad they needed Internet Explorer 6, his dad said, "Oh so you won't need me to teach you anything. Sounds great."

When he was a junior, he decided that he needed sports for college, but jocks always gave him shit about messing up his pretty face. He liked soccer, but Frankie told him he was too tall for it. Soccer was Frankie's thing. What Brendan wanted to do was water polo, but he'd have to wake up at 4:30 a.m. for practice. He weighed the pros and cons and decided to man up and do it. He was okay, at first, and got even wider shoulders than before, but he started falling asleep during sixth-period English. Mrs. Luppino failed him.

He would tell me that part like the punch line of a joke; sports to get into college, the sports fucked up my GPA. Wocka wocka. In the early days, when each of us would urge the other to monologue about themselves, Brendan would get this far and try to stop there. The story of how he got to the park, of how he was the age that he was and still doing what he did. But I never saw what he did as less deserving of respect or prestige than whatever (it was now clear) middle-management banality his dad did. I think what Brendan does is the most special job in the world.

So I'd make him go on. Tell me more of the story.

After failing English and quitting water polo, he got bitter. It wasn't that he felt entitled. It wasn't even that he thought he deserved to pass English. He just kept thinking about that printer smell. It was such a small thing to want. Such a small thing. He convinced himself it didn't have to be what his dad did, or law, or even anything specific. He just wanted to find something that he was good at. He decided that he'd work after school senior year, and if it was temping, rather than modeling or selling board shorts at Pacific Sun, then maybe it wouldn't matter if he couldn't make it into a legit college. He'd have valuable office experience. But until he could do that, he needed to find money another way. His friends had begun driving aimlessly for hours and then asking for gas money. Sometimes they pooled birthday money for booze; sometimes they wanted to see the French NC-17 art movies that only played at the small, expensive cinema in the city. Money was part of the equation now, even if he didn't understand the order of operations.

And so he finally said yes to a scout, a thirtysomething woman who'd run across four lanes of traffic to mash a card into his hands at a sandwich shop, and when she left he noticed the faces of his friends. Something in them relaxed: *This is how it should be. Accept your fate.*

A few weeks before senior year started, Frankie got a job in the mailroom of an office with printer ink. Thea, a quiet girl with calluses on her elbows and fingers, appeared on the periphery of their small group, and one day she announced, barely above a whisper, that she'd started working at Staples. Brendan did new work, too. He started to suffer breakouts from concealer and dripped sweat into his contact lenses while holding on to barbecue tongs, three fanned CD-ROM sets of Rosetta Stone lessons, a five-year-old girl looking sad with a thermometer in her mouth, all while cameras flashed in his face. His mother tore the images from catalogues and sent them to her sisters in Tallahassee and Mayagüez. He got a speaking part in a commercial for a soft drink that he didn't know his agent had submitted him for. They ended up dubbing over his voice in the end, but it didn't change his pay. He learned what "usage" and "remittance" meant. He bought a used Isuzu Rodeo. He accepted a truancy notice from his school so that he could drive two and a half hours to San Clemente, where a TV crew was waiting for him. There was some confusion. It wasn't an ad, actually; it was a teen dating show where he'd sit down with a girl and talk until she told him he had to leave. They gave him a line to say about him being a surfboarder, how he loved living an *extreme* lifestyle, after which the dead-eyed girl would say the word— the magic word that was also the name of the show—that meant he had to get up and go. Date over. They had to shoot it twelve times. His *extreme* delivery wasn't convincing.

Girls started doing things to him around that time, when the episode aired. There had been a surge of above-the-waist stuff around the time of bar mitzvahs, followed by a sexless doldrum that sat in strange contrast with a spate of raunchy teen comedies Frankie was always desperate to go see. Movies about virginity pacts and road trips and something called *Frosh Island*, about a horny aviation accident in the South Pacific, which starred an actor who revealed himself to be Irish in interviews. Declan something. All the white girls

Brendan knew taped magazine pictures of him up in their lockers. Around that time there was a resurgence of childhood notions of crushes, now that most of them could legally drive past each other's home, and had the technology to listen to sad music while doing so. Two girls he'd known since kindergarten had to drop out because of pregnancies, but Brendan could never seem to find a way into the world of sex. There were none of the comedy porn moments and there was none of the bodily ease of those movies with twenty-six-year-olds playing high school seniors.

"They're scared of you," Thea told him once from behind the checkout counter at Staples. He'd taken to wandering the aisles, listening to a portable mp3 player he'd bought himself with Noxzema money. He'd do it whether she was working or not, but it was better if she was. "I mean not scared, but like, they think you must have a supermodel girlfriend in the city or something."

"That's dumb," he said. "I don't have one of those."

"What, are you like . . ." Thea pushed greasy bangs out of her eyes. "Are you like in the market for a girlfriend or whatever?"

"No," he said. "Maybe." He didn't know how else to explain.

"Start showing up at those lame parties." She set her gaze on a point just behind Brendan's shoulder. "They suck but like . . . we could still go."

"What parties?"

The girls, as it turned out, had been waiting for him at those parties. But he didn't find the ease with them, the kind of ease people probably assumed of someone as handsome as him. Those girls crash-landed on him with meteoric force, because they were only able to do what they did to him after getting blind drunk. Always an urgency, in the dark, twinned with apology, in the dark. They were always girls he liked, who were funny in class, or were good at soccer, or had well-shaded doodles in their notebook margins, who seemed to have lives outside of school that were interesting, enviable, maybe even cool. But after their fumbles in hot tubs or guest rooms beside bowls of potpourri, they would go cold, never speak to him, avoid eye contact in the halls. Some would go a kind of green shade in the light of day. Their blood would drain from their face, a little, and it made Brendan sad.

Frankie tried to help. "They make it hella easy for you. At least there's that."

Frankie liked to punch Brendan in the arm. Bros. He'd seen it in all those movies, but he wasn't very good at it; he'd miss and get the side of Brendan's tit.

Brendan's problem was, fundamentally, that he didn't understand how he looked, and I hate when he tells me about all this. It makes me want to do a tiny violin gesture, which I actually never know if I'm doing right, and Brendan always looks at me a little worried when I try to do it. The thing is, he's not an idiot, so how much about his body and his face did he really not understand? So much of him works like that, though: runs on an internal logic I can't understand. So I believe that he may not have understood it, and that the girls' coldness made him rethink how funny, how enviable they'd been in the first place. But that blind spot of his is the saddest thing of all. He wasn't able to see the simplicity of an embarrassed teenage girl, or five.

That was the extent of his anguish—until Thea.

They started fooling around in the cars on the way to parties, but never *at* the parties, and never after the parties. In their last semester of high school, when the colleges had made their admission offers, there was a party most nights, including Sundays, even if it was just someone's garage. It started when they crowded into an ROTC dork's minivan and Thea had to jump onto his lap.

"*Had* to." I eyerolled when he told me this for the first time. And Brendan went quiet, like he was working out pieces of it, still.

He'd smelled the ammonia off her black dye and kept his eyes straight ahead, but the next time they drove somewhere she sat right up against his side, even though there were six seats for six people, and he let his hand find the fuzzy plateau of her exposed lower back. Then they started getting rides with people they knew less well, who wouldn't interrupt them. She put her hand in his pants while the boys in the front seat swore at the skipping Puddle of Mudd CD, and he tackled her sideways, silently, onto the seat. At 3 p.m. in Dante Lao's moving Dodge Ram, Brendan very technically lost his virginity, without ever knowing if the loss was mutual. When they'd arrive at a gathering of five or sixty-five, in a parking lot or a pool house, Thea ignored him entirely, insulating herself in a dense circle of middling drama kids with hormonal acne, or whichever Levantine cheerleader with rhinoplasty bandages might have Percocet.

This part I hate, but he brings it up every so often, when he needs to go over things, when he's had a bad day, like if a kid has puked on him, something like that. He loved her. I guess it was his first love, which made him unable to see any sort of big picture, any sense of how it might have felt to be loved by him.

He wanted her to be his girlfriend, but couldn't ask, and so he assumed she didn't want to be his girlfriend. It was Brendan's first dip into agony. He didn't know how to write poetry or cause a scene with a boom box or make any other gruesome romantic gesture, so he stayed in bed for a week, claiming diarrhea to stave off questions from his mother, reread the Redwall books, masturbated, and looked at his own reflection very hard for the first time. Yes, there was the smile that looked kind of like an animation smile, white teeth and dimples. Yes, there was the angle of the jaw, the subtle crook in his nose that prevented him from looking too angelic, and all the features that made his heritage unidentifiable. (His agent was always telling him to avoid specifying race stuff with clients. "We don't want you to get pigeonholed.") He supposed, looking now, that shadows always hit him in interesting ways. He knew this without knowing how to articulate it until a lady photographer had said so. There was a mark next to his nose that looked like a freckle but was actually a chicken pox scar. That was lucky. His blackheads slid out easily, and if he didn't wash his hair it only became more malleable, never greasy.

For the first time he was grateful that he wasn't ugly. For the first time he thought about how Frankie might be lonely, even though he'd touched some boobs. For the first time he skipped a meal, five in a row, and noticed that he could change his body, if he tried.

He walked to the second-worst shopping center in northeastern Santa Clarita and aimed for the alley behind Staples. He thought he'd have some time to plan what he was going to say, but she was already there, smoking a cigarette and picking at the crust around her lip stud when he arrived.

"Do you want to be my girlfriend?"

At first she looked angry, then it looked like she was going to laugh, but she still seemed kind of angry. She started to say something, but took a long drag instead. Then she said, "I'll think about it," all calm, but her hand shook when she tried to drop her cigarette butt into the gutter, and it bounced back against her own ankle. By the time she'd kicked it away and examined the burn and fidgeted a little more, she'd made a decision.

"Okay," she said. "Yeah."

This is the part where Brendan gets angry, because I always interrupt him to bring up the timeline. He talks about it like the second-most important relationship of his life, after me, even though this must have been March, and the next part of their story—the end of their story—happens at prom.

"That's like three months," I always say.

"It's not."

"You're saying that all this stuff happened in the last semester of senior year. There was all this time where you and Thea were fooling around but weren't together. So I'm guessing that takes us to like March, and—"

"February. Let's say February."

"Okay, so . . . four months."

"Four months is a long time."

"You dated that set vet for like a year and a half. I never hear a thing about her."

"There's not that much to say about her, and oh my god will you just let me tell the story?"

I always let him finish. I like giving him shit. I know what he means, it's the time-distending thing. His first relationship felt long, even though it wasn't. I don't know how long he feels like I've been in his life. I don't know that I want it to feel that long.

They had sex in a public pool and in her break room. On Presidents' Day he snuck her into his dad's empty office. He felt a little gross about it after. She got a carpet burn on her knee that got infected.

She taught him that you can drift onto the other side of the road, a little, if no one else is around. He stopped going to jobs, and told his agent he should be taken off the books after that summer—he'd be going to college. He got into one. Thea told him she'd been thinking of joining the military, just basic and then a desk job or something. He started going a day or two without eating, in order to see what his muscles really looked like, and what else might be hiding under his skin, but he stopped when Thea said that dieting was for girls.

They didn't go to prom, but they went to the after-party. This time they drove up on their own. In this neighborhood there were gates in front of driveways. Here, dads grew ponytails and tried to cultivate small vineyards on tan, crispy hillsides where once a year a mountain lion would appear. When they buzzed at the bottom of the hill and then made their way up, to park beside a burbling fountain packed with thick koi fish, Thea looked out her window at the house. They'd never walked into a party together. She kept her seatbelt on.

Two girls Brendan recognized from his Spanish class were making a big show of switching into Converse while throwing their heels onto the lawn, groaning. Pygmy palm trees lined the walkway to the door. A half-built colonnade stuck out of the side of the house, leading nowhere, from nowhere.

"I don't want to go out there," she said. Then she looked at him and said it again. "I don't want to go out there."

Once inside, he started looking for the indoor basketball court. It was all anyone could talk about, but when he found it, on the second floor, it was a sort of upper-level garage with two mounted hoops on either wall. There was an old wet vac pushed into a corner.

"This is wack," Frankie said.

"Yeah."

Brendan left her alone for a minute. Twenty, maybe. Then he spotted her across the carpeted conversation pit, sobbing. It took him a long time to get an answer—that Madison Jackson had said something about Brendan being out of Thea's league, and one of the gay band kids tried to comfort her by saying, "Madison's only saying that because she gave him a hand job last Halloween," which was true but not helpful, and after that the only words Brendan could understand from Thea's mouth were "two-president-name bitch" and "I knew it" over and over.

She knew it: It had been a bad idea. It had been doomed from the start.

Brendan tries to get into detail about that, about the end of them, but I find it tedious, and frankly I wonder why he wants to talk to me about any of it. I don't tell him about my exes, though there are virtually none. I wait for the part when he gets to college. When he moves in with the first people who were ever really mean to him: four couples, all women, all from the Midwest, who tease him about his good looks and his longing for corporate banality and how he has no good stories. But of course they adore him. They said the best men on Earth are the ones born in LA, and the worst are the ones who move there from other places. Something about how LA kids grow up near the San Fernando Valley, the porn capital, sometimes with parents working in lighting or in post, and so they see everything there is to see before they're thirteen and then they're over it. Nothing shocks them and they never try to be shocking. Old men on the inside.

He started drinking more, in a good way, in a way the women felt was necessary. When he went out with them, he found that sometimes the drinking turned to dancing and it turned out that he liked dancing very much. The oldest of the women, who worked in a goth shop downtown and was often on the phone with a young child who lived with her parents in St. Paul, lent Brendan audiobooks on corporate leadership. He was moved by her support. He learned to talk more clearly, engage in something called "active listening," and not drink on Sundays.

It seemed to be going perfectly, until Thanksgiving sophomore year. A handful of the women came home with him to Santa Clarita, and one of them had a word with Hank Boteros about Brendan's interests. Hank said something that made its way back to Brendan, eventually, before Thanksgiving Day, and he—Brendan—left. He left the women in his family's home, he didn't answer his phone, and he dropped out of school. He's never told me what it was that his father said.

"It's okay to admit that your dad was being shitty about your prospects and that made you upset, or whatever it was."

"It wasn't that. Not like . . . exactly."

"Then why won't you tell me exactly what he said?"

"I have. A million times. And it's hard to remember."

"Which is it? You've told me a million times or it's hard to remember?"

"Roll over, I need to stretch out."

My best bet is that his dad said, once and for all, that Brendan was better off a flash-in-the-pan catalogue model than an accountant or a lawyer, but that still makes no sense to me. I thought parents supported their kids when their kids had sensible dreams that would help them achieve financial stability. I've never said it out loud, but I thought that was particularly true of immigrant parents like Brendan's. His father is second- or third-generation, and one of his grandparents had WASPy ties to Alaska, or Vancouver—one of those. But his mother had only spent a few months off the island of her birth before Brendan was conceived. I suppose I don't know a thing about their lives, or how their pasts would dictate what they wanted for their beautiful child.

He called his old agent, but she wasn't interested, so he called a new one who was only a year older than Brendan and always took weeks to return his calls. He started taking jobs at house parties in the hills, which weren't described as catering jobs, but which required him to hold plates of meatball-pops and ceviche, and he didn't get tips. He didn't think he looked any different from when he was being stopped in malls, but he found it harder this time around. I don't know what happened when he moved out of the house of women, or what filled the years between that and getting hired at the park. He doesn't describe it as a sad descent into desperation and mediocrity, so I don't think of it like that. Of course I think he's lucky to have found the park. For the park to have found him.

When he tells me about his life like this, it makes me feel like I need to tell him something similar. Something about my childhood, my teen years. How I got here. But there's no story, really. There's what happened to me in the shed in Omaha. Now I wear gloves. Now I'm here.

There's a glow at the end of the corridor, behind me, where Brendan is waiting. There are more murals down here. I can feel the brush marks underneath my gloves. I can feel a little bit of panic roiling in my limbs, so I try to locate Renata Revere's face on the wall. There she is. Breathing becomes nicer. That always does the trick. *She* always does the trick.

———————

The machine hum is getting louder.

Every load-bearing wall down here is curved, tucked under the park's circumference, and I lose sight of Brendan. "Keep making noise!" I shout. After a moment all I can make out is the faint iridescence of my gloves, light bouncing off a waxy patch.

Brendan sings a few notes of the main theme from the Kingdom of the Future, something written during the park's opening by two brothers who went on to write most of the animated film soundtracks for the studio. It's rousing and sweet and has a marching band quality that never fails to work its magic on me. He knows I love it. I hear it and I am excited about tomorrow, about a future that looks less like those brothers' lived future (Carter, floppy disks, VHS warble) and more like an abstract concept of skyward movement, Towers of Babel, bloodthirsty geometries, wily citizenry, pure velocity. It's funny that it never appeared in a film. It was written only to be walked through, here. Just above our heads.

Brendan's humming shifts to a free-form, "Hmmmm hmmmm dooooop," and then a frankly lazy "*Noise noooooise.*"

Even in an employee-access corridor, the walls are embossed with delicate murals. It's something for our eyes only, and I've always found that very moving. They've let press down here exactly twice: in 1963, only a few years after the park's opening, as part of a photography exhibition for the Tri-State Panoramic Trade Show in Long Island, and once in 1999, as a behind-the-scenes news special giving viewers a glimpse at the Land That Wasn't. It was an oddly bleak name—and oddly prescient—for what was effectively an extension of the unnamed Edwardian section, something that we might now call *steam punk*, French-inspired, fin-de-siècle, much of it in silent film monochrome. The signature item in its promo was a two-storey model of the grimacing moon from *A Trip to the Moon.* If you stood beside it, there'd be grotesque meringue ripples, dwarfing you.

They did some filming here, I suppose to give the impression that it was just about to be constructed aboveground, installed by plucky crew members, but of course it was all designed and built in the desert. The studio. The Imagination Ranch. Along with the moon tower and some other dazzling nineties concept art, they announced that the long-beloved Peter and Wendy ride would be moved and revamped for the new millennium. The TV spot that filmed down here was accompanied by a soundtrack from *our* Peter and Wendy ride. A classic. Some of the more telegenic engineers, all male, all under forty, spoke about how excited they were to see a Peter for the modern child, perhaps a more human Peter than the previous iteration, who, through the lens of hindsight, seemed totemic, too much a cryptid to be as boyish as he sounded, the feathers and claws giving his black eyes a kind of sinister bent that he wouldn't have had if he was simply a boy. But of course the star land features were the ones steeped in that Gilded Age nostalgia: The can-can canoes. A jeweled zeppelin half-parked inside a hangar too big to comprehend. The undersea adventure, guests in glass orbs, captained by a Victorian purser—you're diving for lost inventory, and then whoosh, you're sucked into the center of the earth.

But the land never materialized. No one knows why; at least I don't. There was no announcement about its cancellation. It was only the early days of the internet, so the fans couldn't really demand answers. Elements of each attraction got butchered up and served to other lands: a chandelier in a Fairytale Grove palace and the spoke of a giant steam train in the tunnel panorama. But I'd guess that most of the props and parts are stored in the desert somewhere, in some air-controlled locker. Truth be told I'm glad that they didn't change Peter and Wendy in the end. I like it just the way it is.

Why is it my favorite? Because I think it might be about how time works in Neverland. It's at a standstill, in a way: Peter fighting the same villain forever, the Lost Boys being boys, not men, for some length of time we can't possibly know. And yet, none of them go insane. None of them crave anything different. It's aspirational.

But maybe it's Renata Revere. She didn't speak much English when they shot it, so she's dubbed over when she speaks. It's a little jarring, but she makes up for it in her sloppy smile and the little leaps she makes when she's traversing Neverland's wild terrain. When she peers into the lantern that Tinkerbell sleeps in, we see her whole face up close, as though she's a giant and we're only pixie-sized, and you feel so close to her, the friend you always wanted, when you were young. Someone who was a child, but also a little bit of a mother, someone with mischief and warmth and, also, secrets.

Brendan's saying something now, but I'm too far away to make it out. The curvature of the corridor makes his words sound suffocated. Above me I faintly make out the section of ceiling where tile gives way to a kind of sleek ceiling tarp. It dips to fit the lake's outer shell, above our heads. The lake's belly descends into these underground corridors, and our arteries of hidden pathways fit to its perimeter. If I sat on Brendan's shoulders, I could touch the curve now. I've only been in the middle of the space once, for a tour of the soundstage, where audio cables as thick as rainforest vines allow the people helming the pyrotechnics show and other parades to make announcements to the crowd, if need be. There's also a small foley studio, for ad hoc effects. That's where I've been. I also understand that it's mostly servers at the center, which is why I'm so hot now. There's a drip along my lower back. It must be even more claustrophobic in there, where the dip above my head is at its lowest point—all that water aching above your head.

I can feel the hatch nearby. There, yes: a square seam about as tall as me. They point it out to us every six months when we go over new safety protocols. There's a smooth lever built into it, but I'm able to jimmy a gloved finger underneath and pull. Nothing.

Then, using all my strength, I pull again, and something clicks and swings outward.

"You're absolutely loving that your whole teacher's pet thing is paying off!"

He must have come closer. I wish he wouldn't. The idea that we might not find our way back to the main corridor makes me feel suddenly sick. But how would that happen? A corridor only runs two directions: forward and back.

"Emergency preparedness is no joke!" I try to laugh.

He answers with something too quiet for me to hear. I can't even make out my gloves now. I feel my way inside the whirring contents of this cupboard, and I know that this means the gloves have to come off. But I only pull off a finger, exposing the skin, and my ears start to ring. A crash of dread makes my guts heavy.

"You okay back there?"

I can't answer. I take a long breath, and try to hold it for the same length of time.

"Just a second!" I shout back.

I don't go finger by finger now. I pull the whole thing off in one, my left hand exposed. My skin gives off a clammy smell. I feel the contours of the generator now: the canister, the amp window, a monitor that glows so dimly I can't tell if it's powered at all. But yes, there's a faint humming coming from it, the gentle suction of air.

"Fuck it," I say, and I start mashing.

"Any luck?"

I don't answer. All I've managed to do is make the dim battery light on the control hatch go off with a click. There's a little tightening inside my chest. I reach into a crevice around the main cube, inlaid into the wall, the thing's haunch. My breath is still coming to me short and incomplete. There's a switch. I flip it.

Above my head, a cascade of warm, dim light dominoes its way toward Brendan. Something cool ekes into my organs, and I take an easy breath. I hear Brendan hoot. I close each small door to the control panel quickly, return the lever to its place, and dash back to where he is, just a few paces from where I left him. I cram my hand into my glove while keeping my eyes straight ahead of me. There he is, squatting, neck wrenched upward.

"Handy Rust Belt girl!"

"Omaha's not the Rust Belt," I say, trying to hide some of my relief. There's half-light above us now. It's only backup, but better than nothing.

I take my time getting to him. I want to air out my sweat. But I wrap my arms around his middle, reflexively, when I reach him. He rests his face on my scalp.

I point to the floor panel. "Who did that?"

It's where he's been squatting. A little outline in the floor. A camouflaged compartment, like the kinds that run along the walkway track of the dark rides. They're usually just filled with gaffer tape and a flashlight, but some have leads into a power system. This one looks like it's been jimmied open, sloppily. One of the hinges is warped.

"Did what?"

"That looks like someone fucked it up. Like, on purpose," I say. "Let me see."

"Nah, I think it's always been like that. I remember tripping over it." He crouches down and tries lamely to fit the hinge back into place.

"I've never tripped over it."

"No need to brag."

"No, I mean . . ." I can already feel him losing interest. "That's—that's pretty serious, right? That and the fact that the lights were out down here in the first place."

"Just a blip, someone probably missed an item on their *Action Plan*." No cast members have an Action Plan, beyond incorporating lines about the Hong Kong park into their accepted dialogue with the guests. "And on the plus side, if we'd hurt ourselves in the dark, we could have sued."

I roll my eyes, but it makes me nervous, even joking about that while CCTV is still running. He reaches an arm out toward me. I pull his hands and, grunting, make a big spectacle of helping him to his feet. He knows how to do this so that my gloves don't get yanked down.

"And anyway," he says. "Before you got here I tried flagging down tech, but they're all on the river, I think."

"Weird," I say. "So there's really no one down here but us?"

He frowns at the quiet of the distant, locked doors beyond where the dark corridors start to curve.

"I think they're dismantling that hippo today," he says, and I can't help but notice that he's changed the subject.

"Yeah," I say, following him toward wardrobe. "I saw."

I change quickly, and tie my hair back sloppily. It's okay for my costume: intrepid explorer. Brendan touches up the spots where his makeup has congealed into little lumps. It's too dim to do much more. In my locker, my phone is lying facedown. *Strange*, I think. Did I leave it there yesterday?

"You ready?"

"Yeah," I say. "Sure."

I touch Wendy, on the mural, on our way up. Renata Revere.

It was announced as an animated film, only the second that the studio made, and the story is famous: They couldn't find the right model for the animators, and one of the artists, a Lithuanian émigré who made his name sketching atrocities just after the Second World War, told stories about the most beautiful little girl he'd ever laid eyes on, from his home village. She sold ducks, both live and strung up like garlands. The Lithuanian shared his fleeting memory of her again and again, to anyone who would listen, so often that one of the studio founders sent a scout to the village, with virtually no useful details about the girl. The paleness of her eyes and her dainty feet, and somehow, they found her. They brought her back to California, fed her and taught her to pose on a soundstage in the desert, where they'd recently established the Imagination Ranch. And before long, the 2D film became live-action, and the girl was formally cast as the little English rose: Wendy. I don't know what her name was before, but when she left the studio, it was Renata Revere.

And after that? I'm not so sure, which I'm ashamed to say, given how obsessed with Wendy I always was. She was in just enough films that she might appear on Turner Classics or some lineup of forgotten mid-century comedies once in a blue moon. I can recall a poster of her with a chimp. Did the chimp talk? I couldn't say. She must have lived well, surely, but didn't become so famous that anyone outside the studio, the park, the rabid adult fandom would know her by name.

When we reach the top of the stairs, the door within the tree trunk, Brendan stops and pushes some hair from my face.

"Just a few more weeks." He kisses my glove.

"A few more weeks," I say back. An echo.

I take off my shoes to climb up the temple room. It's the first of twelve rooms in the Caves of Chirakan, not counting the large central rotunda with all the lava, just beyond the platform where guests board. In this one, three sections of wall, encasing a track, are parked partially inside one another so that they can expand and contract like a telescope, stretching to give riders the vertigo feeling of ascending to a height and watching, ahead of them, a backlit vista of ancient Mesoamerica spread out before their eyes. But it's also—quite accidentally—an Ames room, a type of optical illusion where a person's size becomes distorted as they walk upward on a gentle incline; the room gets bigger and the person gets smaller, while the show scene remains unchanged. A static box, at least to the brain. This ride is a smooth machine, and it rarely breaks down; if it does, this trick of the eye can be especially disorienting. We've been trained to only ever evacuate guests from behind, despite there being more convenient side exits which have been carved into stalactite and guano shapes, all made of fiberglass and fire-resistant resin. Getting them to file out in reverse saves them from seeing someone, perhaps someone in Lycra shorts, suddenly appear huge to the naked eye, and to break the careful illusion. It would be too jarring for words.

From around the bend in the track, back from where I came, I hear the faint din of conversation. They haven't let anyone in, have they? The other operators aren't here. The music isn't even on.

I retrace my steps, past several stone renderings of enormous cobras whose eyes blink every few seconds, past a dry ice valve hidden behind wild vines, past a Snickers wrapper which I hadn't seen before. My knees click when I lunge to grab it.

Back at the loading platform, there's no one in sight. False alarm. Hearing things. The garbage can is gone. Had it been there before? I mash the wrapper into my pocket.

At the far end of the platform, I see movement. The thick queue-rope made of coarse bristles and shiny black gunk is swaying.

"Hello?" I call out. Nothing.

I check my watch. Half-past. Andrea or Hery should be here by now. Maybe it was one of them making the noise. I start to call out again, but stop short. I've recently become a little bit wary of echoes. Lately I've noticed that they behave a bit differently here, in the park, than elsewhere.

I noticed it first on a maintenance call. It was a flume pump. It was out of action in the Barbary Coast Merchant Mania log ride one afternoon in October, when the Colonial Outpost crew were running emergency drills somewhere beneath the archipelago. Over walkie-talkies, a breathless manager instructed me where boots could be found, wrenches fitted to the troublesome valve, and instructions for the dual keypad and needle, which would let me onto the access pathway that runs alongside the ride. I'd never been to an area of this security level. There was the keycard, which reads both a digital lock and your skin's own signature—something more reliable than a fingerprint, something in the carbon you shed—the needle, which requires that extra bit of dexterity, then an additional access code.

Over the walkie-talkie: "*khhch* code is three—you taking note of this?"

"Yes."

"*khhch* Three-seven-seven-oh."

"Three seven-seven-oh."

"*khhch* This is classified as a minor fix and we'll need to reclassify it if you require additional assistance. You understand?"

"I understand."

"*khhch* No one likes extra paperwork, rookie."

"I understand."

The music was shut off in there, and I heard the sounds that all those limbs make on their own, when they move. A chorus of gentle clicking. They were old bots, all of them, back then, almost all of them animals. I saw how their eyes didn't meet one another's, even when they were meant to be in conversation. That's something nice about the new-gen bots, I suppose. They're programmed for basic facial recognition. They make eye contact with the guests.

Even though I was walking in the water, ankle-deep, encased in a tunnel of plaster tree roots of dark mahogany, I felt that sickening feeling of seeing something from an angle it's not meant to be seen from. I kept my eyes down, made my way to the pump, tucked behind the flume's rubbery casing, where moss camouflaged drains and brakes, and did my work quickly. It was a size L child's T-shirt, still with soggy tags attached, that had clogged the pump. I tried my best not to think about the lights coming on as I yanked the thing out.

Before I left, though, I found a gap, just behind the curvature of the water track that guests floated on, where a gap didn't belong. Dead space between flume and maintenance walkway; too much space. But my flashlight revealed nothing about what this space might be for. There were footprints there, though. Dusty. I gently lowered myself, and then the scene of the bots in the room was truly askew, which made my stomach twist a little: I could see the wire mechanisms beneath each hare and catfish, and where they melded with the wall. I shuddered and kept my eyes down.

I suddenly became distracted by the sound of rushing air, and some kind of echo. There must have been a vent running far below, to ground level, or even to the C&C corridors, because I thought, for only a second or two, that I heard a female voice. She was speaking to someone, and was given a response, though that was much more faint. And somewhere in that cascade of soft sounds was a pattern I couldn't quite decipher. A series of clicks—scratching clicks, as if coming from a walkie-talkie. I'll never know if I imagined it, but I thought, perhaps, faintly, there was a different female voice. From the little I could make out, it sounded a bit like my own.

Now, waiting for Andrea and Hery, I decide that I'll check in on the Fairytale Grove during my lunch break. It was the first of the lands to be properly closed off some weeks ago. Entirely shut. The rides go unridden, the ground goes untrodden. I don't know when they'll start dismantling it. I wonder where all the set pieces—small, frightened gnomes, ultraviolet lights, candy-colored cars with the weighted fronts, swaths of scrim and mesh—will go. The Imagination Ranch, the desert, probably. It makes me sad to think about, so sometimes I just ride the rides, even if I'm not supposed to. We know how to boot them up. Brendan and I do it every so often, but I haven't told him that I do it almost every day, alone. Sometimes I ride the Peter and Wendy ride four times in a row.

I need to run checks on the rest of the rooms in Caves. Engine grease tends to build up along the base of the ziggurat. After the guests arrive, I'll be here for four hours and fifteen minutes, then I'll take my forty-five-minute break. After that are Action Plan duties: today they involve doing passes through the closed attractions. No time to spook myself.

I return on my course along the track, where monkey idols and Easter Island heads loom over me in the dark. I flick the manual control switch for the green laser that illuminates from the cobras' blinking eyes—all good. Ten minutes later I'm searching for the haptic patch that interacts with the vehicles' chassis at the Pit of Immortality, a 3D-projected black vortex that's meant to hypnotize the holy cave's intruders, luring them into the land of the dead and forcing the cars to vibrate in a push-pull, levitated way. It's great, when it works. But more often than not guests simply get a little break in motion, and watch a black blob fluctuate on a screen for ten seconds. I hit a button on my control panel and the additional sound effect overlay kicks into life: There's an imitation Wilhelm scream and the scurry-scurry sound of rat claws on earth, and a punch in the score that's playing, a quick crescendo into an eastern scale.

I watch the swirling of the black vortex on the wall. My head feels heavy, and my mouth feels dry. I keep thinking about the voices I heard, just now, the swinging dangle of rope. I can't tell which is more comforting: the idea that I'm alone, or that someone else is here with me, just out of sight.

Think happy thoughts, I tell myself, violently.

Sent from:
Catherine Moser-Towe
2227 W. Catalina Blvd.
Los Angeles, CA 90027

Hello. All right. Where to start?

I'm only writing back because I'm very worried. Not about the new land opening, but about you and . . . the state you're in?

The kicker is that it's taken a great deal of therapy to practice <u>not</u> worrying about you. To break that habit I've had for the last, what . . . twenty years? So all I'll say is that nothing bad is going to happen at the park. If that's what you meant. I mean, you'd know better than me, but in the absence of you giving me any actual reason to be concerned, I'm going to tell you to take a breath and make sure you're socializing and getting exercise and generally being well.

Also, to sound like Mom for a second: They don't want to get sued. Right? So whatever you're worried about . . . like, no one's going to get actually, physically hurt? Can't you just tell me what you're talking about?

And there we go! Here I am! Writing out words of comfort when (1) it's not my responsibility to calm you down, and (2) I don't even know what you're specifically worried about. You can't just fish for concern like that. I'm not going all conspiracy theory with you, even if that's your preferred mode of coping. I have a life. Shocking, I know! And I've actually been looking forward to the land opening. As tacky as a theme park premiere party is, it's the most glam I've had in a while. We've had in a while, I should say.

And Callie is bringing her stylist round to our new place to try on some park-friendly looks. Like Callie Petrisko, the star of Nebuland. Did I mention how we've gotten really close in the last couple of years? Shared trauma, maybe, between her and Declan. Hah. I shouldn't joke about that, throw that word around. But production on the movie sounded rough. You've probably heard.

Should I go ahead and pretend that you asked me about that? About my life? Like any normal brother would? Should I assume that this frantic letter is a veiled attempt to reconnect with your sister after drifting apart for, like, years? Sure! Let's do that.

I'm great. Declan is great. We just moved and I already feel so much better than I did in the old place. I can't remember how much you and I spoke while we were there, but it was so high up in the hills that entire days would go by without me hearing or seeing another person, or even hearing cars. You couldn't walk anywhere (I know! That's just LA, right? Har fucking har, people love telling me that), but at least now I can open a window and feel like I'm somewhere, geographically, on a map.

Not that we're supposed to be opening windows. Are you seeing the news where you are? Is any of it visible from the desert? No, you're too far out, but the fires are everywhere here, little ones scattered, mostly coming from the north. There's the big uncontainable one up in the Bay. Part of it hit Cotati yesterday. The place where we took driver's ed burned down. Tragic, right?

Mom and Dad feel safe by the water, but all the houses in Benicia feel weirdly old, and made of practically tinder. When did you last see them? I'm asking that from a place of real curiosity, not trying to be shitty and passive-aggressive. You were the one who insisted on handwritten letters, and if I was typing this I would have been able to delete it. Anyway, you should call them.

It's amazing how we just get used to these things. The sky turning orange for a whole week. Whole towns evacuating. Losing power for days on end. Maybe people will be flooding the desert soon, like where you are, where the Imagination Ranch is (lol), starting little communes, away from anything that can go up in smoke.

Well, in the process of writing this I've become less annoyed. So, to summarize: I'm not changing plans unless you give me specifics about what could possibly happen in the park. And if you're being dramatic as some kind of ice-breaker in order to catch up . . . well, don't fucking do that. Just tell me what's going on with you. That would be nice.

—Catherine

P.S. I forgot to say, we joined a church. Long story.

CHAPTER THREE

My happy thought is about someone nice I met, once. The night before I first stepped foot in the park. Yes. That was a good one.

I'd felt a little funny then, too, in a budget motel five miles from where I now stand. I thought I was being watched then, and I was right. It was some men down at the bar, at ground level, on the other side of the reception desk. I knew I shouldn't try to buy a drink because I was only eighteen and didn't have ID on me, but the bartender didn't ask for it, and I only wanted one anyway. A beer, and then later I'd order Italian. Maybe a calzone, which I'd never had, and had only heard about on TV. I'd been thinking about it for hours.

There were four men, two very drunk, one on his phone, and the other looked tired. The two loud ones wanted to talk to me. I didn't like it, and knew the best way to get to the end of talking was to start doing it, to seem like I didn't mind. They asked me where I was from.

Nebraska.

They asked me why I was here.

An invitation from the studio founder himself.

They asked me if I liked to lie to guys like them, who were just trying to be nice.

I said it was just a joke.

They said something about shaking my hand on the way out the door, then added "Oh man! Never mind!" and cackled. That was their joke. It was before I had my gloves.

I looked over my shoulder when I got back to my own door, upstairs, on the second floor overlooking a parking lot. The walls of the motel were painted either red or white, candy-cane colors. I tried not to let the idea of rowdy men put me on edge. I'd wanted to eat and plan my first day in the park. I didn't want anything tainting that. But sure enough, there was a knock on my door.

I crept on the softest parts of my feet, the sides. Through the warped peephole I saw someone I didn't recognize right away, because he hadn't caught my attention. The man from the bar who'd looked so tired. Looking closer now, I saw he was plenty awake, and that the bags under his eyes may have just been part of his coloring. Someone in my seventh-grade class was diagnosed with rickets, and their eyes were just like that.

"Sorry," his muffled voice came through the door, before I'd had time to open it. "You don't have to . . . I just wanted to apologize for—"

I slid the chain away and opened the door a crack.

"I'm sorry, I just don't know those guys well and they were being dicks."

I didn't know what to say. "I mean, it wasn't . . ." I trailed off to nothing.

"I'm just with them on a work trip—" He gestured to the banister. "I'm just being paranoid. I was about to go to bed, and I just wanted to make sure no one had like . . . followed you, or . . ."

He rubbed his face. There was color in his cheeks now. He laughed at himself.

"Wow, now I sound creepy. Hey, never mind! Sorry to bother

you." He got several paces down the walkway, almost to the ice machine.

"Wait," I called out.

He stopped.

"Do you want a calzone?"

He stayed in my room that night, on top of the covers. He told me about his recent promotion, given to him when he was interviewing for altogether new jobs in a different state. His wife convinced him to stay, just for another year. He said he got so miserable on the new team that his wife moved out, and I told him that I bet it was more complicated than that. He said yeah, it was. They'd gotten married when they were still in college. Neither of them could remember why.

We looked through the movies on the TV. *Singin' in the Rain* and *The Day After Tomorrow* and something called *Frosh Island*. The one with the plane crash and the island hijinks. He said he'd watch it if he knew there would be cannibalism in the first ten minutes. I said I'd never walked out of a movie theater before. He said that a Milk Dud once pulled out a barely loose molar when he was a kid, but he was afraid of getting in trouble so he didn't say a thing. He just let his mouth fill with blood until his mother looked over at him and screamed, and that's the only time he'd left a movie theater with the movie still playing.

We talked like that, about small things, inconsequential things, until he touched my arm and told me I felt kind of buttery. I said "eew" and then "thanks" and he didn't try anything more than that. In the end I'd had to lurch up to kiss him. We did that for a while, but nothing more. He seemed distracted by something I couldn't pinpoint. I asked him how old he was, and he answered twenty-eight, and when he asked me the same I said twenty-three, even though that sounded wrong, and I did mental math about my birth year that I couldn't quite finish. Then I flipped onto my stomach and he did the same and we both fell asleep.

I woke at 8 a.m., a full two hours later than when I'd planned to wake. He was on his phone. I barely caught the end of the conversation—a "Thanks." That was all. I assumed I shouldn't ask about it, and I stayed quiet until he decided to say something.

"Hey, this is gonna sound really deranged." He was angling his head at me strangely, I think to keep his morning breath off me. He pushed his hair back. It looked like it had grown two inches from the night before. "But after that one calzone I wanted another calzone. I can't explain it." He looked gravely serious. "I don't normally like Italian food all that much. I honestly kind of think it's overrated. But I just called and told them to deliver it here, but I can absolutely call back and change it to my room."

I smiled into my pillow. "Are you crazy?" I said, barely audible through the fluff. "Like I'd let you escape with my half of a morning calzone."

While I walk the rest of Caves of Chirakan, I try to recapture that exact feeling as best I can. I've never told Brendan about that man. I've always kept it for myself. After eating with him, I had gotten to the park at 9:30 a.m., the perfect time, because what I didn't know then was that every park guest has the same idea about getting there when the gates open at 8. It's a madhouse, those first few minutes. Yeah you don't have to wait in the queues, but that's really just good for the first ride you hit. It's not worth the hot, rushing bodies along the midway so early. So the man who'd seemed tired did me a favor. I wished I could tell him, but I never saw him again.

I've always been lucky that way, with men. I've only been involved with very kind, very clever guys who, if nothing else, listen when I talk and can identify when I'm hungry and can recognize unkindness when they see it up close. I suppose I've really only had two boy-friends, in addition to the man at the motel and some high school friends who got a little moody and handsy, but they have all cleared a bar that I now know many men don't clear. And I was lucky enough to be born without that receptor—that radar—for whatever radiance bad men can emit that pulls so many sensible, healthy people into their orbits.

I think it surprises people. I see their disbelief when I say that I've never really had any bad boyfriends, because I know what those people think when they look at my hands. They jump to conclusions, a horror story. They think some terrible man must have done that, but they're wrong.

It was a good man who did that to me.

———————

I traverse the park aboveground, playing back my favorite maneuvers with guests. If a kid doesn't want to buckle their seatbelt, you tell him that the Sorcerer of Chirakan is crabby and won't come out of his tomb if there's an unbuckled child anywhere nearby. The ride would be super-boring without the Sorcerer; it'd be like Planet Song, the musical ride for babies that everyone hates. (I didn't say that last part and I actually love Planet Song. I cry every time the Mongolian fiddler shoots fireworks over the Taj Mahal at the song's climax.) The kid will let you buckle him up quick. The mother usually winks at you.

Outside the start of the Caves queue, I can sense the sun accumulating on the packed, earthen paths throughout this land, the Colonial Outpost. Some plants are wilting, and a few of the huge tropical leaves have dropped onto the ground. They have a tortured quality, and I kick them out of sight, into the carefully manicured brush where you can peek through and see the part of Kipling's Katamarans where a baby elephant and a young Bengali girl splash each other. Maybe I can imagine that water phobia, after all. I wouldn't want to peek right now. I wouldn't want to see the girl's bottom half.

I reach the entrance to the haunted house. It's still open, technically. But just looking at it so underpopulated feels wrong. No, more than wrong. Sacrilegious. When I started out, the wait for the haunted house was often two hours or more. Before the firings, the haunted house crew were always cliquey and self-righteous because the one ghost pirate (the one with the big belly) was sort of an emblem of the adult park fandom. Over 25s with season passes always get colorful tattoos of him, and those guests seem to think C&C are dying to see them. We're not allowed to tell them we don't want to see their tattoos, and that they should put their ankles and their bellies away. We certainly wouldn't be allowed to show guests any of our tattoos, if we had them.

Beyond the house is a little model souk. A maze, meant to be Morocco or Algeria, positioned on the gentle incline of a hillside patch, roped off from the curious hands of the guests. If you stepped into it the reddened walls would reach halfway to your knees. Small mechanical merchants and little tin animals swivel through the maze, willy-nilly, automated to turn around only if they collide with a dead end or with one another. I think the idea is that watching it from above, at this scale, makes you feel like you might be riding a flying carpet, an oddly executed concept if true. It's been here since the beginning. The Beignet Grotto stands where the Colonial Outpost and the entrance to the big midway meet, farther from the lake than the gates to the other lands. It's empty, but still smells like caramelized sugar and wood smoke. The sun beats down on my neck when I bend over to look at a trail of red leading round back. I squint. It almost looks like a stream of oil. But the stream is moving uphill, toward the beignet hut. The one where we stave off tropical diseases.

There are thousands of them: tiny red insects climbing over each other in a rush to get around to the dense, squat shrubs of the hut's crowd-facing façade, where wrought iron lattices masquerade as nineteenth-century New Orleans, or some other Reconstruction-era Xanadu. They're smaller than ladybugs and bigger than gnats. When I squat, I see one vibrant red pouch emerging from each hard little body. Just by looking at them I can imagine how they'd sound when stepped on. I can't identify them, though, but that might just be yet one more alien feature of this state, and this coast. There are things about California that I'm still surprised by, even after all these years, like the small earthquakes that no one cares about.

But as I follow their trail, I understand where they must be headed; I step over the low hedge and follow the hut's lake-facing wall to its far edge. Tucked near my feet are a small hydrant, camouflaged in green paint, a gas meter, and—yes, there . . .

We need to trap the mosquitos, to protect from an encephalitis outbreak, and for the simple nuisance of them, especially at sunset. These mesh nets release carbon dioxide, just like the guests' countless exhalations, which attracts the mosquitos. These nets also put the insects to death, and then the sacks are collected and brought into some lab to be tested for a range of viruses. Normally we wouldn't coat the park in insecticide, so if there's something really nasty going on with the bugs, we bring in cats, small predatory birds, even new, more aggressive ducks for the lake. Of course there are complications there. A cat slaughtering one of the ducklings, say. We offer a free park pass to whichever child might have seen the violence unfold, just after their parents sign a few forms, but normally CCTV catches those feline mishaps before anyone else can spot them.

"Oh wow . . . ," I find myself saying. "You've really done a number."

The tiny red insects coat the outside of the mesh net, like a moving shell. Beneath that, I see that they're mixed in with the leafier bodies of both mosquitos and mosquito-eaters, which I've always been frightened of even though people love to tell you how friendly they are. Deeper still is a mélange of thorax and humming, feasting, death, a compost smell. It's been left here God knows how long, despite the remaining crew, who I know are diligent and driven by their Action Plan, though I guess not as much as I am driven by mine.

I arc my arm very high above the mass and pinch the fixture connecting it to its post. No one likes anyone stepping on their toes, workwise. But it's the least I can do to keep the park's dignity for these last days.

I approach the large garbage cans concealed by gothic latticework beside the ice cream parlor. From here there's a flickering in the corner of my eye, and I can make out the shine of the entrance gates. The sun always bounces off their enamel in a funny way at this time of day. The gates are a long way down, and a small figure is hovering just beyond them.

I take a step back. It looks like a child, separated from its mother, but I recognize her as the very old woman from before. I'm very quiet, and I don't move a muscle, but I watch her turn and look down the grand, palatial pathway, to the spot where I stand. She looks like a doodle, legs of quick single lines, wide set, no hips, all of her obscured by layers of cotton and the familiar warping of the park. Little illusions in every curve and corner. But I feel certain she's looking at me.

Then she's gone, and I've lost track of time again.

I'm desperate for shade. Casita Claw will do.

I get there via the unnamed Edwardian section, past the gently angled hillock meant to be Seurat's *Grande Jatte*. I think, sadly, that without the cast members or guests acting as those straight-backed ladies and loungers, it's just a lawn. Across the water there's that one small archipelago where punting boats used to take guests for brief journeys. There are no boats anymore.

Zoetrope Alley. One of the more recent lands, built as a celebration of the studio's earliest cartoons. They include it in Brendan's circuit every so often, even though his prince was hardly one of the earliest (he was a Technicolor-era prince, with sea-green jodhpurs) and he said that even children seemed confused to see him.

Casita Claw is the walk-through home of one of the oldest cartoon villains, although villains don't stay villains long in the park. Their faces go on T-shirts, and their bent, towering frames become porcelain saltshakers. Exhausted parents play our movies on a loop for their infants, in their homes all across the world, and a baby can't tell a good guy from a bad one.

"Hello?" I call tentatively, as I duck my way in, seeking out my favorite patch of shade. There's no reply. Why would there be? This section has been closed off for weeks.

Brendan's prince slays a dragon in the final act of his movie. It crashes to the moat of the castle with a well-timed lightning bolt. The prince wakes the sleeping princess with a kiss on the hand and some magic gibberish words from her fairy friends. A happy ending. But the story was adapted from a fifteenth-century Bavarian fable, and it doesn't even have a prince. In it, a beast tries to sire an heir with a local maiden through both cunning and violence, but villagers fight it off using a wad of hexed sheep's wool. There is an addendum to the original text that's longer than the story itself, about whether the villagers were allowed into heaven, given their use of witchcraft. The beast is described as a huge and devilish marmot, the size of a house. The studio turned him into a dragon, and now he's sold as a plush toy in the shops by the exits, and outside the Miss Muffet Cruise. During certain seasonal nighttime spectaculars, that dragon glitters and sways on invisible wheels driving around the lake's perimeter. In the final act, it—along with a stadium-length sea serpent and a fast-talking capybara, from their respective franchises—leads the crowd in a round of nondenominational carols.

I touch the walls as I walk, and think of the thousands of children who've touched the same spot over the years. An image comes to mind: photos of Callie Petrisko with young fans, blocked off from the red carpet they set up leading into Nebuland, that day that it opened and she rode the lagoon ride. She squats and poses beside the kids, patiently waiting for their hapless child fingers to press the right buttons, her smile never wobbling into inauthenticity, the gloss on her lips remaining perfectly set. She had a mole a few inches from the tip of her chin, and occasionally she'd cover it with makeup, but not that day. Where have I seen that image? Would it have been published in magazines, after everything that happened?

I pass through painted plastic molds of Cornelius's home belongings, a pile of old newspapers dropped sloppily beside an old-timey television, beset with dials and antennae. Yes, Cornelius Claw is a villain, but more of a foil for the studio's core animal pals. He's a mean old cat, but it's been a long time since the studio released a cartoon of him being truly cruel. He likes to sabotage picnics with chili peppers, or dress as a lady-cat to confuse the studio's hero-dog and rend a rift between him and his wife, a curvaceous but pious goose named Gwendolyn. Gwendolyn has long, feminine lashes, a shorthand of which appears around the park: two lashes at a diagonal.

))

This marking can be found in the concrete walkways between lands, in patterns around Fairytale Grove, in stained glass and carved into gazebos. A little nod to the sweet, motherly goose who gets into scrapes, incites wild jealousy in Cornelius and the dog, but ultimately honks sense into both men, lovingly and with a wink.

The mischief that Cornelius makes is nothing serious. No blood spilled, no war crimes. In the Zoetrope Alley, which is entirely overlaid in the style of the studio's earliest shorts, you can visit the homes of main characters. There are three homes: Cornelius's, Gwendolyn's, and the dog's. I like Cornelius's best. Casita Claw.

There are recesses, alcoves, odd nooks, the kind you don't get anywhere else in the park, because here everything worth looking at is roped off. For viewing only. (Don't worry, Cornelius has an interactive treehouse with a slide just outside.) Just past the room with the television there is a trapeze and two parallel cords, at the end of which hang gleaming rings, all tied to a huge beam at the highest point of the ceiling. This is where your cartoon friends do calisthenics.

Cobwebs hide in the corners. You'd need to look close to find them. Along the far wall there's a shelf that holds Cornelius's knickknacks: cats in terra-cotta, imitation bronze, a cat as the Venus de Milo, and a cat as da Vinci's *Vitruvian Man*. I feel a sudden call toward the kitchen, where I'm met with a hanging gridiron, a frying pan, and a waffle maker oozing plastic batter, as if to say, "You just missed them! They would have made you breakfast if only they knew you were coming!"

I find the large, penned-off square toward the back of Cornelius's home that used to be the ball pit. Now it's empty, and its floor is a polished concrete, that same concrete that must be living under every surface of this house. I won't stay here for long.

I wish I'd gotten something other than a bitter croissant from the stand where the path around the lake turns off to the cluster of smaller attractions behind the unnamed Edwardian section, Spring-time Canyon and the train, but I slide to the floor, rest my back against a wall, and try to recharge. I let my mind wander.

I heard they're making a live-action version of Brendan's movie, his prince and the dragon who is no longer a marmot and no longer a sexual predator. They're probably filming in Hong Kong soon, on those new soundstages beside the new park. I wonder who will play the prince, and how Brendan will feel about it. The original only came out two or three years after *Peter and Wendy* did, so the studio might give it a fresh and modern feel. In the original, you can feel that half inch of mid-century transgression—*Peter and Wendy*'s score is entirely choral, women warbling in states of dainty ecstasy, which also comes across as a little jingle-ish, like they might be selling you women's hair gels and instant coffee while you're watching those children fly into the night sky. Or maybe it's that it's Christmassy, even though it's not a Christmas movie. In the movie with Brendan's prince, there's a song where he answers riddles from a fat sea nymph, and the song she sings is pure Dusty Springfield.

I let the song play inside my head, and hum it a little bit, and all at once I feel that musing must be finished. I don't bother look-ing at my watch. I get up too fast—something shoots down my hamstring, and I steady myself on the thick porthole glass. I shake out the leg. I hear footsteps outside. The sound of someone's tread changing speed.

Shit. I'm not supposed to be here. But then no one else is, either.

I duck very slightly to get through the child-sized door leading out, loosening some flecks of paint from the frame as I go.

A man steps out from behind the carousel, some distance away. I don't recognize him.

His hair is either silver or so blond that it's silver in this light. He's wearing a black sweatshirt that looks too small for him. He's holding on to a messenger bag with white knuckles.

He's dragging something behind him with his other hand. Something heavy. I take a few cautious steps in his direction, nothing to seem like I'm approaching *him*, just perhaps his path ahead. I imagine all the ways I could startle him—rolling my ankle on the ground, stepping on a twig, sneezing. But none of it comes to pass, I'm good at being quiet, but I must have summoned it into being; he must have heard my thoughts. He stares straight at me.

I stop, without meaning to, and he starts to close the distance between us. One foot in front of the other.

I slip away into another place altogether while he comes toward me. It starts with the sudden, loud thought—so loud I hear it above the sound of my suddenly frantic heart: Callie Petrisko would have made a great princess in the live-action remake. Those eyes! That mischievous point to her chin. She would have nailed it!

Callie could have worn huge princess skirts, but also some good boots, so that she could fight and tumble. She would have done both so well—the damsel-ing and the ass-kicking!

I so badly wish I could un-watch the Callie Petrisko video. I hated seeing her so scared on that boat. That first time I saw it, I hadn't known what I was watching. Brooke called me into her room, pulled out her laptop, and simply pressed play. I hardly knew Brooke at that point, and I didn't know that she liked this kind of thing. *Macabre* was the word that she used.

The man is not smiling, the man is not slowing, the man is almost in front of me now. I go back, to where I was.

I watched it, the video, there with Brooke, all six minutes. I did not yet know that Callie Petrisko was dead. Of course we all know that now. That's what makes the video so cruel. That we did nothing. That we couldn't have known what would come next. That she'd set herself on fire outside the park gates at dawn.

Sent from:
PO Box 5538
43824 20th St W
Newberry Springs, CA 92365

I can't respond to all that + you're right, I should have been
more specific. But after or during + before you go off on the
whole I'm-being-over-the-top, I-was-always-the-special-
child-with-the-unusual-brain+it-messed-up-your-childhood
thing, I urge you to put aside your therapist's voice just for the
duration of this letter.

There are a few of us here together in this section of the
Imagination Ranch that no one has ever been to before.
You'd never guess it was connected to any of the other work
spaces. Part of it is this derelict hotel + then this weird stretch
of buildings that have these empty conference rooms + then
there's just desert. They have us sleeping in the hotel, if that's
what you wanna call it. They gave us this memo about how
we're here for training. None of us are super senior, but also
none of us need training.

It didn't take long for us to talk + figure out that each of us
saw some very strange shit happen after the new animatronics
were made. You know the super-realistic ones that they've
been cramming into the old rides + that Nebuland is gonna be
full of?

One of the guys from the Hong Kong team saw something
unsettling in a proof-of-concept video that we got. We didn't
know there was a concept to prove. Like we thought we'd be
developing the new bots, in the desert,
we always do. But no, this whole fleet of them were already
made. They told us they were manufactured for the foreign
parks, with a contractor outside of the US + they wouldn't
answer more questions + management was just being cagey
about it. It was fucking weird. We're the developers +

they weren't answering questions about development. Again, I'm not all that senior, but still.

But the other weird thing this one guy saw in that proof-of-concept video was someone he had studied with at art school in Singapore. Some girl, lady, whatever, about his age. He knew her + in the video, she's working on the skin of this big new bot + it was her. The <u>bot</u> was her.

The guy told me that he thinks it was made for demonstration purposes only, like, what a quirky fun thing for this video, the artists get to make themselves in bot-form, as practice or something. A cutesy PR exercise. Who knows. So she's doing this, in this video in a studio we don't know about, one I don't recognize + she's not doing a lot of talking. She's only on screen for 10, 15 seconds max + they don't talk to her or anything. She's like, background. B-roll. But this guy who's here with me, here in this compound, he says that she looks off + that when he knew her she had really bad insomnia, but she was embarrassed to talk about it + would always lie about it + by day three or four of her not sleeping she'd get this look in her eyes, but when it got really bad she'd need to go away, to this rich aunt's house + she had come back all full of amphetamines + tranquilizers +
it was just kind of a cycle like that. It happened a few times.

Anyway, he says he sees that in her face for just the briefest moment in the video, the look she used to get right before she'd need to be taken away + seeing that, on the video, it makes him sort of shiver. It prompts him to reach out. He hasn't been in touch for years. So he calls the last number he has for her + the woman's aunt picks up + it turns out the woman, his old friend, had died in a plane crash. <u>Died</u>. Just a few months earlier, right after the proof-of-concept video would have been shot.

+ the first thing he thinks to ask is if she'd been sleeping well + the aunt is confused, but says she'd been treated for that a long time ago. She slept good, in the last years of her life.

So naturally this guy gets curious + looks up the plane crash + it turns out it was one of those tiny planes + it slammed into the side of a mountain en route north, to like, British Columbia, despite there being no high winds on the day. He searches all of this on his work computer + within two days he's here, here in the desert, given no reason or assignment other than to "liaise with QA" + plan the rollout.

Okay fine, so someone wants to reconnect with a girl from his past + finds out she's dead + he spirals a little bit + finds himself on a mismanaged work assignment. Maybe that's not too weird to you. Mainly at the start of all this, I'm not gonna lie, I was mostly just confused + pissed off because I thought we were developing the bots + they waited till the last minute to tell us they'd been outsourced, like, almost finished by the time we even got the memo. They called me in to some late-round motion capture day. As a DevOps guy I always get to those early, really early, like six thirty or seven most of the time.

When they wheeled those bots in . . . I don't know how to describe it. It was like looking down at a compass + the needle is spinning all around. It felt like I wasn't where I thought I was anymore. I don't know how to describe it. I already said that.

When I arrived, I saw that a small group was already there. I don't know why but something was telling me to stay quiet. The room is massive, like the Citizen Kane warehouse kind of massive + I pull up a chair sort of in the middle + watch Kendra + Nattson, these corporate blow-hards + some of their team, go in + out of the little display room where the new bot models were kept. It's weird that it's not anyone else from my team, or engineers, but the Kendra + Nattsons of the studio. Seems like one of us should have been there.

I'm sitting so that I don't look like I'm spying on anything, like

I could have absolute deniability about sort of not making myself known, not saying hello. I'm just on my phone, but of course I'm watching + then I see this man + woman come in + I don't recognize them at first, but now I realize that they're the mom + dad from one of the studio's afternoon shows. Some kiddie sitcom. The two of them narrate one of the storybook rides. I don't know their names. I can hear some talk about keeping a few of the old animatronics intact in the Fairytale Grove, because anything too realistic will scare children. It's a discussion that's been going around for a long time. But that's just the thing: They won't scare the kids. The kids will think the robots have been replaced with actors. That's how real they are, Catherine.

But they must have experimented, made models of this TV mom + dad, because these actors are going into the display room + then the woman comes out + the team from corporate are behind her. They're close, at first. I notice someone is always touching her elbow. Then they take their eyes off of her for one minute, one fucking minute + she goes straight toward a wall. She hits her face on it, like she didn't even see it was there + there's this horrible clunk + it's not like she'd been running at it + smashed her skull, it wasn't gruesome like that, it was almost worse in a way. She just walked, at normal speed, toward a concrete wall +
hit her face, didn't flinch, didn't cry out. Then she turned back, a scrape on her face that started bleeding a little bit + then started bleeding more + then she just started pacing. Just pacing.

That's it? Maybe you're saying. You saw a clumsy lady go into a room + come out pacing? A few things. The first is that the other guy didn't come out. At all. I waited. I waited till after they left. I didn't see him again. + second, I couldn't stop thinking about you. About when I got to know Declan, on set however many years ago, fucking Frosh Island. How smug he was that he befriended a lowly production, runner, smoothie-

deliverer, set bitch like me. The runner with the weed. How
it must have humbled him. Seeing that woman pace, I was
thinking about how he always talks about that party I took him
to, when you were in town, how he saw you for the first time +
he says that's the moment he fell in love with you. Maybe you
enjoy that story the way he tells it. I don't know. Because what
I remember about that night is that you were outside on that
shitty deck, in the cold, pacing. You were nervous for the party
to begin. He thought it was some cutesy trait of yours, that you
were nervous about meeting <u>him</u> + every time I tried to tell
him, "She's always paced, since she was a kid, it's not nerves,
it's just that she likes to be in motion, especially on the phone,"
he didn't listen. He thought it was about him, but I knew you
were pacing because you're you. I shouldn't have let him talk
to you that night, is what I keep thinking. Play the protective
brother role. I bet he's the reason you're not willing to listen to
what I'm saying now. He's probably telling you that I've gone off
the deep end. That it's got to do with me getting a cushy job with
the park + abandoning <u>cinema</u>. Something stupid + European
like that. Is Ireland Europe?

Anyway that afternoon TV show with the mom + dad actors
got canceled. Gone.

Wait, another thing. I'm thinking about that shooting at The
Standard last year. That was a Nebuland actor, right? Maybe
that's a reach. Half of Hollywood was in Nebuland.

So we're here, in the desert + no one knows what we're
supposed to be doing + we all are kind of disposable + we
all saw things + talked about it. Like, there aren't henchmen
keeping us here. I know where my car is + everything, but it
still feels fucked up. We all have this feeling that something
bad would happen if we really tried to leave, so we haven't
tried it yet, but I can feel that point fast approaching.

So, Cath, my argument is: If these bots are making people's
brains go haywire or something, if they're making people . .

. I don't know . . . behave dangerously? then don't go. I keep thinking about the plane crash + also the other thing, the blood trickling out of that woman's head. I'll give you this: When I wrote the first letter, I was agitated. I hadn't slept, I was dehydrated + we'd all been sharing these stories of ours. So maybe I did sound dramatic. But I still don't think you should go + if you can't promise me that then at the very least . . . I don't know. Keep Declan away from his bot.

—Bro

PS: What the fuck? A church?

CHAPTER FOUR

W hat's that you've got there?"

The man has an accent, but I can't quite place it. His hair is lank and knotted and there are slivers of gray in his stubble. There's a dot of dried blood on his neck.

"Who are you?"

He doesn't answer. Instead he looks at my hand. "I asked my question first. Why are you holding that?"

I can feel myself looking stiff. I look down at what I'm holding—funny, I'd forgotten I still had it. "This? Just something I found." There are one or two insects crawling up the white sack, still. He's fixed on it, can't quite seem to unlatch his gaze from it, so I keep talking. "I'm taking this to get looked at. We look at sample mosquitos. Just normal protocol, keeping everyone safe." I'm suddenly embarrassed using that word—*everyone*—in front of these empty cartoon homes.

Something is positioned just behind his legs. A garbage can. It's left tracks along the footpath. They're heavy; I've tried to move one on my own and never managed it.

"Do you work here?"

"Yes," he says.

"I've never seen you. Do you work with Sam?"

He looks at the garbage can. "Yes. Sometimes." Then, seeming to count the pores on my face as he speaks, "But Sam's old. He doesn't always remember me."

"Ah."

"You seem very awake," he says.

"What does that mean?" I start to think that I might know him from somewhere. I can't quite place it.

"Nothing. Never mind."

He seems comfortable there, in the quiet that comes, looking straight at me. He doesn't blink much, and in this light I can't tell what color his eyes are. Blue, green, gray eyes. I wonder if he's the type of man who would correct me if I described their color wrong.

I can't bear the silence.

"I had less coffee than usual this morning. I was actually feeling pretty dopey just now, in the cat house."

He steps closer. I think he's going to say something, but he's watching my face, not as a whole, but its components, one bit after the next. The garbage can makes a painful scream when he comes close, metal on pavement. I wince. That only seems to fascinate him more, and now he's close enough that I could reach out and grab one of his hoodie's drawstrings.

"Sorry," he says. "Awful noise."

I try to chuckle. "I'm a little sensitive to noises. Funny choice to work somewhere with screaming children, right?"

"My wife was the same way," he says. "You should go."

"Oh. Okay."

"We're clearing some of this out."

"Um . . ." Something drops in me. "Are you one of the demolition guys?"

"Demolition?"

"Or whatever you're called. *Disassembly.*" A sting on my arm by my elbow. Two moving red dots. I guess they bite. I brush them off. "I didn't realize it was starting so soon. While guests were still here."

I can feel my skin become hot. It starts to itch.

"Don't worry," he says. "We'll be very quiet."

––––––––––

Where's Brendan? Where the fuck is he?

It's all I can ask. I know I'll be late back at Caves. I'm leaving my other Action Plan duties undone. But he needs to know about the man with the garbage can and the plans to start dismantling Zoe-trope Alley, but the thing about a popular park prince is, there's no telling where he might be.

The train hasn't been running for weeks, and walking down its middle feels like bad luck. It's dark here, but cool, an escape from the heat. I veer closer to the glass. On the other side of it, the mechanical men suspended against a cliff face show their expressions of shock, of fear at their height. Their faces are static, each just a single piece, pivoting gently, though one of them has stopped moving altogether. These models must be close to fifty years old. They're little more than dolls, really. They dangle on there while a flimsy stream of dry ice collects on the floor. There's meant to be more of it. You're meant to see only cloud-top, and a little rascal goat looking down at them from a ledge, but the tan tiles on the floor are clear as day, from where I'm standing. In the back of the panorama, someone's dropped something. A rag. A sock? I slow and look closer: a mask. Eye mask. For sleeping. Some fabric and a strap.

I drag my gloved fingers along the glass as I round the curve into a stretch of dark, holding my breath until I reach the light of the next panorama, just up ahead. It's still meant to be a vision of Nepal, just like the last staged scene, a great wonder of the world, but in the Mesozoic Era. The terrain is flatter, and where once was a pastel-blue painted backdrop of a morning skyline, there's now a ruby-red dusk, and a fleet of triceratops. Nothing in this room is in motion. It's all been turned off. There's just the doom-and-peril soundtrack playing on its loop, and the sound effect of a bird cawing, although it's surely meant to be a pterodactyl.

I pause at it. The spotlights are on, but the bulbs are mostly burned out, so some huge reptilian bodies are hidden in shadow, some illuminated. Their soft, outermost layer of paper-thin rubber ripples beside a vent. You'd never notice if they were all in motion, all together.

No time. I check my walkie once more, and nothing. It's never been connected to Brendan's earpiece anyway. I don't know what I was expecting. Between Nebuland and the canal district (gondolas, piranhas, Channel Tunnel luge) there's an elevated track where a race-car speed ride used to be. It broke down so, so fucking much, but it was almost entirely outdoors, so evacuating guests was easy. There were ladders everywhere, and even an elevator for disabled access, camouflaged as a support column. From there I'll be able to see a huge section. From there I might be able to spot Brendan.

Yeah, I knew about the demolition schedule. So did you. They've been over and over it. How could you have forgotten?

Was that what I wanted to hear from him? No.

There's been a mistake! They're not supposed to start till we're gone, days from now! Out of the way, I'm going to kick some ass!

Not quite that either.

I'll talk to them. Don't worry. There's probably been a misunderstanding. Someone will be able to sort it out. Get back to Caves. Get back to the guests. For you, I'll go in search of answers.

There's a screech of breakage from somewhere in the distance. I come to an abrupt stop, loosening some smooth pebbles along the path. In the silence I try to listen for the wind at either end. There's no light coming through; I'm at the dead center.

This time I feel the vibration before I hear the sound again. And again. The crash. From behind the tunnel walls, the park's outer perimeter. The Cemetery.

These exits, the ones hidden behind the train car's route, are new to me. The key panels don't glow like they do elsewhere, but I make out the small box shape, the key reader, and cross the tracks. I check, instinctively, reflexively, that my needle is still attached to the delicate little loop that holds my keycard.

The thing about the needle is that it's not pushing something deep within the mechanisms of a lock, like you might need to open a smartphone. There's an RFID chip, smaller than I knew chips could be, somewhere in the needle's tip. I always wondered why they did this, and the best I can figure is that it's a fake-out. If someone wants to try to break their way into these more secured parts of the park without knowing about the chips, they'd try to use something long and sharp, poke at a button, and what? It would buy security time to stop them? I suppose I've never seen that, so I don't know. There were more security problems back then, maybe, when they introduced the needles. Is that true? Were any decades particularly turbulent? People aren't such a problem now. I have nothing to complain about.

A needle and skin—skin with that carbon signature—on the keycard, pressed flat. I slip the needle in. Skin on card. Nothing. I try again—waiting for that almost-silent wisp and release. Still, that music behind me—the crooning of a wounded stegosaurus.

I push the door with my shoulder and something gives. One more time—I almost hit the ground. When I regain my balance, I'm in a white corridor that's utterly stark, nothing like our passageways belowground with their calm glow. This one can't have been used often. The trains never broke down.

It's a short passageway. The hall ends, and I'm forced to go left, then there's another end, now right. I'm making that same shape as in Omaha, in the sheds that were once my birth father's, then became Whit's. He never hesitated in taking over that small bit of property from the once-man-of-the-house. Whit loved to say, "You snooze, you lose."

Another door, another push of my body weight, then daylight and nothing I want to see: an expanse of long, tan grass. Barbed wire fencing and a dense row of feeble trees and a taller concrete wall. The Cemetery. We call it that because it's a vacant lot, overgrown with mostly-dead grass and tangled shrubbery, dirt clots and herniated foundation rock, where old props and parts are put if they're not valuable enough to be archived, or sold to collectors with the means to fix them up. It's where bits of the park go to die.

There's a section of wall back here where people usually try to climb into the park. It's one of a handful of spots along the perimeter that's carefully designed to seem ideal to anyone skilled in urban exploration, or to more serious trespassers, as a lure. An ex-marine even tried to hop it once. It's a little bit like the needle, maybe. A trap. There are curated breakages in the wall's blocks, and a seeming absence of cameras. Then, when they've made their way to the packed earth on the other side, smiling security in their plain clothes will be waiting for them, with cuffs. We have a jail cell somewhere underground. It's decorated in the same color scheme as the hotel room inside the castle.

I hear a sound, like a joint clicking under the earth, packed soil unpacking. I almost call out, but hold back—I wait, but hear nothing at all, not even the highway beyond the parking lot. But I can feel it: an unmistakable thickness; a presence.

"Hello!" I allow myself to call out. I'm impatient now. "Is someone there?"

Faint footsteps.

"You can't be back here!" It's an embarrassing half howl.

I know I'm fucking up. This isn't how we were trained to speak on park grounds, especially not to guests who have done wrong. Jesus, how were we trained to do this? When you issue instructions to guests, you must make sure your words are *Clear, Kind, and Final.*

"Let me help you find your way to an exit!" But my voice sounds scared. I'm rattled by the man dragging the trash can, yes, but also by that corridor. Whit. Sheds. All of that. I try to steady myself.

The Cemetery is organized in very loose sections. There are the swaths of seasonal décor—sacks of crispy tinsel and nutcracker heads dripping with plastic icicles, meant for the moving mechanical wall in front of Planet Song. There's the hardware, which is mainly rotors and enormous sections of flooring, the unrecognizable cogs and pistons that go unseen in the park, and then they come here to rust. And elsewhere are various ride cars that have long since been upgraded, some with Gwendolyn's lash marks,)), painted on in flaking gold. There's a very old model of a trolley car and a ski lift and some glass orbs that I can't quite place. I recall the undersea journey in the Land That Wasn't.

"Delph?"

I jump.

It's him. Just him. He's in makeup, the costume with the puffy white sleeves from the waist up. Below that he's in the same jeans that I saw him pull on this morning.

"Jesus Christ, you scared the shit out of me."

"What are you doing back here?" Brendan asks.

"What are *you* doing back here?"

"Looking for leggings. Mine are sweat-stained." He's got one arm inside a steel cage on broken wheels, lined with transparent boxes.

"Gross."

"I think they stopped dry-cleaning. I only noticed like an hour ago." He touches my waist. "Help me look."

"Did you check for more, underground?"

"No," he says, deadpan. He slips his arm out from around me. "No, instead of looking in the large room called *wardrobe* I decided to rummage through a garbage dump like a mile from where I'm supposed to be."

"Okay, fine, but . . . hey, so I think they're starting to take apart Zoetrope Alley."

His arms, under their white puffs of prince blouse, drop to his sides. His fingers start fidgeting with one another. "Who is?"

"I just saw one guy. He was getting started. I think. He looked pretty rough."

"What do you mean, rough?"

"Just, like, definitely not C&C. A contractor, I think."

I watch Brendan watch me, waiting for me to say more, but I can't focus when he's half-prince like this. It feels like a crude joke, and for a moment I think to ask him if he's been walking through the park like that.

"There's no way they're gonna start dismantling stuff when guests are still here, right?" I continue. "Do you think he's, I don't know, not meant to be here?"

"Are you sure it wasn't Sam?" He's looking past me, over my shoulder, back toward the dark entrance to the tunnel and back into the park.

"I know what Sam looks like." I try to sound convincing. "This guy was tall, skinny, dressed kind of weird. Like in sort of teenage clothes. But he was older."

"How old?"

"Hard to say. Like, forty? Forty-five? Fifty?"

"That's kind of a big range."

"Can we just—"

"Wait, and what do you mean *teenage* clothes?"

"Hoodie. Jeans." I find myself making strange pantomime gestures as I go, fanning my hands out toward my thighs.

"If I see Eddie or Jun I'll ask them later. Are they working today?" He doesn't let me answer. "And I mean if it's just Zoetrope Alley I wouldn't worry. . . ."

"Yeah, I know."

"Sad, but . . ." He shrugs. It's no one's favorite spot. Everything out here, in this crescent-shaped hinterland, is static and dull, beige from being baked under a constant Southern California sky, or from gathering a nameless sandy dust that might come from the distant mountains. "I'm done out here. I'll keep looking."

"There's always Peter and Wendy."

"What, his leggings?"

I smile. "Yeah, the old-school bots don't have their costumes glued on, do they?"

"Some don't."

Brendan straightens his back and arches till something clicks. He makes a thoughtless little grunt of relief, and my eye catches something behind his legs: a cardboard box, missing its top half, bright colors inside.

"Okay I'm sold! Let's rob Pan of his Peter Pants."

"Wait, are you serious?" I find myself moving toward the box.

"Peter's not gonna need them for long."

I still can't tell if he means it or not. The box has my full attention now.

"Where are you going?" He grabs my arm; I twist away. "You gotta be back at Caves in like twenty minutes, right?" he says, at my heels.

"What is that?"

"What? Just some ancient merch."

"Brendan, stop grabbing at me."

I free my arm and crouch beside the box. Thirty, maybe fifty copies of a DVD, wrapped in plastic, called *Santa Swap 2*. The front cover is busy: On either side of a pane of glass, perhaps a mirror, Santa Claus and a reindeer look aghast. The reindeer is wearing Santa's red clothes, and Santa has only a towel wrapped high on his thick waist. I feel the faintest stirrings of memory, something about the first straight-to-video *Santa Swap*, the actor playing Mr. Claus himself performing as a reindeer transplanted into his body. Behind the two figures on the cover are an array of men, women, children, elves, and Rudolph's cruel siblings.

"Who is that?" I flip it around and hold a copy close to my face. A tall woman with dark eyes, tan limbs under a long-sleeved dress with green-and-white boa trim, and thick black hair down her back, flipped up at the ends. Her arms are crossed in front of her, brow lifted. A printing glitch has made the pixels stand out over her cheek.

"God those must have stopped selling years ago," and then we're moving, his feet and mine. He's holding my hand very gently, but I'm almost tripping over my feet.

"That woman."

"What?"

"That woman on the cover."

"There's no woman on the cover. It's Santa and a reindeer."

"No, there's one on the back."

"How do you swap bodies with a reindeer more than once? Like, what kind of God would allow that?"

"She looked familiar, right?"

"Is Santa a god? Who does Santa pray to?"

"Brendan . . ."

But I know to leave it. I know better than to push it when his mind is occupied. Brendan sincerely regards himself as a good multi-tasker, but I've seen people try to engage him when he's lost in a train of thought. It's embarrassing, and it's why people assume he's vain. How lucky that I know him better than that. He spaced out for the entire new-gen bot replacement meeting, an international teleconference where all on-the-ground staff were placed in identical amphitheaters and walked through the new technology of the characters who would be introduced across the park. They played a video, actors in motion capture bodysuits, and our breath caught in our chests when the woman in the explanatory video revealed herself to be one of them—one of the new animatronics, one of the new bots. Brendan didn't look up from his hands, and kept letting out heavy exhalations that I recognized as his snore, but at the woman's reveal he said, "I totally called it," though of course he hadn't said a word.

I can see ahead of us that he's planning to get back into the park through a different door than the one I used to get here. I feel the Mesozoic panorama waiting just within those walls, its pinkened pool, which usually bubbles with volcanic heat, lying stagnant in the dark. But out here it's too bright, migraine bright, and it seems like the decaying bodies of The Cemetery are jumping out at me whenever I blink: There, a dead quiz console with a shattered screen from the Lux Pavilion, the enormous atrium where sponsors rotated seasonally, displaying their newest tech to adult consumers with fructose-fueled children desperate for all variety of interactive demos. There, a cold aqua bench, from a food court. There, some type of pod large enough for two riders, which attached to the end of a huge robotic arm and ran a simulation of a roller coaster—one of your own design. I remember this one. It, too, belonged in the Lux Pavilion, and the company that made this simulation game also built the air-to-surface missiles used to suppress a short-lived coup in Yemen. I once went in that pod with Beth, who was still in her Madame Lily costume, a few auburn tendrils escaping her chignon, and even though we were in Gentle Mode she got nauseous.

But before we leave The Cemetery behind, I make the mistake of looking at something large, propped up against a grate: the Sorcerer of Chirakan, all nine feet of him, an old model. And this one, leaning inanimate, at a scarecrow angle, is missing his face. It's a punch to the gut and I look away as fast as I can.

I don't think Brendan saw it. I let myself shiver and try to forget.

"Pan?" says Brendan. The door is open, just an inch. It's been propped open with a rock. Brendan pulls it open and lets me pass. He pockets the rock.

"Sure," I say, letting the cool and the dark wash over me. "Why not."

Sent from:
Catherine Moser-Towe
2227 W. Catalina Blvd.
Los Angeles, CA 90027

First of all, that's the least generous read of the night Declan and I met that I could possibly imagine. That's really how you see him? Some raging egotist who saw me pacing out back and thought I was swooning over the idea of him? That was the end of your friendship, when he—a grown man!—showed interest in your sister, who you'd never been that protective of in the first place? It's wild to me that in the space of a few weeks, after not seeing each other for a year, that you'd think you could tell me where to get up and go to, and how to totally reimagine the history of my marriage.

And as far as the other stuff . . . I'm going to burst your bubble here, so get ready. You're scared because you've seen one person come out of a room and act weird? Am I missing something? She's a sitcom mom, she's probably on some cocktail of speed and matcha and she went into a fugue state. Your coworker lost a friend in a plane crash? That's very, very sad and awful. The robots are hyperrealistic? Good. That was the point, right? When was the last time you were in the park just as a guest? Those rides are old. They're dated. There's still that 3D movie from like 1987 with the soundtrack that sounds like a Rush cover band, and not in a good way.

I want to be sensitive to you, but my mind's going straight to: Oh, it must be so hard being a promising young man in STEM, an innovator at the most influential entertainment studio in the world. You're not disposable. You get paid shitloads to do something you're good at, and yeah you had a weird time working on movie sets in your twenties, but you got a thriving second career before you turned thirty. You know how few people achieve that? It must be so hard having found one thing that you love, that makes you respected. That's sarcasm, to be clear. All this sounds too mean, I know, but I've just been thinking a lot lately about how things might have been different if we were kids now. Like present day. How if you'd been, you know, properly diagnosed with something then, I would have had a more normal childhood, instead of following you around the neighborhood, apologizing for you, stopping you from experimenting on those lizards you always tried to gut, making sure no adults saw and branded you a serial killer in the making. How I wouldn't have had to stay home to watch you if Mom and Dad were out. How many kids watch their siblings, when there isn't much of an age difference? Something I think about a lot is, if things were different, I could have been a weird kid, too, covered in lizard blood. Just in my own way.

We've talked about this, I know. You've apologized, sort of, on occasion, I know. I don't mean to sound bitter. This is a digression. I guess what I'll say is: You know this new technology better than me. If something seems off to you, then you're probably right that something is off, but I'm not going to buy into this whole idea that it's <u>catastrophically off</u>, like going to be dangerous for me and my family. And I know it's taking a long time for both of us to send and receive these letters, but I do actually want you to update me if you get any clarity on what's happening—but again, not because I'm worried about myself. I never worry about myself. I promise no one's gonna go throw you into a ditch if you use your cell phone. Just call.

I had to get up just now. Callie came by with her assistant. She'll do that sometimes. Bring her people here for meetings or fittings. She's great. Did you meet her while doing the animatronic stuff? The more you get to know her, the more her baby face is this hilarious joke. She's so dry, really smart, dark, just so, so funny. An old soul. And I know she comes over a lot because she wants to make my day more exciting, because she thinks I'm bored, not because she thinks I deserve pity. A lot of people approach me with pity. Oh, your husband is this actor and you're just you. It must be so hard!

Callie was doing prep for the thing you don't want me to go to. I didn't mention it to her. Should I have? That's a question I'm asking myself, not asking you. She wanted to arrive together, get her driver to pick us up. She and Declan and the rest of the cast get to go through some park entrance no one knows about, like through this weird roped-off area that used to be a park-run campground in the sixties, and now it's just this empty field, and I guess there's a tunnel that's only used for VIPs. Like the employees of the park don't even get to go there. Wild.

I asked Callie if she'd seen her bot yet. She said only in photos. She said she thought it was going to be weird. I said maybe. I probably sounded weird myself. So I hope you're happy. You've gotten into my head a little bit. I don't know if it's much comfort but all this stuff with the animatronics, with the launch of the Nebuland-land (how are we saying that, by the way? Nebuland-land? or is the land just called Nebuland, like the movie title?), will be over soon. Just keep that in mind. Make it your mantra. It will be over soon.

Oh, and the church. Hah. Yeah. So Jon Yule, the big bad guy from the movie (of course you know who he is), really took a shine to Declan when they were filming, I guess, but he tried to push this Jesus stuff on him, which, as you can imagine, Declan didn't love. But when they were doing the mo-cap late last year they got to talking again, and I guess Ol' Yuley maybe wants to help fund Declan's next project. His idea is to do this whole trippy reimagining of an Old Testament story, Jacob fighting that angel, they beat the shit out of each other, J gets his hip messed up, angel gives him a new name. Do you know the story? Anyway, Declan's vision is really specific, like, nothing literal, totally abstract, very Gaspar Noé, he says. My theory is that it's a means to an end for his old raver friends in Dublin to do a soundtrack.

So Declan thinks he can convince Yule to come on board, and maybe come to some understanding about it not being all that Bible-ish, but Yule suggested that we start coming to their church "just to network," and you can imagine how I reacted to that. But Declan wore me down. He said it wasn't a real church, it was a <u>celebrity</u> church. He was pretty sure Rick Ross and the guy from Highlander show up sometimes. It would probably be funny. We only have to go a few times. So I agreed.

It was Yule's backyard, on this steep hillside. We didn't go into the house itself, though it looked nice and old—that kind of self-built seventies thing that people go crazy for here. Not opulent. A little dusty. The path around the side of the house was full of spiderwebs, but Yule led us down the hill and onto this zigzagging path beyond his back fence, until we reached this thicket of trees. It was nice. Kind of a magical feel, I'll give it that. Nothing too manicured, and you could make out bits of the valley. We were some of the last to arrive, and there were maybe thirty or forty people there. I half-recognized almost all of them. They had these faces I know I'd seen somewhere. And tons of them were twins. It was this compounded déjà vu, seeing double and having the vaguest recollections of the commercials they'd been in, the little bit parts in shows they'd had. How much of our memories are made up of people we know nothing about? God, I'm just remembering: One of them had the)) Gwendolyn Goose lashes tattooed on her wrist. Mega-fan, I guess. Still, seems like a weird move for a jobbing actor, right?

There was this guy doing dumb stunts, but kind of only showing off for the really young women there. Like the sixteen- to twenty-year-olds. Which is whatever. Not criminal. Just a little gross. His whole thing is that he can balance a bunch of heavy shit on his forehead, and also he does motocross or something.

Declan became tense early on—I think because most of the people had had background roles in Nebuland and he was the most recognizable person there by far, aside from

Yule. At the start it was just that classic LA thing of everyone reeling off their last five jobs. Cringe. Most of them talked about their commercial work and their corporate voice-over jobs like they were things of the distant past. After Nebuland, things were really gonna turn around for them, even if they'd just been credited as like Crab Nymph #6. Some of them said they'd sold their likeness. I didn't know what that meant. They described it as modeling work, but one teen boy kind of rolled his eyes and said it wasn't anything like modeling, that big companies prey off normal-looking people this way. Get the rights to use a person's image for "boring stuff." He said the park did it all the time. I wondered what that meant, and . . . Well. I won't even speculate. I don't want to feed into your "fears" about the animatronics.

But then everyone got to talking, and there were these little performances, like this one woman burned some Palo Santo that she'd "scavenged in Cancun," and someone else read this poem about this type of fern that only grows out of shit, like human shit, and that was actually pretty cool and funny and put me at ease. But then Yule took over, and brought it back to bog-standard Jesus stuff. Pop-Jesus, I mean. Teenage Soup for the Born-Again Soul, that kind of thing.

And this metaphor about tapping, tapping the rhythm of a song, and no one understanding what song it's meant to be, but maybe some people understand? I didn't quite follow. So I don't think we'll be going back. Declan can find other producers.

I need to go soon if I'm gonna get this to the post office before it closes. It's annoying to do, but I gotta say, this feels retro. Look at us, letter-writing. Just a couple of Brontës. But look: Robots aren't making people badweirdviolent, the desert sounds boring, and I love you.

—Catherine

CHAPTER FIVE

I hadn't been living there when my birth father finally left. I was with another family then, the Macphersons, and Mom being on her own might have had something to do with why she was suddenly able to petition for guardianship again. But I never really asked. The last thing I remember of my time with that family is hiding in the pool. The only evidence that it had ever been swum in was an outline of black mildew around its rim, where rusting hook-bolts wove together aluminum and torn lining. I remember there was the *put-put* of a game-show prop sound coming from inside the house.

Beyond the fence, the neighbor's screen door lay flat on the lawn. Dandelions grew out of it now. I remember that, too. I went over there one afternoon and picked them out of the mesh, and later, when I was moving back into Mom's, now Mom and Whit's, I'd find traces of their spores floating ghostly in my bedroom and in the hall, suspended in the light.

I lowered myself step by step down the inner ladder, which shook and creaked, even under my weight, which was almost nothing. Mr.

Macpherson shouted into a wall-mounted telephone. He liked to look at Mrs. Macpherson when he shouted, even if he was talking to someone else entirely. She was probably sitting on a kitchen chair, a beeping plastic device that let her play five-card stud sitting in the hollow of her groin. The Velcro on one of my shoes had come undone, and I was thrilled that I'd get to pull it tight again. What a treat. Also, it took me no time at all to see a bug; I saw one before my feet touched the ground. I was too happy for words, happier there than I remember being in my childhood, to be in this new place, just me and some bugs. Maybe I'd never have to see anyone else ever again.

I toppled onto my knee when I landed, but it was okay because it didn't hurt and I never cried, as a rule. But once there, I noticed that the bottom of the ladder was far above my head, farther than I could reach. It didn't matter. I'd worry about it later, after I chased beetles and tried to revive dead cicadas, some almost as big as my fist. Maybe I'd take a nap. I was always told that I was a good sleeper.

The sun didn't stay in the sky for long. I was quickly exhausted from the wars I was enacting with piles of leaves and baby spiders and calcified chunks of chlorine, which were so easy to shake out of their little container, which once orbited the pool like Sputnik. I remember thinking that everything was backwards: The night was heating up the way that day was supposed to. I wrapped my arms around my middle and let my eyes droop. The last thing I saw before the hollering of the neighbors just after dawn was a smear of iridescence across the sky. A little shooting star, nothing more. But I hadn't known they were real, really real, in the same way that Californians both know and don't know that fireflies are real, and I thought of the videos I'd sometimes watch. The cartoons. Princes and singing animals and water nymphs and boys with their shadows sewn on, pulling children across the night sky. I slipped into a bliss. There was so much I didn't know. And if I was able to look up and explore this wonder of the cosmos while stuck in a pool, three feet shy of my way out, then who was to say what I could find once I was back on land?

Maybe that's why Whit's addition to the shed was intriguing. It was so dark in there, and he was always making light.

First, Whit had moved his equipment into what remained of my dad's sheds. Then, later, he added a mini fridge. Mom came out to check on him at odd hours, between her shifts, but she only asked "How long you been out here?" or "What are you going to say if the neighbors complain?" She never asked specifics, and I don't even know if she even really knew how he made his art. I never asked; he began showing me gradually over the weeks and then the years. I always knew I loved neon, mostly in signs, but I never knew it could be real art. Whit's was mostly abstract—a lot of reds and yellows in wobbly formations that looked like claw marks—but occasionally he'd play around with military imagery, a boot or a helicopter, and he always found buyers for those because people found them to be ironic, but neither he nor I could quite understand why.

I hate what people think. I hate what they must have thought before the accident: a grizzled old man luring his stepdaughter into a sinister shed. It doesn't sound great. But I've maybe never felt more safe with anyone. He never touched me, never so much as a hug. I got a slap on the back if I'd been particularly helpful with the fire and glass, or if I did good on a spelling test, but that was about it. After the accident, there was no defending him, though. Everyone made up their mind. And he didn't correct them. He wasn't able to, even if he'd wanted to.

In Belgravia Mrs. Darling is being physically chased by her suitors. Tiger Lily is looking scornfully upon Tinkerbell. Carvings, along the queue for the ride. And just below them are dark banisters that over a million hands have touched. I've felt every crevice, both with gloves on and without. Brendan always wants to skip the queue and I refuse. Walking through it is part of the whole experience. I say I'll meet him on the platform.

Sometimes I move extra slow, going through the motions of the ungodly wait time the ride always had in its heyday. It's got a tiny load capacity. The vehicles are Peter himself, belly-down, his boy-claws extended by our side, in flight. Riders mount his back, two at a time, and slip into seats carved out of his body. He is the boy who never grew up, and also, very technically, a kind of bobsled.

As a prince, Brendan never had to learn to work all-in-one ride operation systems, but he's proud that he figured it out, with almost no instruction from me. I don't have the heart to tell him that the control unit on this one hasn't changed in forty-five years, and it could be run by a reasonably intelligent ten-year-old. You pull a lever and the whole contraption, the woven tree roots of gears and electrics that control the Peter and Wendy ride, whirs into life without the complex choreography of distinct power units that the other, newer rides need. Its own power source is nestled at the center of its largest showroom, right underneath Skull Rock. Brendan lights up when he ducks under the calligraphed, pastel-painted *No Entry* sign at the very front of the queue and takes hold of the console. The vehicles don't need to come to a halt while loading; they slow to less than a mile per hour. The restraint bar, anchored to the rod connecting Peter's thoracic spine to the overhead conveyor system, lowers automatically once you begin your flight, an ascent toward the steps to the Darling home at the end of the platform. We let a few Peters roll past. I'm still in no hurry, not when I'm here, in the space itself, even if my break is running long. Hery and Andrea will be fine.

By the time we're loading ourselves into our Peter, though, I'm letting the unhappy thoughts in. The disassembly man. The faceless bot in The Cemetery. I settle into the harsh plastic contours of my seat, and Brendan thumps himself down beside me.

He puts his arm around me and plays with my light canvas sleeve. "You okay?"

"Yeah," I say. "It's just a little sad."

There's a click and we tilt upward. We gain speed, and the speakers below our feet start the cheerful, iconic harp riff of the main theme. Those women, warbling.

"Don't be sad yet," he says. "Let's enjoy the moment."

"I know." I rub my face and become more alert to the scene unfolding: a Pepper's ghost, reflection-on-reflection, dance of John and Michael wrestling just below us. At the key change we pivot toward Wendy, who's watching the horseplay shaking her single-piece head, a little bit like the stacked Sherpas in the Everest panorama inside the train tunnel, disapproving.

Brendan whispers, "I'm going to figure out what's going on with that guy, whoever you saw. So don't worry about it."

"Thanks. I'm not worried. But thanks."

Our Peter slows while the interlocking sections of wall in the next room prepare themselves for us.

"You're sure you'd never seen this dude before? You're really sure?"

Subtle clunking, and then the odd change in the soundtrack's midsection: the sudden switch to the 3/4 signature, a waltz.

"I told you," I hiss. "I didn't recognize him. How many times do I need to say it?"

"Delph—"

His softness makes me sharpen, involuntarily, in a way I almost always come to regret. "What happened to *let's enjoy the moment*? Just forget I said anything."

He leans back and removes his hand from me. "Fine."

The speed of our vehicle again, maybe three miles per hour now, tilting upward. My body knows every movement. A panel slides away, and we're in the narrow slip to the first dark showroom: black wall on all sides of us, the only time in the ride you feel constrained. You move slowly, with only a few faint woodwinds as soundtrack, trilling and tense. And then—like a gunshot—lights everywhere, illuminating the cylinder you're in so quickly it's the same effect as the dark: no sense of where the walls are, only blinding starlight flickering in a seemingly endless astrosphere. Countless glowing dots scurry toward a point just behind you. They call it a *stargaze corridor*, but this one stands out because of how long they let you sit blind. They let you live like that for several breaths. I like that. Rapture has to be acclimated to, or else it's just a cheap sparkle effect.

Then things get a little messy, I'll be honest; the story's events start to appear out of order. I understand why. *Peter and Wendy* is kind of a slog. Both book and film, but especially film. Action never really ramps. The only act of heroism comes from Tinkerbell, and isn't addressed in any meaningful way after the fact. The whole thing is a series of exceptional peculiarities and sherbet-colored vignettes on celluloid, but it's part of my DNA now; I'd die for it. But the story has its flaws, and its sinister omissions. Core moments are there and gone before you know it. The shadow ordeal, for example . . .

Well, never mind about that.

The ride needs to be arranged differently in order to finesse the emotional journey, so we go from the stargaze corridor to a mirrored, ultraviolet kaleidoscope room (literally—a mirror-ball turbine, almost like an enormous telescope with each third rotating in an opposing direction), letting us know that we're flying into an unnavigable place, where up can be down and the only way through the chaos is to barrel straight ahead. Then our Peter, where we're seated, twists in reverse, giving us a last glimpse of London, a forced-perspective cityscape of Buckingham Palace, and Tinkerbell dropping fairy dust onto the Thames so that it lights up green then yellow then red then purple. We swing back, facing the right way again.

Brendan's looking at me.

"What?"

He looks away. There's heat in my chest.

"I know you're thinking that I spaced out on a memo or something," I whisper.

"What are you talking about?"

"The guy I saw. You think you're going to find out that that guy and his team are totally meant to be here, and that I actually knew that; I just spaced and I should have remembered." I'm hissing my words over the music. I know he can only hear every other word.

"That's—" He exhales. "That's not even remotely what I'm thinking."

"You keep asking if I recognize him."

We swing low, jolting for only a second or two, a slight gut-drop while we pass over the elaborate Lost Boys tree forts. A solar glow behind their lean-tos and catkins. Curly is bashing a tree with a hammer, and Nibs lounges in a swaying hammock, running his hands through his hair.

"You don't need to take it personally," he says. "It's just hard to keep track of who's coming and going, and I wouldn't blame you if you got mixed up."

"That's very sweet of you. To not blame me."

"Delph, what am I missing here? Why are you so pissed?"

I wish I could tell him. I wish I could understand why today his kindness feels like a hand around my throat. I say nothing. I try to focus on what's next, the spookier bit of the ride. I try to muster my normal wonder.

We hit a bend and a distant vision of Skull Rock hovers and disappears into thin air. It's a cool trick, and easy to do. Just a well-placed mirror.

The words suddenly come to me. "I'm doing the best that I can. And all you think is that I'm going to fall apart."

"When the park closes, you mean?"

My mouth is dry. "When the park closes, I mean."

We loop around a larger-than-life pirate ship, with a coiffed James Hook at the helm. A strobe effect gives the impression of wild action. The strobe catches Brendan's face in momentary blasts of perfect stillness, like Polaroids being shot off. His voice comes out smooth, but out of sync with his flashing flipbook of expressions.

"You know you're allowed to just be sad," he says. "You don't have to worry about what *I* think about how well you're doing. Just be sad. Everyone's sad. And you and I haven't sat down and made any real plans. For after."

"I don't want to talk now," I say. "I'm trying to enjoy the ride."

This is the part that always scares very young riders. We tilt downward again into a fresh darkness, and a tense shift in the music vibrates from underneath us. The ground actually shakes. Then Skull Rock looms so close we could almost touch it, atomized fog obscuring both its top and its bottom, giving the effect of it having no beginning and no end. We come closer and closer until we're inside his eye—his left one, illuminated with firelight. There's the sound of crackling wood. A channel of rocky dark, and little scenes play out through the gaps in the cave wall. Tiger Lily hides behind an outcrop and sharpens a shard of flint attached to a long piece of driftwood, the blood of her enemies smeared under her eyes, while pirates are distracted by an angry, shrieking flock of Never Birds, swarming in brilliant rainbow flashes. Cold air blasts from vents embedded in the set piece. And then the ticking: the crocodile looms.

We can only see his shadow moving quickly along the firelit dripstone. In the movie he wears the sneer of Captain Hook's grandfather, a cruel cannery baron from Swansea, who met his own terrible fate at the hands of the beast, which allows for an extra layer of psychological torture. In the ride they've toned it down; when the crocodile eventually peers out, it's nothing more than a haggard reptilian monster, sort of nondescript in the face, but with a great illuminated belly and scales.

Brendan rests his hand on my thigh. I dip my head onto his shoulder, but I know that I'm not done. Whatever heat was inside me is still there. It's just resting.

"I love this part," he murmurs and leans forward a little.

It's the ride's crescendo. A new room. There's some of that mirrored turbine kaleidoscope once more, and the Jolly Roger keeling along an invisible track just as we emerge from it. Then Tinkerbell soars, fairy dust covering every surface so that it's like someone's cranked up both volume and saturation. It's pure delirium, a symphony of mermaid song and tribal drums. The crocodile leaps, swinging from one end of the room to the other on invisible wire, crashing onto the pirates, and all the children that are left standing start to take flight. Our car pivots backward once more and there's Peter. It's the first time we actually see him—confusing, as we're sitting on him as well—and he's clinging on to Wendy, locked in a sort of wrestling hold. Both watch the incomprehensible vastness of the magical world below. Wendy's face looks so serene. The face that belongs to that Lithuanian girl, to Renata Revere.

Then Peter is in front of his band of Lost Boys, giving a victory address. Then again, taking little Michael by the hand, and standing on tiptoe, ready to take flight once more, back the way they came. Despite myself, I am covered in goose bumps. Despite myself I want to grip Brendan's hand.

Brendan's gone.

For a second it doesn't compute, and I touch the part of the seat where he should be. I make a little sound. Our Peter is twisting back to face forward, the last room of the ride, the return to London.

"Brendan!"

I'm drowned out by the last of that heavenly homecoming chorus. I twist in my seat. I'm not supposed to see the room this way: There's exposed plasterboard and the back end of the kaleidoscope mechanism, a utility light coming from behind a flap, the ugly turbine, the forced perspective of a tidal pond. It's warped and I wince.

Then daylight. The platform. I'm out of the dark. Ride over.

The bar at my waist clicks and lifts. I trip when I'm getting out and I sit on the walkway's edge, where normally C&C would be directing small groups into their loading section, or to the hat shop beyond the exit. I'm dumbstruck. I don't know how much time passes.

Brendan's got leggings in his hands when he finds me there.

"That was fun," he says, waggling green nylon.

"What the fuck?" I'm hugging my knees to my chest. I know it looks pathetic, but I can't seem to get comfortable. There's a pain in my back.

"What? This was the plan." He's still smiling. "It was your idea!"

"It was a joke. I didn't think you were serious."

"Dead serious!" He sits down beside me. "Wait, you're not really upset, right?"

"So there's just a Peter in there who doesn't have pants?"

"The one talking to the Lost Boys, right at the end. I didn't think you'd mind."

"It's . . . I just ride this one a lot."

His eyes soften. He looks straight ahead, to the old Alpine façade of the Schnitzel Cabin. "I know."

"It's gonna be too weird if he doesn't have pants."

"It won't be *that* weird. It's not like those bots are anatomically correct."

"Those won't even fit you." I grab them. They're small; I could fit into them if I really tried, but it wouldn't be easy. They smell like mothballs.

"Okay, then I'll put them back. Let's go."

"No," I say. "Do it yourself. I don't want to see you down on that . . ." I search for the word. Floor? Sea? Void?

"Come on. One more ride. I won't mess with anything. I'll hop off right at the end and dress your boyfriend and you can cover your eyes and you won't have to see a thing."

"Hery's waiting for me."

A pause. "We always do this twice."

Something catches in my skull. I straighten my back. A cloud shifts just beyond the tent cover of the platform, and I see a brief patch of warm drizzle.

"We always do this twice," I say back. I nod.

Do we always do this twice?

We get to our feet together and we board the next Peter. By the time we're approaching the Darling windows, I've forgotten all about whatever it was that had been bothering me. Maybe forget isn't the right word. I'd stored it in a place where it could become something lost, like a photograph, or a boy.

In the middle of the night, I pull my comforter around me tight, denying Brendan the ability to put his skin against mine, but I need to feel encased. There are heavy blankets that make people calmer. Those weren't around when I was small, though I don't think I would have liked it then. Whit might have. He had bad nights. There were nights after long days where he'd drive me to the VA but his buddy wouldn't be there, or the pharmacy couldn't process his prescription, or they could but his loyalty card didn't give him a great enough discount to be able to take anything home. After those days sometimes I'd see him out back looking at the shed. Sometimes he might be on his brick of a cell phone, calling up his son, Daryl, who answered one in thirty times. Sometimes he'd smoke a cigarette. Sometimes he'd leave the door to the shed open so that some moonlight let me see its shallow depths, where the huge containers full of shattered glass and old blinker boards and spare gloves sat. If I joined him outside, he'd tell me it was too late, I needed to go to bed—and it was among the few times I felt more like his child than his sidekick, and although I didn't like it, it felt like comfort, too. I'd go back to bed, and rest my nose on my windowsill and watch him, his hands shaking as he looked into the night, into the shed, planning the light he was going to craft. I hope that's what he was thinking about.

Leaving the park last night was strange. Brendan got the way he sometimes gets when we're off the clock and he doesn't see anyone around. He gets ideas, before we reach the gates. I shouldn't say that they're his ideas entirely.

"You can't wait till we're home?" I asked.

"Do you want to wait?"

I thought about it. "Not really."

We went into the gift shop. I told him he didn't need to use anything. I've been on the pill for forever and he knows it. But it was like he didn't hear me. "Better safe than sorry," he'd said.

It was the last gift shop in the park, right before you hit the pay-by-the-hour lockers and the station to get stamped for reentry. In terms of raw dimension, it was the largest shop in the whole park, but of course it was designed in crafty angles and a selective palette to be almost invisible when entering the park, and unmissable when guests were trying to leave. There was a whole floor devoted to home furnishings. He made us a kind of nest out of a Gwendolyn Goose duvet-and-pillow set, but I tried to shuffle us into the stockroom to avoid CCTV.

"What are they gonna do, fire us?" he said while descending on me, after wrangling an ancient condom, hungrier for this than I'd guessed. We were half on the warm shop floor, half in a cold aluminum inventory cupboard stacked with lockers and boxes. At one point I lost focus and thought about that Christmas DVD again. The woman on the cover.

But Brendan lifted me from my ribs and carefully placed me against the door frame. I reached backward and held on to him, and he finished only moments after that. Or I guess I thought he finished; when I looked, he was a few feet from me, on his knees still and bent over at the waist. When I reached to pick some stray down off his damp skin, he shuddered, and I realized what was happening.

I said I thought he'd already done that. He said no, he was just being cautious. I asked why.

He said I should just leave it, and he wrapped me in his arms.

I didn't want to sound dramatic, but I felt a little robbed. It's a feeling that hasn't left me, even this morning, as I count koi. I don't often feel bitter about those kinds of things. Sex is the Wild West. Lawless, by design, I had thought for a long time, until I understood that of course it couldn't be.

Before coming to California, I was used to an extremely unremarkable type of boy or man who was in a perpetual state of anger at not being remarked upon. They often had a singular point of focus—usually it was someone lovely and busy—and they put them through rigorous examination every few hours: She listens to the wrong music. If she let me, I could fill her mind with much better music. She only cares about looks. If she was less shallow she'd wonder why she didn't have the ability to read my thoughts, just the same way I lament not being able to be inside her mind. She's been failed by a society, by parents, by even shallower friends, which is why she's with that guy with the long torso from that other school. An equitable world would make her endlessly curious about me and me alone. That kind of thing.

Of course, I found myself near these boys, because they were the only ones around. When I was in junior high, a goth friend named Angela told me that all the jocks of the world are rapists and everyone knew it but me, so my world became a little bit smaller. I didn't clamor for close friends anyway, the way other girls did. I stopped doing that after going to stay with the first family that wasn't my own, not the Macphersons, but the one with the daughters who cheated at MASH, and who didn't let me go inside their church, even though I'd wanted to.

These boys, though. They didn't talk directly to me, even if I'd sit near them on grass or go watch them play video games in silence for hours. And yet I'd pick up on their speech patterns, their slang and cadences, the same way I might overpronounce for someone who lip-reads. They made me overly kind, and the moment I was out of their radius, the moment I became absent from them, the moment I let literally anything else in the world catch my attention, they let me know that I'd failed them, that I was like the shallow women at the heart of their struggle—the only difference being they didn't want to touch me.

I was days shy of thirteen when a boy first called me a bitch, and for my birthday Whit bought me three things: Dr Pepper–flavored lip balm, a clover charm for my stackable bracelet, and a Browning Black Label .45.

"Learn your way around that thing and then we'll line up some scrap glass."

"How do I learn my way around it?" The gun was heavier than I'd imagined.

"All those books and you can't figure out how to use that?" He snorted.

Mom started listening and said, "What the hell is wrong with you?" to Whit, but only at half power because she was also reading oven instructions for a pile of frozen pierogis. I made them all the time when I was alone, when Whit was at his meetings. I told him I never wanted to shoot a gun, but that I wanted him to show me his tools for making neon.

"Fine," he said. "If it'll keep you away from shitforbrains boys." I loved how quickly the words rolled off his tongue. Every day he cut down his Thorazine substitute, there was more of him to hear. More deftness. I wanted to hear everything.

Brendan was remarkable and expected nothing, and so I didn't prepare myself for him, and every time we'd find ourselves the only ones in a group laughing at the same thing, or resting our elbows on the sticky surface of a bar in the same way, it was a spark-shock. I didn't make any effort for him, and he didn't mind when I went quiet on him for a week or more. He liked whenever the last thing I said to him was deeply uncool because he knew that meant I'd be coming back. No one would let their last words to a handsome man be "Tomatoes give me heartburn," or "You shouldn't be rude about flyover states."

By the time we realized we were in love—by the time I already understood his tendency to fixate on developing short-lived skills and hobbies, and after I'd explained to him why I know so much about helium and bombarding-transformers—we'd unlearned how to love a person any different way. Ruined for anyone else. I never got jealous. So why is last night like a bruise?

Now that it's morning, I decide I'll find Old Sam Ybarra and say hello to him first, to make up for not recognizing him yesterday. I've just got to keep my eyes peeled and walk with purpose. No one's here yet. I can't see any janitorial staff. I make a circuit up and down the midway at the entrance and stop to catch my breath.

The lake at the center of the park stretches out in that way that makes you dizzy, and the barrier presses a hash shape into my flesh. I think about the bottom of it, that pool-bottom tarp that dips into the earth, into our underground C&C terrain. I find that there's a coffee in my hand. It reminds me of my one and only plane ride. It had been shockingly bad, then. The coffee, I mean. Decaf. When we'd started to descend, a recorded message played overhead: *The bathrooms can no longer be used at this time.* For some reason the wording, *can no longer be used,* rather than *should,* or a simple request like *please don't use,* had been so, so goddamn funny to me. And the more I thought about it, the funnier it became.

I try to see the bottom of the water, where it dips. I make out nothing but a few scaly flashes, fish, long-term residents. I can only count two. It must be too early for them. And anyway, I don't have time to count fish. I stretch my spine and knock back the rest of the coffee. Today is the day I close down Ben Nevis. It's part of the long plan, the Action Plan, and though it's not actually in my territory— so far from the amphoras, swaths of nautical nets, and souk contraptions of the Colonial Outpost—the task somehow landed in my lap. The ride itself hasn't run in, what, a week? But its tunnels are still lit. Its deepest power sources are still surging, tunnel after tunnel of glacier texture, patterns of blues and whites. Safe. Nothing that would give me a fright if I saw it backwards. Filled with natural light, for the most part. I'm not fearful, like I can sometimes be. There are tracks and spotlights and only two animatronics: an angry stag threatening to lunge out at riders from its cave, and the Loch Ness monster, in a shallow, burbling pool. Nothing to make me shiver, nothing to make me dizzy. No parallax, no looming sense of an illusion done wrong, that summoning-a-beast feeling when the lights come on.

The first few groups of guests, just three that I can see, move in.

"Hello," I whisper.

I check my watch: just after seven. Now that so little remains open, they circle in and out of the same rides, no longer trickling out of the exits in a daze, but pivoting with purpose back inside again, on repeat. Devotees. I can just about make out the front of the space coaster. The guests are only little dots, but on my left, farther, there are the tips of Nebuland's most popular attractions. The lagoon ride.

The one I can't think about. Its structure pierces the sky and seems much closer to me than it really is.

My foot touches something. The stuffed white bag. The bag of red mites and dead mosquitos. *Oh.* I don't remember leaving you there.

"Hello to you, too," I whisper.

There's something mournful about these last remaining guests. Would I subject myself to one last park visit if I didn't work here? If this place had been a beloved family routine? I don't know that I would. It would be too much responsibility, to have the perfect farewell. I can't let that idea infect me, though. Can't think like that. I can't even picture the word, the letters that constitute f-a-r-e-w-e-l-l, or something inside me will unravel. I squint at the guests, try to settle on their outlines and their little movements. Three of them. One little group. They're hovering. Looking lost. Sad. It doesn't help that they're all wearing black.

Yes, all three of them. All three are wearing black.

There's a hand on my arm. I jump.

"Sorry," the man says.

I laugh, a laugh with an edge, and say, "No, sorry, hello again."

The man, the one who'd been dragging the bins in Zoetrope Alley, scans my face. "I'm here to help you. I'm going to shut down the rides. You don't have to worry about that." He looks bleary. The type of skin grease that only comes from an all-nighter.

"That's . . ."

But before I can respond, he starts to fumble through his pockets and pulls out a card that looks exactly like mine, but with a label stuck to it and no needle. He only holds it in front of my face for a moment before pocketing it again, and his thumb is covering the label—a name—that's been scribbled in Sharpie. It reads *Hery.*

I squint at it. "You're not—"

"Ben Nevis," he says, firm. "Ben Nevis is on the plan for today, right?"

I work with Hery every day. We wear the same cargo shorts. "Right, but—"

"Which manager assigned that to you?" he asks.

I try to feel where anyone else might be—Sam Ybarra, Brendan, any familiar face. "I'm sorry, can you remind me exactly what you do? I just hadn't seen you till yesterday, and I've been here a long time."

"I help management."

He has an accent. I can't quite place it. It might be Canadian. No, not that.

"You help management," I say back.

He nods, and then he begins to walk, a contagious pace that makes it impossible not to walk alongside him, unthinking. Before I know it, I'm leading the way, to the mountain. I take the long way, though, collecting my thoughts. Ben Nevis sits between lands, and the Nebuland gates distract me when we pass by. I don't often open myself up to Nebuland, revel in its details, its theater. It's Callie. It's the same reason I don't look at the spot just outside the park gates. I swear there is still a mark where she was, if you look closely. Never look too closely.

There's an immensity to that land, Nebuland, the new one overlaid on the old one. It's a veldt of glossy white structures, somewhat militaristic, patched onto the Space Race stuff that the park originally opened with half a century ago. This is nothing like the Fairytale Grove. Nothing like the unnamed Edwardian section. Here, there's not a single cardboard cutout, and none of the baked-in impurities of the Colonial Outpost. The ground in Nebuland is sloped gently upward on all sides; guests enter at the base of a kind of bowl, making its outer boundaries appear to spill outward and upward, toward some brilliant horizon.

I watch the gates as we pass, but the man is locked onto them with a great deal of focus. He's trailed farther behind me, so far that I wonder if he'll lose interest in me and simply disappear. He's clutching something. It's a shoulder bag, the same color as his hoodie, draped with a strap across his chest. After some time there's the tired clip of his shoes again, and then we're in Ben Nevis's shadow. It's looming cool and blue-white. I'm still leading the way, this time to a set of concrete stairs. Out of sight from the front queue. He watches closely while I use my card, then the needle, and slip the key away. I wonder if he sees me put it into the little pouch inside my pocket, where some of the C&C keep little snacks or Adderall.

I hold the door for him. He almost looks surprised. I'm surprised, I suppose. I know he's not who he says he is. He's not Hery. But he's here.

The old woman comes to mind again. The one with the very thin legs, and the face that looked so old it was almost melted. I want to ask if he knows her. Two strangers must know one another. But I don't. I follow through the door, into one dark, sterile corridor, and then another. There's a rot smell that comes from the loch at the center of the ride. It's always there; thankfully guests are moving through the air too fast to notice.

Then we slip into the innards of the mountain, where the track lies in a gutter just below our feet. When was it last operational? I wasn't part of that team, the team for running it or the team for starting to shut it down. *Starting to.* No one finished. Layoffs must have cut the shutting-down short. There are sound effects—a *drip* and some bleating—still running on a loop, but there's not that jaunty score that I remember. I cross my arms while I walk, and I dictate the plan to myself: three control stations, at three points in the mountain. Run checks. Pull the plug.

And let this man . . . watch? Do whatever it is he says he was sent to do?

"I'm not Hery," he says.

"Yeah I know."

"I didn't steal anything from him, if that's what you think."

"Okay."

We've begun walking up the spiral ramp, and I can already feel the effort in my calves.

"You don't seem scared."

"Why should I be scared?"

"Because I'm not who I said I was."

He has a point. Maybe I should be scared. I can't muster it, though. I start to pick up my pace, and I hear him start to breathe a little heavy.

"I *am* here to help shut down the park."

"I've never seen you before."

"I was only called in recently. How long have you been here?"

"Long enough to know that most contractors don't act like you. They keep to themselves."

"How long, though?"

"A few years."

"That's not very long. In the scheme of things."

He says *things* in a way that tells me he's not Canadian. He's Irish.

The ramp gives way to a flat platform that forks off from the coaster, curving outside along the mountain's exterior before it will eventually loop back into a different section of dark, full of moss and LED midges. We walk into daylight. There's no railing here. Straight below, glass beads are mixed into the white paint. Realistic, glittering snow. But some of the beads have cracked over time, so if someone were to fall it would be bloody, which is also realistic, in its own way.

"Do you like this ride?" he asks.

"It's fine. It was always a guest favorite."

"But not yours?"

"I don't like sudden drops."

"Really?" He smiles. "I love them. Reminds you that you're inside a body."

"You need reminding?"

"Sure."

We both put our hands on our hips as we look out, accidental choreography. "And it doesn't go fast enough," I say. "*Didn't* go fast enough."

"So you like speed but not drops."

"Yeah," I say. From somewhere far off, I hear the gentle sounds of movement. I can hear braying. "Are you developing a theory about me?"

I think he shakes his head.

After some time, we reach the first of the three control rooms. My work is quick. Today the touchscreens and panels, the little generators and patched-on sockets, feel like the contours of a rare animal, and under this man's gaze I feel my own mastery. He's followed me into this room. It's round and lit from above, those work lights casting almost yellow shadows on our skin. I try not to look at him, but he looks at me so brazenly as I work, as I make each bit of machinery go dark.

"You're switching off the electricity?"

I look over my shoulder at him and finish my last screen stroke. "You really don't know anything about this."

"The kind of work I do doesn't have anything to do with electrics."

"This isn't electric. Not all of it." That's not fair, I suppose. It's *mostly* electric. But I want him to admit it to me. What he thinks he knows. Who he really is.

"Everything here runs on electricity. That much I know for sure."

I shimmy past him, out onto the walkway, where the air smells like plaster, beside the two parallel rails. I'm not sure exactly where we are. There are a few gaps in the craggy wall where a little shot of ice-blue would have been lit up, giving the impression of vast hidden chambers of ice and water within the mountain. You need less detail on coasters. Just smears of color.

"Well," I start, not quite sure where to begin. "When it comes to a lot of the park, sure, it's the twenty-first century and all that. There's a lot of electricity keeping the main infrastructure going. But when it comes to the rides, and the bots, it's more about how you choose to . . . you know. Bring something to life."

Once more he falls into step beside me. "How many ways are there to bring something to life?"

"Three," I say. "Hydraulic, pneumatic, and electric."

Before long I notice that he loosens when I'm speaking. Something in his gait. He likes the sound of my voice, and I like being able to share my knowledge. It's more than that, though. It's like a blister being lanced. It's like a release of some dam, water that had been festering. I explain to him how big movements happen with hydraulics. Something enormous pivoting from the hips, in the finale room of a dark ride, or maybe in a parade if you can get the right vehicle, arms the size of studio apartments, moving in rhythm, giving the impression of orating to a crowd. Hydraulics push the heaviest. You need to ask fewer questions about inertia, about mass—how heavy is this armature? That kind of thing. Those are embarrassing questions to ask of hydraulics. Those are questions for electricity or air.

When the stretch of track, our stretch of pathway, changes palette, and the little gaps in the outer wall start to appear, letting cool air in, I start talking about pneumatics. How pneumatics will make a muscle flit. It's how the new bots look the way they do. A small release will mimic the facial movements so small we wouldn't notice it if a friend were doing them from across a table. It will use the state of a valve to dictate springiness. It will give you a droop or a nod, and the fragile balance of pressure can signal fault or failure: It's how the coaster in the Kingdom of the Future knew to shut down. Something blew out.

When we're close to the second control room, I start to explain electricity. I tell him that it's always funny to hear the engineers say "the future is electric." They say that a lot, like it's a new discovery. It makes them sound like they're in a fin-de-siècle farce. But electricity isn't actually everywhere, not in the park, not like you'd think. For one, they don't make electric motors as small as you'd need to make those tiny movements. Look at a small animal figure if you're in a park anytime soon, in Hong Kong perhaps, and notice how their ankles and their wrists never flex. Pistons can't make a gesture, but they can do the *stop start* of those larger movements like nothing else, and when *stop start* are your only options, it makes sense to make them perfect.

Stop start. Linear and rotary. In and out.

"I hope I'm making sense," I say.

We hear a gentle hum and I press open the door. This time it's more camouflaged with the wall, and only a faint seam and an impression of heat within makes me think that the second control unit is here. We approach the clot of machinery at the center of a room. This time the space is the size of a two-car garage. It takes a minute for me to recognize the type of control unit, the processor, and to guess where the most important panels might be. It's old, so there will be some lever-pulling. Behind it, someone's made the *))* marking. Seems like it would be lost on us, the mech people. Real commitment to the Easter egg, I suppose.

It's a different kind of light in here: clinical and medium bright. The man seems hesitant to come too close to the thing, the thing at the center. He hovers along the wall. I get a clearer view of him in the dimness, and I understand why he might be used to being allowed anywhere. He's handsome, in profile. No. *Striking.* That's the word. And unlike most everyone, the harsher light makes him look younger, like he might be in the bathroom at a discotheque, a rave, or what I guess discotheque-rave bathrooms might be like.

"Delphi," the man says from above me. "Why are you still here?"

My hands stop. I meet his eyes. His arms are down straight by his sides.

"When did I tell you my name?" I ask.

"Well, my name is Towe."

"Towe," I say back. "It's sort of rude to ask someone why they *haven't* been laid off by their employer." I try to laugh, but now my neck is prickling. Why have I let this man come with me? We're utterly alone.

"I just mean, so many of the others are gone."

"Sure," I say, trying to sound at ease. "And not us. Reduced staff but not *no* staff. I don't know what to tell you."

"Do you think it's because of the guests?"

I blink. "What?"

"Do you think it's because of your people skills? How well you look after the guests. How you take care of them."

"What are you talking about?" I can't hold it back. His body blocks the way out of this room, this room that seemed unusually big a moment ago, and now seems tight. Towe steps out of the doorway's silhouette. He must feel the shift. He's showing me the way back to the track.

"Never mind," he says. "I don't mean to make you uncomfortable."

I slip past him, onto the path, the strange light and the sounds of horse pain echoing close. One more control room.

We're in a rotunda now, where two sets of tracks double back on each other, so that riders get a glimpse of other riders, and even fear that they might collide. At the narrowest gap between the two tracks stands the angry stag. Without knowing why, I hop down to track level and step over the bars. I stand at the base of the thing, close enough to touch. It's braying and raging, moving as one unit with its hooves flailing. Its antlers are enormous, almost the size of its entire body. Eyes are wide open, red, angry. I've never seen it this close up. Almost no one sees it this close up, for this long. It doesn't even look frightening; it looks sick.

He's beside me again.

"Delphi, I'm trying to tell you this without scaring you: You need to leave."

I stiffen. Without touching them, I can feel the stag's teeth moving. "I'm going to carry on with this. I think you need to go back down." I can feel the empty space where my walkie should be.

"Delphi, there are people in the park who shouldn't be here. They're watching you. And it's not safe for you or Brendan to be here anymore."

I take two steps back and almost trip over the curve of metal. "How do you know his name? Who the fuck are you?"

It's a strange thing that happens next. He's thinking, choosing his next words, choosing how to avoid the question. His jaw is readying for speech. But something slips into place. I suddenly know who he is. I take another step back. I really look.

"Oh my god. You're an actor. You're that guy."

The shitty movie on TV in that motel. Irish.

"You said your name was Towe. You're that . . . from like years ago . . ."

"Declan," he says.

"Yeah. *Declan Towe*." My spine is tingling. There's a rumbling from far off, from the top of Ben Nevis, but I hardly even notice it. "You're definitely not a disassembly guy."

"No."

Something else starts to form together, motes clotting midair in some hollow part of memory. "You were in *Nebuland*, weren't you."

The princess liked to call the lieutenant Airman, a funny joke, because of the whole rank thing, an airman is nothing compared to a general, and there was Garra, Airman's war-hungry half-brother. He falls off a cliff in a stupor just before the final battle, sending Airman into a violent rage. I remember now.

He nods. "It was the last thing I was in."

"How do you know my boyfriend's name, Declan Towe?"

"Why don't I tell you both when we're out of the park?" he says, but he notices it now, too. The rumbling. "I think we should both get out of here."

"I'm not gonna keep telling you, I'm not leaving unt—"

"I knew her, you know." His voice is tired, all charm drained out. "Callie."

My stomach clenches, and the part of my mind I can't control plays part of that video. I see the dark spot in the parking lot.

"What does she have to do with this?"

His eyes scan mine. I can see that he didn't know what this, what Callie's name, might do to me. A long shot. His eyelids are red. I can make out the capillaries as if he's being lit from within.

"Delphi, do you ever feel like you're being watched?" he almost shouts, over the rumbling, which I feel in the soles of my shoes.

"I . . ." I can't do both. I can't look for the source of the noise and process his words, give him answers. "I'm always being watched. It's the park."

At the same moment we see it coming. A cart, running backwards, careening out from a bend beyond the stag. We leap to the edge of the floor, bodies up against the wall of the walkway, its edge cutting into my breastbone. Towe is cursing, and shouting something.

"There are people in the park! People who shouldn't be here! They're a church! Leave them here! Let them have it!"

A blast while the cart screams past us, missing us by no more than a foot. It's impossible. The mechanism was shut off. There's no way the carts could be released.

People. People are here. A church.

The clatter of those scraping wheels dies down. I watch the tracks, waiting for more.

"Delphi, did you hear me?"

I try to catch my breath. "Who do you mean? Who's here?"

"People who are after the same thing that killed Callie. They think it won't kill them. They think they can master it. But they're dangerous. They're dangerous now and they'll be even more dangerous after, if they make it out . . ."

"Out *where*?" He's looking at me so pityingly that I imagine slapping him. Something in me twists. Who is this guy? This actor? He doesn't believe I have a job to do. *I have a job to do.*

I clear my throat. "You said there's something dangerous in the park?"

"Not in it," he says. "Under it."

A blast, deafening. I slap my gloved hands to my ears. Music. It's piercing, too loud even for a coaster in action. The stag is still bucking in small jolts just beyond Towe's shoulder. He's almost doubled over, one hand covering an ear, the other trying to hold me back, back to the platform edge.

I wriggle out from him—*Got to find the nearest control panel*—but no. It wouldn't be coming from there. This music . . . it's not anything that belongs to the ride. Trumpets and cymbals, Americana. Something old. Then I place it: the old theme from the Kingdom of the Future, before it was Nebuland. Rousing. Deafening. When the marching band drum line comes in, Towe comes close. He's mouthing something that I can't make out. I keep an arm out, don't want him close. He leans in, shouts again, but still, I hear nothing. He leaves my side and starts to touch the walls, starts to pound his fist and feel for something. A door. An exit. He's looking for a way out. When I start to lead the way to the nearest one, when I pry it open, when the music starts to diminish, I finally hear what it was he was saying, now coming out in little breaths, a pained and empty mantra:

"It's too late. Too late. Too late."

Sent from:
PO Box 538
4381 20th St W
Newberry Springs, CA 92365

More. A man I've never seen before arrived to give us a talk about new data protection policies, it was extremely weird, the AC didn't work in the room + we were sweating + so confused. There were windows in the room but they were tinted that kind of gray-green like you get in minivans + at one point we saw an actual tumbleweed tumble past. It was too much for us to handle. We all felt insane. Eventually this guy starts talking about NDAs + uses all this sinister legalese + we're just sitting there. I spaced out + when I came to, it was clear that the whole meeting was this thinly veiled threat, like they found this boring administrative way to tell us we couldn't talk about anything. We ask if it's okay for us to leave + the guy says he thinks we're still needed out here.

But then they leave us. They leave us here where we can talk to each other + wonder what would happen if one of us just left, or if they'll assign us to something new. They build everything out here, just a few miles down at the Ranch. So why not put us to use?

Speaking of the bots: I was clinging to this idea that the bots weren't all modeled after real people. Some of them had to be imagined, totally from scratch, right? The Nebuland + Lagoon Ride bots are based off actors, but not the other ones. Not necessarily. Sure, I've heard stories of the artists, even the engineers, crafting their bots into their exes or spouses or favorite cousins or whatever. Even if they did each have a living source, a real body, a real face that they're replicating, those living people might never step foot in the park, so they wouldn't be at risk of seeing . . . themselves.

But then I start thinking about the plane crash that the guy from the Hong Kong team talked about + the shooting that you didn't even respond to. I've been trying to do the math about how much harm a few people could do if, all at once, they slipped into that . . . mindset? State? Curse? Catherine. Just don't go to the opening. Don't let Declan go either. If I know him, he'll be desperate to get a glimpse of himself in there.

There's a really old guy here. His name is Oliver Candler. He was one of the really really early animators. Some kind of child prodigy, got into the studio as a teen, and somehow hasn't retired yet. I don't even know how that's legal. But yeah, he worked on everything. He worked on the first Gwendolyn + Cornelius + The Dog shorts. He worked on Peter + Wendy, like with little Renata Revere + everything. He'd been around for that whole crazy story about finding the little girl from the war, from Poland or wherever. He's Black + I guess he was the first non-white animator at the studio + he got written about a lot, way back when. The studio liked to show him off, pat themselves on the back + then not hire any women or non-white staff till like 1985. He seemed less angry about it than I was which made my anger seem showy. The point is he showed us little clippings in his wallet. He carried everything in his wallet. Old parking stubs + a key to an apartment he'd lived in in 1965 + a photo of his nieces, these two twin girls. It was so sad, to me, I don't know why it hit me that hard. Or maybe not sad. I don't know what to call it. He just had so much pride in being involved in a studio that would lock him away in a derelict room in the desert. Though he has a clean bed. Ours have gum stains on the frame.

He didn't know about these new bots. He spends his time out here mainly now, in the Imagination Ranch + he didn't see them getting made. I was confused about why he'd be

here, but then I started asking him more about the early
days of the studio. He spoke about the handful of execs
who took charge of all things <u>creation</u> (that's what he said)
because The Founders were just some Illinois bond brokers
who came into money after the war + didn't want to attract
any attention. No interesting story there. But then there were
the handful of men who led and pieced together the studio's
vision, the vision for the first lands of the park + the first
feature animations. They were into all sorts of things. Like
maybe they were swingers + got obsessed with the secret
drugs that got developed during the war + kept trying to get
their hands on LSD, before it really existed + got into that
esoteric pagan revival stuff. Do you know about all that?
It seems like something they might have made podcasts
about.

A guy called Thomas/Tomas/Tomasz (the one who rescued
Renata Revere from postwar wherever, that whole story)
would throw these parties that would start off as totally
normal parties + then at the end he'd reveal that he'd
arranged the buffet in such a way that guests had been made
to walk the outline of some Kabbalistic rune, just because of
how the buffet was laid out or whatever + everyone would get
really pissed off, or think it was kind of funny, or be terrified.
It's funny to me that this wasn't a one-off thing, like, he did it
again + again + people kept coming to the parties over and
over.

We talked for a long time. Oliver is cool as hell. In the 80s
he did most of the concept art for that new land that never
got made, the really old-timey kind of French one with all
the glass + gold + zeppelins. He said something about there
being a new vision for Peter + Wendy in that, some ride where
you're the size of Tinkerbell. A shame it never got made. The
whole conversation was nice. It made me feel calmer. He said
there were more parties he'd heard about, from the early days

that he'd tell me about later, if he remembered. It felt kind of spooky, the way he said it, but I think he's just an old guy wanting to get his debauchery off his chest.

So I was feeling good, more calm. But then, just as I was going to leave, he asked me a question.

"Why am I here?"

And it was like whatever had calmed me down had been totally purged from my system with a few words. I said, "I don't know." + he asked me if it had anything to do with his nieces. The girls in that photo. I asked what he meant. The sun was going down by that point.

But he said: "I drew them."

So I said, "Okay."

+ he said: "If I drew them, they might get copied."

+ then he sort of drifted off to sleep + I felt more on edge than ever. It was such a strange thing to say. When I got back to my room, I emailed Kendra + Nattson. I'd done that when I arrived, too. No response. I haven't gotten an email in days. Not from the studio. Not from anyone connected to the park. I checked + no one else has either. No one knows if we've been cut loose. No one knows if we still have jobs. I don't know why they're keeping us here, but as of this morning my car is still in the lot. I can still drive to Newberry Springs to mail these. I'm going to sit tight just a bit longer, until I can get a response from someone, or get a sense of how I would even go about leaving. But Catherine, if more than a couple of weeks go by without you hearing from me, in . . . Well I guess I don't know. Start asking around.

I have an idea. I like the idea of you going to hang out at the cabin for a while. If Declan made you go to a weird C-listers forest-church session, then you can get him to take you to the cabin. It just sits there. Mom + Dad never go. (Oh, to answer your question, I talk to them plenty. We talk when we want to talk. It works for all of us.) If you don't want to get away because of all of this, then go to get away from the fires. Wildfires don't make it there.

- Bro

P.S. Seriously that church sounds sad. Yeah, Declan can find producers somewhere else. Jesus, what an idiot. Wait, you said some of them were in Nebuland?

CHAPTER SIX

J ust before my birthday Whit drove us into Omaha for a neon exhibit at a gallery. He knew some of the artists, he said, and it seemed to make him genuinely happy, holding my mother's hand, and occasionally mine, through those dark corridors. I loved seeing the light in there. I was used to watching hot glass underneath Whit's hands in the shed, for hours sometimes, but seeing it here reminded me what it was all for. I ran up to a few pieces and got scolded by seated gallery attendants, but I barely heard them. Neon feels hedonistic, such a bare manipulation of the senses, such an unnatural pleasure that there's almost shame in it, in a way that makes it all the more precious.

But on my birthday, Whit went back in. A voluntary hold that turned involuntary pretty quickly. Mom assured me it was only temporary. He'd be back before I knew it. I asked her what it was that made things hard for him again, and she said that it just happened sometimes, with his condition, and it wasn't her fault, if that's what I was asking. I told her it wasn't.

"They keep showing the goddamn footage!" she shouted when she got back from her first visit to the hospital. "On the TVs, the towers, over and over the same thing. How is that meant to help anyone be less crazy?"

Whit's son, Daryl, drove from Colorado Springs during that time, and after his first visit to the hospital he had similar things to say. "Dad keeps asking them to change it from the news but no one'll listen to him. It's like a sick joke. All that burning metal and the fucking skyline. They're all freaked out and the staff think it's important for them to see."

Daryl spat a lot and it almost seemed like he was going to spit on the kitchen floor just then, but he didn't. I remember thinking I would pay to see what my mom would do to him if he had.

Daryl stayed with us for almost two weeks, but he slept in his Camaro and went in and out of Whit's shed most days. I got worried he might be touching the setups or taking things. Everything would have to be dehumidified—I'd have to ask Mom for money for new vacuum gauges. He started moving boxes into the shed, brown boxes and a couple of duffel bags that rattled a little bit.

I came out of my room one night when Mom was working and found Daryl on the couch with two other men I didn't recognize, watching some TV movie and counting something in a box. One of them wore a ski jacket even though it was summer. I watched from the hall but didn't come into the living room, even though that was the only way to the bathroom and I had to pee. I held it till Mom got home, and when she did, the men had already gone, as if into smoke, and Daryl didn't say anything about having people over. That night he asked if he could crash in the living room. Mom offered him my room, said I'd sleep on the couch, but he said he was too big a guy for a kid's bed. He'd be just fine on the couch.

I started to be out when Mom was out. I started staying after school and got in the habit of asking my teachers, especially Señora Kennedy, if they needed help grading papers or something, but they never did, so sometimes I'd just do laps around the school, looking like I was going somewhere, until the sun started to set. Then I walked over to the library and sat in the entry area even though I didn't have a card. I knew I could get one if I showed them a bill or a letter with our address on it, but I remembered Whit saying, "You don't owe the federal government one iota of your time, you never run their errands," and even though I knew libraries were civic, really, not like the IRS, I got worried he'd find out and be disappointed. Mom always told me it was worse to be disappointed than to be mad.

Eventually the nice girl who worked at the desk started giving me whichever books weren't re-stockable. It took a lot for a book at a public library to be discarded, she warned me. Either loaned so many times the pages were almost mush, or if they'd been severely damaged. She had a twin sister who worked at Sun Mart who was kind of famous for being not nice, which I found very funny.

While Whit was gone and we couldn't make neon in his shed, I did almost nothing aside from reading those thirdhand books. I read *Wayside School Is Falling Down* and *The Sum of All Fears* and *Deenie* and *Empire* by Gore Vidal. I read *To Kill a Mockingbird*, *Chicken Soup for the Golfer's Soul*, *American Psycho*, *Dianetics: The Modern Science of Mental Health*, *The Ladybird Baby Names Book*, *Visionary Experience in the Golden Age of Spanish Art*, *Dune Messiah*, the novelization of the 1992 film *Scent of a Woman*, and, of course, *Peter and Wendy* by J. M. Barrie.

That one was in particularly bad shape. It had a hard embellished cover, but the last third had been torn out, so I focused on the story's beginning. Even after I found out what happens later, all the stuff in the Darling children's bedroom was my favorite part. There's something in there about a kiss box that I didn't understand, and Peter's appearance is actually very gradual. Then there's his shadow. It's misbehaving. Peter tries to catch it. It continues to misbehave. It takes trickery to catch hold of it. Trickery and then stitches.

One day while I was waiting around in the library, I saw Daryl out the window. He was talking to another man, and he had one of the duffel bags I'd seen him move into the shed. He gave the other man something from inside it and took some money in return. The girl behind the counter saw it, too, but she didn't say anything.

Another time I was in the kitchen.

"Heyheyhey!" Daryl barked. I didn't know he was in there. I'd seen an arm with a cigarette sticking out of the Camaro just earlier, but I didn't know if it was him. His friends had been coming and going a lot by then. He got up close to me, and I noticed that a little chunk of his ear was missing. "That's not for you."

Only then did I notice the water bottle in my hand. Mom always got huge cardboard stacks of them, plastic-sealed, from Costco. I'd grabbed it from the kitchen table, but this one didn't have a label. I don't know what came over me. I was angry at those nights when the men came over and I couldn't pee, and the fact that my mom had almost handed this man my room. Maybe the brave feeling came from nowhere at all. I wrenched it back from his reach and opened it, took a whiff. I knew what booze in a clear plastic bottle smelled like. This wasn't that. It smelled like something different altogether, a chemical smell like when you walk into a pet store.

He lunged for it, but it was just like in a movie: My mom walked through the door that very moment. I left the bottle on the table and mumbled something about not leaving stuff around if he was gonna have a conniption. I don't think he heard.

Between the time with the water bottle and when Whit got back, my mom and her work friend Tenitra took me to Lake Okoboji. We never made it to the lake itself; they loved the motel's indoor pool. I remember braiding together three pool noodles, wrestling with the top part so I could get some give on the strands, when I heard my mom and Tenitra talking to a couple of men in the hot tub. "She reads all the fucking time but she never talks about what she reads. Should I be worried about that?" my mom said.

"Maybe she's got that thing," a man said. I think he made a gesture because the rest of them made overlapping "hmm" sounds and little strained laughs.

"She ran away once. She hid in an empty pool for sixteen hours.

You ever hear about a kid staying in one place for that long without shouting?"

On the long drive home I read *Number the Stars* by Lois Lowry and *Bad As I Wanna Be* by Dennis Rodman back-to-back and I didn't say a word.

When Whit got back, he started to train me—really train me—in neon-crafting.

"Tell me everything you know about glass," he asked, skinnier, one day in September.

"It's hard. It breaks."

"What else?"

I thought about it. "It's fancy. You can see through it. You're not supposed to touch it, really, like most of the time, and if you step on it you might not feel it at first but you feel it later, in the middle of the night, when you're trying to sleep, but it's not something you can wake up your mom for, it has to wait till the next day."

"Did you know that fire can make it soft?"

"Yeah. Yeah I think I've seen that on TV before." I felt stupid for having said that it was hard. I never said it was hard *all the time*.

"Now tell me everything you know about fire."

"You shouldn't touch it."

"That's it?"

"Um. I think so."

"Did you say that because you think it's what I want you to tell me?"

"No."

"Well," he said, sticking the end of a murky rubber tube between his teeth. "That's not very imaginative." He handed me a pair of long gloves.

The vacuum pumps, the manifold pressure, the practice argon. Arranging the slim torches in a semicircle, so that they faced each other at an angle. From above they look like the maw of a terrible beast. The ribbon burner like an upturned janitor's broom, releasing a thin horizon of Bible-light, pale blue, hissing like a garden snake. The moment you place your glass on it, the color changes.

Whit snapped in front of my eyes.

"I lose you there for a second?"

"No. I'm fine," I said. "I love it."

Our electrodes came premade, and though I didn't know a ton about how they worked, I was able to attach them to two ends of two lengths of glass using the blow hose to keep things cool and intact while molten. Once, when Whit was walking steady laps around the reservoir behind the 76 station, getting air despite a recently herniated disc, I went into the shed alone. I got the seam to meld perfect on only my second try. Then I used the hand torch. I liked how it looked like a tool for making s'mores, a little square frame at the end of a long stick. I started bombarding without paying attention to the pressure gauge, which made me feel like a real dummy, but nothing got messed up. I clipped the lead from the bombarding transformer onto the electrode, made sure power could get to the circuit, and before flooding the whole thing with gas I decided to play REM from the dinky blue stereo that Whit kept around, because he liked that and I was missing him, in there. He liked "Stand" best.

Underneath the stereo I saw a few more water bottles without wrappers. Someone had draped a blanket on top of them. An empty duffel bag sat beside them.

I planted the rod I made on the sticky checked plastic sheet covering our kitchen table. It was only about a foot long, with hardened bubbles at the seam, but it worked just fine.

"Where'd you learn to do that?" Mom asked, poking at it.

"Whit lets me help him."

"That's what goes on in there?"

She rolled it one more time, and went back to her magazine. She snapped half a rice cake into fourths with a quick maneuver of her fingers and ate two pieces.

"I'm gonna watch TV," I said. I left the neon beside her. I hadn't even plugged it in.

There was a news segment about a new land in the park, one that had been in the works, in one way or another, for over a decade.

There would be all kinds of things that I'd read about—France and ear trumpets and funiculars and the starlets of silent films with their hemophiliac skin and diamond-shaped lips—and things that were both unknown and unknowable. Park secrets too delicious to reveal just yet. But there would be a new Peter and Wendy ride. I sat inches from the screen. They cut to an ad for a daytime show, meant for people my age, starring a girl about my age named Callie Petrisko, who had a birthmark sitting near her nostril, and who had sharp teeth, toward the back. That made me smile a little. I didn't think about my lonely length of neon left unnoticed in the kitchen. I didn't think about my mother and how little she knew, or cared, about me. And when the ad went away, I touched the screen with my fingertips, longing for the images of the park and the images of the girl to return. But all I felt was hot glass.

There's an emergency exit that leads down the side of the mountain, along a narrow path meant for acrobat cast members who did the daily flight show along fishing line between lands. I think Towe's not quite agile enough to navigate it as I am. But I must be clumsier than I think. He's just behind me, shouting about how some people must already be at the central park controls, though he couldn't possibly know where those are, and how they're looking for something dangerous, something about the new animatronics. My heart is in my throat. I've got to find management. I've got to find Andrea or Hery or anyone else. I've got to find Brendan.

"I let them in here."

It sounds like Towe is just over my shoulder, but I venture a look back: he's full feet up from me, but the sight . . . makes me wince. The top of the mountain is just there, as well, the illusion of it narrowing into a great height ruined from this vantage point. He's as tall as the last ice ledge just below the pointed peak. "In exchange for something."

What does he mean *let them in*? Every guest has paid for a ticket, or a season pass. There's no sneaking in, no sneaking out.

"You need to leave," I hear myself say.

"*You* need to leave, Delphi. Let them take it."

"Guests," I say between little lunges down the steep path. "Gotta evacuate."

"What guests?"

I stop in my tracks. Turn around. He slows to a halt. He's sweating. He looks scared.

"What do you mean? Those guests." I fling an arm at the empty space below.

"There are no guests here, Delphi."

I want to laugh. This man is deranged.

"There aren't guests in the shut-off sections, if that's what you mean." I know it's not. "But there are guests on rides. On Caves. Brendan is entertaining guests as we speak."

That sad look again. "Delphi, there's only me and the people I came here with. The ones . . ."

Something over my shoulder. I twist—there. I see what he sees. A little figure. This time I really do laugh. "You were saying?"

And I bound down the last third of the mountain to the concrete below. In my haste I step through a begonia bush at the base. I barrel through the empty queue and launch myself over the outermost barrier post. My feet ache from the climb, but I'm filled with helium, something that makes me light, and then the guest is before me.

I recognize her. The very old woman.

"Oh—" I stutter. I start again, coming closer in happy little steps. "Hello there! There's no cause for concern, but we're going to help you exit this section, as it's shutting down for the season." How we've been trained to say it.

She doesn't move. Her hair is a small white cloud framing that puckered flesh. She wears glasses on a chain, a tank top that looks like it belongs to a teen. Her arms look featherlight, the texture of paper that's been balled up, thrown in the trash, salvaged, and balled up for the garbage once more. Her feet are planted firmly, but her hands shake where they are, dropped by her sides. Her pants, worn cotton, are stained.

"I'm sorry, ma'am, did . . ." My voice comes out shaky, and I can't right it, can't will myself to speak calm and clear.

She keeps mouthing something, and I feel Towe behind me, and I look over my shoulder for not even a second, and then she's gone. There's a panel swinging from a faux stone slab near a hedge, underneath an awning that normally shades the queue for churros. I pull open the panel: stairs and the distant echo of small footsteps.

"Who was that?" asks Towe.

"I . . . How would I know? A guest . . ." I see the hinge has been broken. The key reader has been battered so that the plastic has come away like a layer of skin. "What, you don't know her? She's not one of your mysterious danger-guests?"

He says something in response, but I don't wait to hear it. I don't know these stairs, this corridor underground—it's not my normal section—but I fling myself down the stairs and do my best to shut the panel door behind me, yank it a few times so that, even broken, it might wedge into place.

Another section with faulty lights. There's not even a flicker here, just damp air and a wall that feels wet with condensation. I shout a few times.

"Ma'am!"

And then, "Hello?! Anyone?"

And I half-trip over something that rolls. I feel, clumsy and frantic, for a moment before I find it. A flashlight. I look for the switch—it's not there, there's a rubbery button instead, like I'm pressing into bruised fruit. It's not one of our flashlights. But it works. The beam reveals a sign reading *SECTION 4B*, which orients me a bit; it lets me know that if I've come from just east of the lake, I'm moving north, toward the castle, Fairytale Grove, and Nebuland.

There's rust on the walls, signs of poor upkeep, no murals, no cast changing nooks or lockers, the little dorm-like comforts of shared employment, communal life. Ahead of me there are a few piles of clothing. Not costumes, not uniforms: gray gym shorts, checked Vans with doodles on the soles. I crouch beside a small velvet top, which might have been gold once, but now bears veins of mildew and a patch of moss. When I poke at it with my boot, it reveals an underside of wet black.

There's a clang from just ahead, and I'm on my feet. A door with the same injuries to its hinge as the entry hatch. A door on my right, and a door beyond it. A heavy curtain. Something's coming back to me: a soundproof curtain.

I've been here.

They gave us a tour of this room early, just after I started. Mostly for the live show team. The pyrotechnics guys, the parade crew. Sometimes they needed to do effects on the fly. God, the memory feels like a dream.

I push past the heavy curtain. The room is an asymmetrical network of shelves. The floor is sectioned into neat squares, like looking at farmland from a plane. Yes, they walked us through here in small groups. We skirted along these segmented sections: a patch of concrete, one of fine sand, one of wood planks, then brick, loose soil, gravel, Astroturf, and one smooth, polished stepping stone. Oddities on the shelves: one devoted to car parts and to vegetables, musical instruments. Shelves of cloth. Shelves of empty plastic containers that were damp from the inside with condensation.

I approach those shelves now. They're almost exactly the same. But where vegetables were, nothing. I spin around and let my flashlight slice through the shadow.

I remember from that tour, years ago, there were also several different types of walls and ceiling, overhanging panels of felt or a dense wood, and a few little square huts. I guess all of that careful placement, alien density to the surfaces, had to do with resonance, if that's the right word. Reverberation.

I shout into the dark, one more time. They're not words anymore, but a little groan, maybe an attempt at orientation in the dark, bat-like, to get a feel for the dimensions of the space, in case I get lost. Some imagined voice is telling me that I've already become lost.

"Half rock salt, half baking soda," a sound engineer had explained, back then. He held something that looked like an animal's stomach, and he was twisting it. The top was knotted with the deftness of a young father who'd tied off thousands of balloons for countless birthday parties. "And, of course, a condom."

Some of us laughed. We didn't know if we should laugh at condoms in the park.

The man disappeared for a second, and when he returned he had a small mic with a pop-shield clipped onto it. I felt relief when he reappeared; I felt like without him we'd all have become lost in tchotchke phantasmagoria and drowned in countersunk screws and piles of paper party hats.

The man crouched down by the condom filled with salt and baking soda.

"Can I get a volunteer?" he called out. None of us said anything, even the showboats among us, the ones who'd come straight from Groundlings or musical theater. We felt ill at ease. It was a stage, but it had no audience, so we couldn't figure out how to perform.

"You." He pointed right at me.

I made a sort of *Mm* sound, caught halfway between a coy *Me?* and a cool *Nah*.

"Yeah, you!" he insisted. "Come on up!"

I did as I was told, though there was no "up." There was only the segment of floor on which the horrible lump sat. A few sarcastic woops and claps came from the rest of them.

"Step on it."

"Will it—"

"Step on it."

I put a small amount of my weight on the lump and then pulled back. The thing looked intact. I did it once more. And then, there, the sound.

"What we have just made, young"—he looked at my name tag, machine-fresh and sparkling white—"Delphi Baxter, is—"

"Snow," I said. "It sounds like snow."

Now I'm retracing my steps, spinning, waiting for my light to land on the door I just entered. Panic hasn't quite consumed me when I find the curtain, barrel toward it, power through. I'm back in the main corridor, and I'm hollering *Fuck it* inside my head, searching for stairs, stairs up, stairs out, any stairs.

I'm staggering up, my hands slapping sandy strips on the stairs. Then the rush of air, the drug release of natural light on my face. The sun is waning, maybe an hour from setting, and there's a mist over the park, one that isn't really visible, that I suspect only I can see.

Someone's running toward me. I'm doubled over, hands on my thighs, breathing shallow, and then there are hands on my back, my shoulder.

"What happened are you okay what happened—"

Brendan is in the prince's shirt and his jeans. He's got black marks on his face and a few on his legs. There are other stripes. Spots, too. A smear of magenta.

"There are people in the park who aren't supposed to be here," I manage, still bent at the waist. I can see some gnarled, geological excrescence. The glittering, breathing gates to Nebuland. "The disassembly guy is one of them. He's not a disassembly guy."

"Where is he?" Brendan asks, serious.

"I don't know. There was this really old lady—"

"Where did you last see him? That man."

"I . . ." I can't tell him about Ben Nevis. What would I say? "I—"

"Tell her."

Brendan and I both turn toward the voice.

He's still clutching the strap that holds a bag. He looks thinner, somehow, even though it's been less than an hour. Towe comes toward Brendan, fearless, jaw clenched. "Tell her what happens when you try to leave."

Sent from:
Catherine Moser-Towe
2227 W. Catalina Blvd.
Los Angeles, CA 90027

Why won't you just call me, or answer my calls? This whole conversation could be done in under an hour if you just called. Do you still think they're bugging your phone? Do you have any evidence of that whatsoever?

And why not just leave, if your car is there, and you're already driving out to send these letters, and you think this studio is so evil? I'm not saying that because I think you're in any kind of danger, but it sounds like you're not getting answers, so . . . I don't know.

You said I didn't respond to the shooting at The Standard thing, and that's because . . . Jesus, that's just really dark. Why does anything like that happen? People are sometimes mentally ill and anyone can buy a gun in this terrifying country and I don't think it's got to do with the robots that you're so suspicious of. Sorry if this is sounding dismissive again, but I'm feeling kind of bitter. I had to go up north and get Mom and Dad out of Benicia. Did you know that? A whole chunk of the San Pablo Bay is gone. No one's not aware of the fires. They evacuated Mom and Dad's neighborhood and still not a word from you? Cool.

There was obviously a problem with the power grid in the Bay Area, and time that with fire season, I guess no one (including you) could have guessed how fast the surrounding area got torched. And everyone's safe. But when I got to their house, before we drove south, they had all these scented candles laid out around the floor. There'd been a blackout for three days. And they didn't have flashlights or anything. God forbid they follow common-sense advice about natural disaster prep, but yeah they had like objectively way too many candles, all the ancient ones they used to keep inside the skinny closet with the towels in the old house, like the ones that had been around since the early 90s. It looked like a séance. Fire inside, fire outside. Mom and Dad are at the Zuckermans' now. And on the way back to LA, on that last stretch of the 5 where you start to think maybe you're in a Twilight Zone episode and that the freeway will in fact never end. I saw that glow over the hills, from off in the distance. More fires. SoCal fires. How can it be everywhere?

I'm glad you made a friend. I want to know more about these sexy occult parties. Oliver sounds great. That is a weird thing for him to say, worried about his nieces being . . . duplicated? . . . but remember when Grandma was always asking about mesothelioma? Over and over, do I have mesothelioma, for like two years before she died? Sometimes old people get like that.

And yes, to answer your question, a lot of the church members were in Nebuland. I'm kind of embarrassed . . . Declan actually convinced me to go back. And I think I get it a little bit more now. Like, it's not any more appealing, but I think I understand what's bringing everyone together. They all seem to have done something to sabotage their careers. The stunt guy, whose real name is Lander, if you can believe it, fucked up the bones in his face doing the stunt that he's famous for, balancing concrete blocks on his forehead. Something came loose and it almost broke clear through the bridge of his nose. He has a gnarly scar. I don't know how it works, but I guess when you mess up that bad in stunt work everyone hears about it fast. So he got really into bodybuilding while he wasn't working, and then that made it even harder for him to get work. You can't look distinct, can't be some beef-cube of muscle if you're standing in for relatively normal actors, which I guess had been a lot of the work he got in his early days.

Someone else, this nice lady about my age, was saying that she'd booked two speaking roles on some premium cable series back-to-back, and all she did to fuck it up was get pregnant.

She'd been married for like three years, and when she was twenty-six she had a kid. She lost the weight, but every casting director said she'd missed some crucial window just after her episodes aired. She said they said that to her a lot—the words "crucial window." She had the energy of someone really wonderful, like just beautiful eyes and a genuinely nice vibe about her. But she also seemed so, so sad.

The woman with the Gwendolyn lashes tattoo lost a role because of it. You don't get IP tattoos, I guess, if you ever want to be on camera.

One guy slept with the sister of the roommate of his agent's assistant, and never got work again.

All these people have lost their hold on their own futures. They've missed some opportunity and feel like their lives have been defined by it. But they won't just come out and say that. They all kind of perform. If it's not some kind of group breathing exercise performance, then it's singing to the ash trees. Or it's weeping during prayer. Or it's hugging the hardest, having the quirkiest interests, scavenging the rarest shrooms in the most obscure corner of the world. One white guy did Mongolian throat singing he'd learned from an on-set tutor while shooting the Any Which Way But Loose reboot.

Yule's sermons still have the stench of Christian summer camps. He rarely talks about God directly anymore. Instead he speaks about how all of us are so very different. (Different from what? Unclear.) And only in building this community will we realize what we were created for.

He was also in a terrible mood because he had some scenes cut from the movie. And I guess he might have his bot pulled from the ride. So there ya go. One less maniac to worry about. (I kid.) Oh, and of course afterwards Declan totally abandons me to talk development with Yule. These women approach me to chat. They're twins, and they explain why there are so many twins around, and in Hollywood generally. It's the child labor laws! How virtually every child actor you see on screen has to be a twin. I'd never put that together. Children can't work full adult workdays, so if you're a stage-mom you've struck gold if you have twins. They flock from every state, every country, to get their two kids on set playing one kid. But there's a particular population of sad, failed adult-actor-who-used-to-be-a-child-actor. A whole population of sad twins.

So yeah, these women just started monologuing about Declan, like about how he was so good in the movie and he was definitely going to get the relaunch of his career that he wanted. He'd definitely spoken to them about those desires. I didn't want to listen; they were just huge turds with matching pointy jaws that looked like they could chomp through steel and fuck em.

I hate saying anything bad about Declan to you. I don't want you to say I told you so. But it just seemed like . . . he understood how sad it all felt to me, but he brought me along anyway. He couldn't go alone. He just wants this film of his made. He just wants two hours of red lights and ambient music and sinewy men wrestling and insects pupating, endless arthouse bullshit, all so everyone forgets Frosh Island.

That took a turn. Well . . . thanks for letting me get that off my chest! You said to wait a few weeks if I haven't heard from you. What's a few? Three? Bro, I really think you're fine. I saw some stills of the new bots and—fuck. You're right. They're good and . . . almost too good? I can see why you'd be so creeped out by them, especially if you don't know much about how they were made. But remember that's all they are: creepy, not dangerous. Creepy is fine.

Write soon. Despite everything, I'm enjoying this.

—Cath

P.S. Wait, another thing, Callie mentioned that only a few people would be going on the rides on opening day. It'll just be her and her date and some kids. Does that make you feel better? Can I go to it now?

CHAPTER SEVEN

We're forming a triangle: me, Brendan, and this lanky man, whose face I can now place in the background of posters for movies whose names I've long forgotten. Just a semicircular arrangement of young bodies, hamming to the camera, maybe an eyebrow raised. I can faintly see his name printed on the glossy pages of a teen magazine. Hear *Declan Towe* rattled off in a string of supporting actors' names during a commercial.

Brendan doesn't look surprised. Not surprised enough. His eyes are only on Towe for a moment before they settle somewhere in the middle distance. He waits out the silence in a way that I can't.

"What happens when we leave?" I ask, knowing that's not exactly what Towe said. He said *try*.

"Nothing," says Brendan. "You know, Delphi. You're there. At the end of every day, we wrap up. We change. We go home."

"This isn't good for her. And now there are people here. It's over, Brendan," says Towe, gently, maybe too gently. "Let them have it."

They share something, some moment of silence, and I do some

quick calculations: the distance I must have covered underground just now (two-fifths of a mile? the length from the entrance of our nearest CVS all the way back to the pharmacy, five or six times?), how many fights I've seen Brendan win (zero), how many fights I've seen Brendan *in* (zero), how old Towe must be (unclear), when I saw Towe's face in the background ether of popular media (the time of Tenitra's son's friend taking me to that Christian rock concert? the time of mustache tattoos on the inside of girls' fingers? Y2K? a royal wedding?). I try to measure from where I am now, these gates to this land, to the biggest gates, the park gates. I try to count the remaining tasks on my Action Plan.

I can't recall a single one.

The men are talking in rushed, hushed tones, but when I start to speak they fall silent, like they've only been biding time till I made an announcement. "Brendan, I think we should just go."

He seems to me then as if he's behind glass, a moving liquid collection of tan and gray and the sickly cream of his shirt. But Towe seems to be watching him with a clarity I am suddenly, incandescently envious of.

"Let's walk first," Brendan says, and touches my arm, and then my tailbone, and moves me deeper into the leafy, throbbing gates of Nebuland. I don't hear Towe's footsteps follow us, but Brendan takes me sharply to the left as soon as possible, perhaps to lose him.

While we walk, while he guides me with a warm hand, I feel my fingers twitch for something: a key, a needle, a flashlight—the flashlight. Where had I dropped it?

And we're on a pathway that runs alongside the main thoroughfare leading from the gates to the land's western side. There's a fenced-off little ramp made for wheelchair-using guests to have direct access to the main canteen, where food items themed after characters can be slopped onto trays for $22. From the topmost point of this little arched footpath, the entire icy metropolis of this place spreads before us. I catch myself breathing strangely. Brendan lifts his hand from my back and rests his elbows on the rail. I do the same and find that I can breathe easier.

It would have been too expensive, too controversial to completely tear down the old Kingdom of the Future, so the existing architecture was adapted here—all the towering Futurist monoliths, cutesy fifties flying saucer sculptures refitted and plastered over with glittering ice and the blues and pinks of the new franchise's palette. They expanded to twice the ground area, so that Nebuland is now larger than some state fair grounds. And unlike other sections of the park, this one is mostly fully visible on foot, without those twists and shrouds that the other lands need to give the illusion of size. It's an open expanse of elegant spires and boldly signposted attractions housed in big rectilinear nodes on elevated walkways like this one, and these are overshadowed by a rim at the top of the land's caldera shape, mainly used for stunt shows and the odd VIP security detail. And when you diverge from the path of the cold, exhilarating cityscape, there are avenues and sitting nooks infused with the warmth of those few scenes where Fiusha and the lieutenant general—Airman—fell in love, dared to touch each other's alien skin, and dug into the planet's cozy depths. All around there are lights-on timers so that day and night become meaningless, and guests are in a constant state of being lit up from above, like starlight, or below, like an alien burial ground. There's a fully functioning day spa and a super-speed track ride and, of course, the lagoon ride. Callie Petrisko's lagoon ride.

"That was Declan Towe," I say. "You remember him?"

"Kind of. He was in the movie." He nods toward everything that sits before us.

"Do you know what he's talking about?"

"He might have gotten in as part of one of the packages. The remaining tourist groups. Like a VIP thing."

"Okay," I start, "and then he had a mental break?"

Brendan doesn't laugh. "No. I don't . . ."

He doesn't finish. I scan the distance and see a faux snowdrift made of odd synthetic material that lets guests press their bodies into it, like a snow angel, but upright, and then bounces back to normal shape. It smells like pennies.

"I think we should leave. Declan Towe is right, even if he's making some stuff up. It feels like someone's fucking with us. Ben Nevis, like . . . someone was in there with us."

Brendan doesn't look at me, but he nods. "Leave . . . ," he says, to himself. "Yeah, we can do that."

When he looks sad like this, I have a full-body pull toward affection, like an animal instinct, and it's almost physically painful to resist. But I can't read his face if I hug him, and I need to read him. I need to understand. We sit in silence. Silence makes sense, here, in Nebuland, but it's more than that. I remember more of what Towe said.

"Brendan, how many kids came up to you today?"

"I don't know."

"Roughly," I say. "An estimate."

"Hey, when you started here, did anyone ask you about The Founders? The whole mystery of who started the park?" He looks at me now, twisting his body in a pose that almost seems graceful.

"Yeah. Some baristas told me about that once. The Founders were real, or The Founders were not real, or the park is like a sentient being."

"What do you think?"

"Why aren't you answering my question about the kids?"

And I think he's evading the question, I think he's being quiet to buy time, to think around whatever he's not telling me. But he's fixed on something. I follow his line of sight. I see it, too. Movement on the edge of the square outside the Lux Pavilion, behind a sculpture. It used to be a sculpture of the solar system, maybe ten feet in height, and it would toss and swivel each planet around its orbit every hour on the hour. Now it's a static stone carving of Do'loyia, the tribal lady-sage who appears before Fiusha and offers sweet words of guidance in an enchanted, snowy glade. And it's moving.

No.

There's movement at the edges. Two bodies, flanking it.

"Do you know them?" I ask. Brendan doesn't say anything. He reaches for my arm, and I startle myself by twisting away.

Then: a sound like carnage. A fiery scream, like metal scraping up against different, more unwieldy metal. I leap backward, slap my ears, and find myself moving toward it. I can faintly hear Brendan call my name. There's a pause, a breath, and then more scraping, like an injured animal. Towe is there, where we turned past the gates, and he's dragging something behind him. A cannon? It seems to be cutting into the flesh of the park. There's a crimson stain where it's dragged against the ground, so visceral and grim that I need to squint. No, it's not a wound—of course not—but it's a stain.

Towe is shouting now, but he's drowned out by what he's dragging.

"—keeping you in!" and "—safe out there! You've got to—"

Brendan takes my arm with force, not a guiding hand, but a pull from someone who's no longer pretending they're not twice your size. I'm almost off my feet entirely.

"What the fuck!"

"I'm sorry," he says, but he doesn't loosen his grip. "We've just got to go."

"Brendan, stop!"

I hear how pathetic it sounds—all that's missing is a lame flailing of my fists—but I don't do that. I gallop, I try to keep up, but he's moving too fast and I can't stop the soles of my feet from dragging, and when I'm finally upright, in motion, pulling against his grasp, I stumble and instinctively reach for him, and for some reason that feels like giving in, like he doesn't need to drag me anymore, though of course he still does. I stop fighting. I can't tell where we're going, until suddenly I can: Lux Pavilion. Back entrance. I've never been through this way. He looks like he knows where he's going, but when we reach the door it's my keycard and needle that he reaches for, right pocket. He slaps it, fits the needle, and hands it back, pressing it to the middle of my chest, where I catch it with clumsy hands.

Another corridor, white with scuff stains on the wall, a decade of large objects—the tech on display in the Lux Pavilion, showroom prototypes and flashy science stuff in pieces, being moved in and out.

It's so dark I can't see the carpet below us.

"You don't need to pull me."

He loosens his grip on my arm, but he doesn't slow down, and it takes a minute for my eyes to adjust. There's a single shaft of light illuminating the otherwise inky darkness of the huge space. It's from a shattered section of ceiling; there are chunks of insulation and ice floes of industrial glass. It's been like that for a while. But the light outside is fading fast—it casts the massive space in hazy hues. It also reveals an elevator shaft, tilted—collapsed and colossal—resting at a diagonal. The Pavilion closed sooner than the rest; it was often shuttered for weeks at a time when they were changing out exhibits or replacing one shiny prototype self-driving Vespa with another. But how could a collapsed elevator go unnoticed?

Brendan's looking for something. He start-stops, trying to orient himself in the dark.

I take the opportunity. "What did Towe have?"

"Just follow me," he says.

"It looked like a cannon."

"There," and he's pulling me again, not as rough as before, now more frightened than angry.

He leads us past the few curved partitions that remain upright. Most of them, especially at the back of the pavilion, are flat on their backs, loosened from the ground. This space used to be a labyrinth of sectioned science exhibits, like any of the static parts of a Museum of Natural History: some gemstones behind glass and a microscope displaying some kind of cell with the word *IMMORTAL* splashed across a nearby wall. Tech was where the real action was: the custom roller coaster simulator, a giant skinless bot head that would mimic your speech, a quick DNA analysis booth that only required a mouth swab. Engineering and math were crammed together along the far end, and into the mezzanine level. Small stations, requiring two minutes or less of a visitor's attention each. An enormous tuning fork. An air blower within a Plexiglas hemisphere, making patterns in waves, delicate or frightening, depending on how much chaos the child wanted to see. You'd maneuver through these "learning points" until you emerged in the wide-open center, with all the room a kid would ever need to run and tumble and scissor-kick on a discreetly padded floor.

I say it again, to myself, what Towe told Brendan to do: *Tell her what happens when you try to leave.*

"He said it was a church that's here. What kind of church could be here? Did you know of any church group that was meant to come through?"

I know he won't answer, but after another minute of tripping over debris and carpet in the dark, he says, with the measured calm of a training video, "Delphi, the important thing to remember is that you have a job to do."

"What does that mean?"

"Just . . ." He fumbles. "The Action Plan. Despite who might be in here. You have your plan. And maybe now what we should do is, like, get ahead."

The words *Action Plan* do something to me. "So," he says gently. "Let's shut down the lagoon ride."

I pull my hands from him. I step back. "What? No."

"Delphi—"

"I'm not going in there. It's the one place I don't go. You know that."

I hear, rather than see, his careful steps toward me. "Delphi, I promise there's nothing to be afraid of in there. I'll be right there with you."

"Why are you talking to me like that?" The tops of my hands start to tingle. "Why are you so afraid of Declan Towe?"

"I'll explain when we're in there."

"Why do you want me to go in there so badly?" I take another step back and start to pant.

He doesn't try to close our gap this time. "Because he can't follow us in there."

Those words land different, and something begins to calm in me. He's telling the truth.

"He can't?"

There's a thump, and Brendan puts his hand over my mouth even though I'm not making a sound. A few faint, resonant dings emanate from the shaft. An object dropping.

Then we're running.

My arm tugs against its socket and Brendan's fingers dig into me, just above the elbow, bare skin. I know where we're headed.

"No no—"

"Key!" he spits.

My hand flutters in space above my hip and he shouts it more: "Keykeykey"—and the C&C door stares back at me. What is this?

"Delphi, quick, fucking now."

I'm fumbling, and the scuttling behind us, along with an invisible vibration of male voices—*voices*, more than one—

I can't even make my fingers work. "Goddammit!" Brendan's hand is in my pocket. Then a click, a slip, a slam: The rotting air is gone, replaced with chlorine. A corridor.

This can't be. We can't be here already. But I work out the distances in my head as fast as I can. The Lux Pavilion and the lagoon ride . . . they feel far from each other, but no, their encasing staging blocks back onto each other . . . This corridor leads . . .

"Brendan, I don't . . . I can't be here."

I see Callie Petrisko on the other end of my TV screen. I see her sharp canines and the pink rim of her always-smiling eyes. I see the birthmark, floating near her nostril. I see her doubled over in her boat as a robotic version of herself dances silently before her.

"Yes you can. Just a little further." When I don't move, he adds, "The doors are locked behind us. There's no going back."

I try to make my joints lock, but it's no use: We're moving. Fluorescent lights. Music from just beyond the door in front of us. From the adjoining room. Brendan's gotten behind me, pushing gently, but he manages to kick at the door that sits between us and the lagoon beyond, and he gives it one more heave, and I'm tumbling through, eyes tightly shut.

Green and gold light warms my lids. And there's that music. It drowns out everything else, even the words coming from Brendan (they sound like "I'm sorry, go go"), in a rush of tam-tams, Levantine cane flutes, stringed Bedouin guitars, intonations that feel Slavic, Serbian, sub-Arctic. There's also an oboe. Always an oboe.

I'm sweating through my shirt, and the smell mixes with chlorine and rust, and my lids seem too thin. Like I can see through them.

"I'm right here," Brendan shouts.

Too hot. Stage light. Lagoon light. Alien light. He slips ahead and resumes pulling me. The strain becomes too great, and my eyes drift open, but I try to keep my gaze down. We're on a platform, another camouflaged maintenance walkway. There's synthetic grass at Brendan's feet, lit by LEDs, and the water runs thick and loud on our left. Boats smack into each other, rubber bumper to rubber bumper. They're each carved, laser-cut with vines and dancing Nebulanders. There are too many of them, like leaves clogging a drain. I think of insects pouring from a tap.

Across the main waterway in this section, a waterfall trickles, and a plunge pool burbles in sapphire. I raise my eyes to it, take in the whole of the scene.

"Are you still with me?" he cries back at me.

"I—" I don't know what to say.

"Keep moving."

"You said he can't come in here?" Another gentle tug, his fingers digging into my wrist. "Why do you think we're safe here?"

"I don't!"

The sickness rises in me. I know what we're approaching. Callie. Fiusha. I remember it from the video. We move closer along our thin platform, closer to the waterfall, its rock formations. I make the mistake of looking closely at it as Brendan crosses the path of a projector and the waterfall disappears. A shadowy hiccup, like a cloud passing over a hillside. The rocks that had been real enough to touch become a black void, empty canvas. A display error.

The next room is a little bit darker, less gold, more silver, and it's full of bots. The new ones. An ecstatic cornucopia of dancing bodies: men and women, small children, animal hybrids swinging from branches and popping up from the water. Echoes of hooting sounds and some canned laughter top the music score. A boy of about eleven, with gills, touches his fingers to the water and strange patterns radiate out from him.

On our side of the water, just over our heads, a bot arm swings from a ceiling mount camouflaged in deep green leaves and black vines, and I see what's going to happen before it does, but I say nothing. It collides with Brendan's mouth. I dodge it, and the thought that it might touch my skin sends chills through me. He doubles over, releases my arm, presses his palm to his lip.

I consider running, but Brendan's hand is sticky when he pulls it from his mouth, and I can't stop myself from coming close, from saying the words "Are you okay?" even though he can't hear them. The bot above us continues with his merry swinging. I can make out tendons straining in his neck, and the tip of an arched nose dips downward with a smile. The inside of his mouth is wet, just as humans' tend to be.

"Get off me," Brendan says, but when he starts reaching an arm out, he doesn't grab me; he waits for me to take his hand. He looks apologetic when I take it, and I feel like an idiot for following him, in step with him now, at his side.

We take a bend and she's on my right.

The spot where Callie's boat once stopped is so close I could squat down and touch it. Her hair levitates in the breeze. Princess Fiusha. Her skin is lighter than Callie's and her hair is darker, a kind of magenta, a *fuchsia*, even. She's crouching low on a kind of lily pad, and then pushing herself up onto her toes, giving the illusion of very careful balance on water. Wherever she's anchored, it must have been very carefully concealed. She's not a stunt bot—she can't walk around on her own, be tossed into the air, land safely. She lives here, in the confines of these dark rooms, with all of the elegant geometry of her originator, Callie. The squared lips and cherub cheeks.

Now I regret not running. I feel sick.

Brendan looks behind us, the way we came, scared, and then he starts talking.

"There's a problem with them!" he starts shouting, still walking, rushed, at my side, crouching a little to get close to my ear. "The bots! It turns out that if you had one made of you and you look at it, it can make you . . ."

"Make you what?"

Callie on the boat. Callie at dawn. The ash stain they couldn't get rid of.

"I don't exactly know! It breaks people!"

Something settles over me. "That's how you know Towe wouldn't come in here!" I shout up at him. I think Brendan nods. There's a new light coming up ahead. A new room. A change of act.

"Is that why they need to shut the park down?"

Another nod.

So it wasn't just Callie, her death. It was the possibility of all the others, anyone with a bot made in their likeness. There were more *Nebuland* actors there on that day. But no, they hadn't been let onto the rides. In the end it had only been her.

Had they known? Had they really known? Who were they, who built the bots, out in the Imagination Ranch, that fucking campus where they made everything else? On top of all of this I find myself overcome with rage. The sickness fades. How could they have let this happen?

I try to watch my feet, but I feel the air shift. A new showroom: soft, cool lights, a humming harmony coming from steely blue rock formations, a cove of jiggling invertebrates like huge crayfish lined up tight like chorus girls, and something like cotton balls with googly eyes, baring teeth.

We arrive at some ice bridges bisecting the room. The boats, if they weren't stuck, would navigate through them. They're releasing gusts of frosty air: Four small AC units are mounted to a panel tucked into the fairy-white structure. The arch itself is meant to look too narrow to get through, though of course it's not, just a trick of the eye, a kind of mobius bend and a wiggle in the track. That's what's causing the backup. Here, boats mount each other's rear. They creak and slow. Two of them have been pushed up and out of the flow. They're upturned. I can see their magnetic bottoms, rusting.

Our path, on the other hand, has become clearer. My shoes catch on sandy tread strips.

There's another Fiusha here, crouched into a deep squat, the lush pelt of some creature daintily covering her crotch. She's preparing stones for a small fire. I look her in the eyes.

It takes a moment to understand that I've been looking at her. Looking straight-on. I feel fine. No madness, no fear, no collapse, but I feel compelled to throw something. To hurl myself at her now, and see if she'd catch me, if she'd tear me apart, if that dry patch on her lip would come away if I peeled at it, if blood would bloom from her face if I scratched at it.

Brendan sees me. "Don't look."

"It's okay," I say. "I'm not scared."

Brendan eyes the path behind us once more, and he looks confused.

"You said he can't come in here!" I say, less loud now, sound softer all around us.

"I know. This just feels too easy."

Fiusha locks eyes on us, and keeps them there while she continues her arrangement of stones and twigs. Her software, the software that lets her notice people looking at her, is still in working order, I suppose.

"We're almost there," says Brendan.

But then we hit neon. A room full of it. I feel the distinct UV heat on my skin. It's the chaos of war—some sort of enchanted light from under the earth and the airships belonging to the military men rocking back and forth, embittered background characters in battle. When the bots slap together in a wrestle, it makes the sound of skin-on-skin, the rustle and thud. But mostly, there's neon.

We shouldn't be here. Neon. Snowflakes, dangling. Neon. A black fog starts to obscure my vision.

"There," says Brendan.

I try to crush down the sick swell. "Where?"

My eyes are clenched tight again, but Brendan takes my face in his hands and gently angles it upward, and there he is. Garra. Declan Towe. He's on the other side of the water. Just a boat's width. He's shuffling, ready to fight, ready for action, fingertips brushing the gun in his belt. Underneath his hair, where his ear meets his neck, he's a little sweaty. His lips are chapped. Still, he's got that same geometry that Callie had. A beauty for screen. He looks different now.

Brendan doesn't waste time. "Listen, now we're here, he's definitely not coming. I can tell you he's right—there are people here, but I think that we can *both* be here and he's going to try to show you something that's going to make you want to leave."

He catches his breath. I can't even muster a question. My jaw is slack.

"But we don't *need to leave*, not now, maybe later, but I just need you to trust me, and once he's gone, and the people do whatever they need to do down below, we can carry on as normal and—"

He trips up here. He goes quiet for another moment, getting something straight.

"And we can finish out our jobs and come away from all this with really good references and this can just be an awful and challenging but ultimately sort of *okay* episode, something we'll look back on and maybe laugh. But I need you to trust me and not him. He doesn't know you."

He takes my shoulders and looks deep into my eyes.

"He doesn't *know you*, Delphi. He doesn't know what happens."

"What happens when?" I can see he's fumbled. Erred. I can see him try to recollect something. "Let's just go home, Brendan. Let's just leave it with the night crew and make sure everything's set and go home and sleep and let this be someone else's problem and see what's going on in the morning."

I'm impressing myself with how sincere this sounds. I want to do that. I do. But I also know that I won't be able to sleep. I won't be able to get it out of my head. How wrong this place has become. How every flash of colored light and trick of the eye has become warped. How I'm seeing shadows I wasn't meant to see. But how, too, the idea of leaving makes something in me grow heavy. Immovable.

Tears start to form in the whites of his eyes. I've never seen this before. He looks so young, like a toddler, but he's also bleeding from the mouth.

"I wish we could do that, Delph."

He puts his forehead to mine. I breathe him in. Then the room goes silent. The lights come on.

I'm crouching. I'm letting out a strange sound. Not this. Anything but this. I wrap both arms around my eyes, elbow crook on elbow crook, anything to drown out the light. I feel Brendan leave my side, I hear splashing. He's in the water.

I roll onto my side and reach one arm out to find the wall. If there's wall, there will eventually be a door. There's the stomach-drop rush of being caught in a lucid nightmare, or needing to run and not being able to. I crawl until I reach the wall and prop myself up. The silence is sick, I can hear that skin-slapping more clearly, but rotors, too, creaking, and it's like instinct, clockwork, it's a sick reflex: I look at the room.

I see grates, vents, ceiling tiles. I see the bases of the bots, where they connect to a port on a block locked into the ground. I see shit at the bottom of the water. I see how filthy the water is. I see a buckle of duct tape keeping an attack helicopter connected to an extension cord. And I see a glass panel that I hadn't seen before, half-reflective, and a man behind that glass. A control room, walled with monitors, a microphone for emergencies, and a chair for whoever's manning all of it. But the man isn't sitting. And the man is Towe. The microphone is clicking ineffectually. And then a door is flying inward at him, and Brendan's in there, and they're everywhere in that room, bodies hitting bodies. I don't know if Brendan can fight. I don't care.

Twice in that flurry Towe makes it to the mic, before Brendan pulls him away by the neck, or shoves him against the wall. In those times, he says:

"Get to the gates!"

And—

"Go now!"

And then I'm back at the wall, counting down from ten while I feel for a door, for a lock pad, for anything. When I fall into a dark corridor, it's an accident. A well-hidden exit that gives way to me. It washes over me, but that bleached light feels like it has left a stain. I don't feel clean again until I'm outside, in the night, panting, in the middle of Nebuland's main square, shapes swirling behind my eyes, and that statue of that old, alien woman looking down at me, her eyes large and knowing.

I vomit on her feet.

Sent from:
Catherine Moser-Towe
2227 W. Catalina Blvd.
Los Angeles, CA 90027

Now you're worrying me. Where are you? Wherever you are you must have heard about what happened at the press day. With Callie. I saw the video. It looked awful. It was almost 24 hours ago now, and she hasn't been answering any of my calls or texts. She's probably just overwhelmed. Some people get claustrophobic like that. But then she'd done all those stunts in that navy training pond a few years ago and she seemed fine . . . It didn't look like a normal freak-out. It must have been so weird. To be stuck right in front of your own face, only bigger, more you than you.

I have to acknowledge that you were right, sort of. I'm glad I didn't go. I'm glad your stupid monotone voice in my head won out. And I had a cold. I would have been puffy in photos. I'm glad Declan didn't get anywhere near the ride in the end.

Christ, the robot didn't *attack* her or anything. But I'm trying to piece together everything that you saw, in the underground studio. Could you tell me a little more about that? That woman you saw come out of the room and walk into the wall . . . that's all she did? How hard did she hit herself?

I'm scared because you're not answering me. I'm scared because something on that ride really fucked with my friend. I'm scared because the fires aren't going anywhere. You must be aware of that.

Do you really think the cabin's safe from fire? The hills? I guess I can google it. I'm scared because people are talking about blackouts. I'm scared because I'm too stupid to understand how there can be fires <u>and</u> mass blackouts at the same time in a developed nation. I'm scared because my husband keeps going to a church that keeps shouting about "knowing how different we are" and something about "a song that we all know how to sing but don't know how to tap the rhythm to." The fucking tapping thing, that I still don't understand. Also that stunt guy hangs around Yule like his henchman now. Some of them have started sleeping over at that house.

Declan keeps reminding me of all the weird shit artists endure for the sake of their craft, for the sake of financing, and all the cults in Hollywood and how lucky we are that this church isn't as crazy as any of those. But none of that makes me feel better.

Nebuland is still opening to the public as planned, soon. Walk me through that math again. How many bots are there on that ride, total? How many were modeled off real people?

What if I came to you? You said you were near Newberry Springs, right? And they do tours of the Imagination Ranch all the time. It's not in lockdown or anything. I could find you. Declan and I. If I can convince him.

Write back. Anything. I'm serious.

—Catherine

CHAPTER EIGHT

The trains that run around the park pass through more than just the elaborate panorama scenes. At one point the trains drive through Ben Nevis and back out again underneath a waterfall where photos of passengers are projected onto a wall of mist. It also passes through the space roller coaster. It's a chance for riders to feel serene and listen to a soundtrack of theremin—except for the rare time that the coaster itself roars past the window dividing train from cosmos. Then, exhilarated by both the thunder of action and by their own luck, guests gasp and lights flash and the whole trainload feels very lucky indeed.

There's a special compartment right behind the conductor that's a private, self-contained box with a window. The glass blocks sound, of course, and half the fun of the train is hearing the action of those rides it slices through, and the sounds of primeval beasts, but the first time I was ever on one of those trains, I asked if I could sit in it. The secret compartment.

It's never guaranteed; it might be occupied, by a small party or by an internet sleuth who feels like a genius for knowing about the box's very existence—but I calmly and seriously asked if I could ride in it on my own, and the middle-aged woman with a ponytail down to her tailbone said, "Sure thing!"

Long ago, the day of my first-ever visit to the park, with the sleep-smell of that nice man on my unwashed clothes, I spent an hour in that compartment. I still smelled like pizza grease. The conductor poked her head in twice to ask where I wanted to get off, but I asked if I could stay just a little while longer, and she said that was fine just as long as no other large parties wanted in. Eventually a young couple ducked in through the little door and sat at the opposite end of the box, some six feet from me. I sat on my hands when they got in. The man used his BlackBerry to take pictures through the glass, and the flash blinded me in the tunnel's dark. I got out at Zoetrope Alley.

It was crammed with young children and their older siblings pretending to be less excited than they were, just like people pretend not to be moved during Planet Song. I kept walking down the main avenue, past the novelty homes and the CoasterTown Blast, a ride devoted to a strange, clumsy animated homage to *Chinatown* from 1976. Guests queued on a red carpet while a cutout of the studio's hero dog, nose bandaged, displayed how tall children must be to ride. I thought about lining up for it, but something told me to keep walking.

I reached the end of the land's eponymous alley, the single road from which all dark rides and shops stemmed. I know now that at that end, behind the eastern limit of Zoetrope Alley, there's a drone storage bank that's blocked off from guests by a painted canvas wall. A trompe-l'oeil. A photorealistic continuation of the road extending into a storybook forest, where it becomes pale and distant. I stopped before it. Families had approached, too, and a few children posed in front of it, some jumping in the air in hopes of being caught suspended on their way to those towering cumulonimbuses, those biblical clouds that had been painted with such care.

I walked straight up to it. I put my hand to the canvas. It felt less sturdy than I'd imagined. I knocked it with my scarred knuckle and it sounded hollow.

I was asked to move. I stepped out of the way once so that a family of four, three of whom were in wheelchairs, could get a photo, but after that I returned to my spot and didn't move. I kept my hand to the beginning of where this implied void should be. Where the illusion started.

"Miss?" someone said to me. I looked up. The sky was dark, almost navy. I couldn't see the sun. "We're just closing up this section of the park. You're welcome to go find a place at the lake for the Thursday Night Spectacular."

He had dark hair swept forward. I would later learn his name was Mitch, and he had a bad habit of emailing us about unions that we were unable to join.

I moved my hand off the wall. He watched me do it, but he didn't linger on my hands. He didn't escort me out. He just smiled and let me make my own way out of Zoetrope Alley.

I'd missed a whole day. I felt a quick pang of sadness, but—no. No bother. I had at least another week in the motel. There was always tomorrow, only a few hours from now. Just a dream away.

I'm trying to run. The pastels of the shop fronts blur. The ice cream parlor, the chemist, the shop—our shop—with the home interiors floor, push me and pull me and slip away. There are the lockers. There's the pet wellness center. And there—the row of turnstiles. The UV stamp booth. The entrance. The exit. How I leave.

I catch my breath at a turnstile, ten feet tall, bars coming out of a rotating spine. I let one of the bars push against my hip, and I press just gently enough for it to move but still push back. I let it keep me in place. My knees become weak. There's a snake of light wreathing around the backs of my eyes, and a pull to go back. From somewhere, nowhere, there's the electric sparkle of blue-edged flame, and the shy smell of argon in my nostrils.

Then, something washes over me like a mother's voice saying that it's snowed. They canceled school. You can go back to bed. Go back.

Snow. Salt in a condom.

I open my eyes and press my feet into solid ground. I push past the turnstile. I make it ten paces before I hit the blockade.

Where the welcome hedges, floral arrangements, sherbet-colored signage, and standing floodlights give way to the ornate front gate, there are cannons, mortar parts, scrap piled to my waist. There's green, violet, black-blue dust, bleeding everywhere, from the mouth of each rocket. Everything is pointing out, to the parking lot, and to the arid stretch of nature beyond. I can't see the spot where Callie Petrisko burned herself alive. It's been buried by sloppy rows of equipment that look like lawnmowers, canisters the size of my torso, and box-things like guitar amps, but read *DYNAMIC FAZE 700*. The barricade reaches as far as I can see, wrapping around the front of the park, almost into the start of the loading bays and C&C parking. I crouch to the nearest smear of green and run the tips of my gloves across it.

Five years before I arrived, the park experimented with a daytime fireworks show. Nothing illuminated, nothing sparkling, but great tumbling arrays of densely saturated chandeliers of smoke webbing across the sky. To make it, all you need is lactose, potassium chlorate, baking soda, magnesium, and industrial dyes. Cheap, easy, unlike anything any park in the world was doing. But for six days and no more, a few stray men and women would watch the show begin, then scramble toward the bathrooms, the exits, dark shaded corners, sometimes leaving their shopping bags, sometimes leaving their families. On day seven someone pointed out that the show looked a whole lot like an air raid, or, more specifically, a missile defense system signaling something incoming, like they'd used in recent conflicts.

This oopsie of triggering guests' PTSD was quickly forgotten, and the daytime show was scrapped. I thought we got rid of that dye. I guess I was wrong.

In the barricade, there are three diggers, the lower half of a crane, an excavator with a needle nose, and one with steel shears. The machinery stretches densely, and I need to crawl over mortar tubes and beefy claw-grapples to navigate my way out. I start to climb, and when I'm squatting atop a wiggling propane cannister, I stop. I shut my eyes again. I feel every pain in my body, the spot where my ankle rolled while Brendan was dragging me, the pulsing in the back of my head like a knife. I can't remember where I parked. I'm trying to spin myself around. I'm climbing down. I'm hopping the turnstile. There I pause, looking out at what lies behind the barricade. I must need water. I look away. I turn back, back into the park.

I haven't been here in years. The train's secret compartment. It smells like I remember. Stale air and the sweet atomized remains of cotton candy, churros, the tips of ice-cream cones. I curl in a far corner behind a bench and drop into a limb-numbing sleep, a sleep of such stillness it seems your blood should stop moving.

When someone crawls in, I open only one eye and accept that it was inevitable. I can't imagine summoning the will to jump to my feet. This box isn't even big enough to stand in.

"Don't be scared," says Towe. He sits at the farthest edge from where I'm lying. I make a noise, a noise that says, *I'm not.*

"I thought you might leave," he says.

"I tried."

"Did you see what was out there?"

"Where's Brendan?"

I hear him rap his knuckles on wood. "He ran off. Neither of us really know how to throw punches."

"Why hasn't he come after me?"

"I think he's looking," he says. "Do you want me to go find him? Tell him where you are?"

I don't answer right away. I roll onto my back. "No."

"Delphi. Did you see what's outside? Out front?"

"Who did that?"

"Brendan. Surely."

I shake my head and sit up and let my head nod toward my chest before I rub my face, surely transferring that green ash from glove to skin. "When?" I reconsider. "*Why?*"

"Couldn't tell you," he says, and I notice that he's still clutching that messenger bag of his. His fingers wrap over a flimsy latch at the top. "But he's desperately trying to keep people out. Why do you think that is?"

"This feels like a question you know the answer to," I say.

He gives me nothing. Another sad look.

"Right." I look at the floor and lace my fingers behind my neck. I want more than anything to be back asleep. "You and Brendan can fight over whatever the hell you're fighting about. Staying, not staying, Action Plan, no Action Plan, dangerous church people, no dangerous church people. I'm gonna get out of here tomorrow."

Then why hadn't I gone? Towe doesn't ask it, but I know it's what he's thinking.

"You're done with Brendan then?"

I bristle. "What? I—no I never said that." He's watching me closely. "I'm just pissed. I don't know what he's doing."

"He took you into that ride."

"Yeah but *you* turned the lights on. That's what fucks me up."

"Why can't you cope with the lights coming on?" He reclines a little. Both of us are steeped in the warmth of the day that's passed, the warmth that's been trapped here in the train, and will remain long into the darkest hours of night. He yawns. Part of his lip has recently stopped bleeding. "It's part of the job description, surely."

"Is there someone you love?"

He doesn't answer. I don't mind.

"You can love someone, and be dedicated to them, and work to keep them happy and healthy every day. Would you like to see them inside out?"

Beyond the windows there's black night, no stars, no moonlight. He watches some patch of it now. I lean on the wall and let my eyes flutter shut. We stay like that, suspended between night and dawn, sleep and life, for a time I can't measure. It could have been three hours. It could have been ten minutes.

"We'll go together," he says, like it's all he's been thinking about. "Out some back way."

"There aren't back ways," I mutter, barely more than a whisper. I know that's not entirely true.

"You've got to avoid them," he says. "The church, I mean."

"They're trying to get down below. They can do that and do what they need to do, and we can carry on about our business. That's what Brendan said."

"Do you believe that?"

"No," I say. "But they're already down there."

"They're somewhere. Underground. Around. But they need to go deeper. They need your key, and your skin-print, for that."

"This place is falling apart. You've seen it," I say. "I'm sure they can batter down any door they need to batter."

"Not this one. And you don't want any part of it."

There's a dim sliver of dawn breaking over the Rainbow Calistoga Geysers, where little children ran rampant, whack-a-mole-ing jets of water from the ground, and adults parked in front of misters disguised as cactuses. I don't think Towe can see it, though. To him, in his far corner, it's still night.

"Get some sleep."

He shakes his head, but arranges his body on top of his bag. To do this he has to move a few inches in my direction, and I find myself shifting, laying my head where my feet were, closer to him.

"What's in the bag?" I ask.

"Letters," he says. "Letters that my wife was sent."

Something stings at the word *wife*. The sting is a surprise. I try to forget it. "From who?"

"From her brother."

I can tell he doesn't like this, having the tables turn. Being the one who's asked questions.

"They don't leave your side."

I think he shakes his head.

"Are you going to give them to her?"

He looks at a spot over my shoulder. "No. They were my payment, from a man called Yule, who leads the church. I helped him get in undetected. I came in through a back entrance, once. For an event."

"So you got your payment. Why are you still here?"

"Because you're still here. I thought the park was empty."

"It's obviously not empty."

"I mean, I thought no one would get hurt. But there you were. Working your normal routine."

"We're all working our normal routine," I say, too defensively, with a whine that makes me embarrassed. "We all have an Action Plan. Those of us that are still here."

The embarrassment lingers, and I can't shake it. The Action Plan. The fact that I was selected to stay on after so many others were made to leave. The fact that this man was worried about me, while knowing nothing about me.

"They must be pretty important letters," I say, to change the subject.

"I'm not sure."

"Are you going to ask your wife about them?"

"My wife's dead."

It hangs painfully in the air. "Oh." Can't just say *Oh*. "I'm very sorry."

I think he might be shutting his eyes. I should let him be. But I'm too awake now, and I've trespassed too far with him. He's the one who followed me in here.

"Can I ask . . . how she . . ."

"She was trying to get out of the city," he says. "She was going to a cabin. She asked me to go with her so many times, and I just . . .

settled . . . into this comfortable idea that she was overreacting. A lot of people were on the road. She stopped to get gas. Something kicked off at the station. Someone killed her there."

"I'm so sorry."

"Yeah. You said that. Thanks."

I'm embarrassed at the tendency to give useless condolences like that, and also at the questions I still have, questions I shouldn't ask, but . . .

"What do you mean something *kicked off*?"

"Something bad happened out there, Delphi."

"What?"

"It wasn't safe, for a while."

"What, like fires? Or do you mean like"—I search my catalogue of West Coast dangers; I feel suddenly alien, unacclimated, a tourist—"crime?"

"Fires had something to do with it," he says. And then, with new sadness in his voice, "She always hated LA. Where I'm from, where I grew up, you can't imagine that as a concept. Someone hating the place where Hollywood was. So I never properly believed her, but then she was the one who got hurt in the end. *By* this place. It's funny, that." There's no humor in his voice, "She was clever and bored and had so much to give the world, you know. She really wanted to give the world something, anything, and instead of helping her figure out what that was, I forced her to watch me take from the world. I made her listen to me talk endlessly about this dogshit art film of mine. It . . ." He trails off here and I don't push it.

"The people from the church think they're gods," he says. "Or something like gods. They think they can withstand the bots."

"They have bots?" I ask. "Of themselves?"

"They're all failed actors. They were in the movie with me. Or they did other work with the park." Then his focus drifts, just for a moment. A muscle in his neck tightens, then releases. Unthinking, I touch my own neck. "They think it's down there," he says. "The technology that made the new bots . . . do harm. But *they'll* do harm," he murmurs, so slurred with fatigue that I can hardly make out the words. "If they're right . . . if it's like he said in the letters."

"What your brother-in-law said in the letters?" I ask. "What does he say?"

He doesn't answer, and we drift into one of those little slices of sleep again. I'm grateful that my sleep stays dreamless, except for a static image of two men, made of shadow, entirely silhouette, standing over a rupture in the earth. I can see no more detail than this, but I know, with unwavering dream-certainty, that the rupture is filled with broken glass, and that if I were to come close, I would hear the shrieking singular note of audio feedback. In the dream, the very old woman is nearby, just behind me, just out of sight.

When I wake, Towe's moved his body closer to mine. In spite of everything, in spite of my exhaustion and the adrenaline hangover, the cold of an uncertain future with Brendan, I wish he was closer still. I wish he'd wrapped an arm around me in the night. I consider wrapping myself around him now. He looks a decade younger in the morning light. Some color has returned to the underside of his face. I check my watch: just after seven. I almost have trouble leaving him there. Almost.

Sometimes if we were alone in the apartment, and I seemed anxious or foggy, Brooke would tell me about a little strategy she had for anchoring herself in time and space. At night, just before sleeping, she wrote: "You are in [city]. You arrived by [mode of transport] yesterday [time of day]" on a small sheet of paper that she stuck to the wall beside her bed. This was during her gap year, whenever she slept in a new country, especially if she was jet-lagged. Doing it in advance made her feel motherly, taking care of her future-self like that, and in turn she was able to feel reassured almost instantly if she woke in a state of confusion and couldn't recognize her bedding. She did this in hostels in Kuala Lumpur and *agriturismo* farmhouses in Sardinia. But sometimes she forgot to unstick the sign from the wall, and the whole thing backfired. She'd have been in Korčula for three days when her bleary eyes would read "You are in Croatia. Your ferry arrived here last night," and for one terrifying minute she'd wonder if she'd dreamt the last few days: the young yacht Brits who didn't wear sunscreen, and the charred octopus tentacle that flaked under her bite like a candy cigarette. The little favor to herself had now done more harm than good, and so, eventually, she gave up on it altogether, stopped writing herself notes, and accepted that she might feel scared in the morning from time to time, but maybe that was just part of adult life.

She was in Barcelona in November, when there were almost no tourists to be found, and she got a six-bed room to herself. Barcelona did nothing for her. The beach reminded her of Adelaide. The narrow streets felt like Portugal, but less intriguing, and the wide streets were like anywhere else on the continent. She cut the trip short to visit a cousin in Dover, but on her last night a woman took a bed in the room. She was Chinese and older—forties or fifties—and she tried to speak to Brooke in Mandarin, in a way that always made Brooke feel guilty. Brooke said, "Sorry, I never really learned," in the woman's language as best she could but got *mei* wrong so that, later, she realized that she'd said the word beautiful, let it float where it didn't belong. The woman switched into slow English and told her: "I have been divorced." When Brooke asked her what she had planned, the woman said, "I am here," twice in a row.

The woman had such nice things. SK-II toner and a hunting knife.

Brooke almost changed her mind and stayed. She imagined walking past the Gaudis with this woman, being honest about how unmoved she was by them, but the cousin in Dover had a charity street-team gig lined up and Brooke couldn't say no. She had enough cash for her bus to the airport, and a sandwich, and not much more.

She packed the night before and made her alarm quiet. On her way out the door she paused and wrote, "You are in Spain. You flew in yesterday," and stuck it to the wall beside the sleeping woman, and only when the bus was coasting around Plaça d'Espanya did she realize that the woman might not be able to read it, that it would be nothing more to her than a string of letters, no more useful than trying to pinch yourself when you're sure you're stuck inside a dream.

———————

It's time to go. The wall out back. In The Cemetery.

I'm shaking when I reach the tunnel's darkest stretch, and the gravel that the tracks lie on top of seems formed to trip me up. I stumble, bleary and almost blind, but I don't slow down. This way, I won't have to say goodbye to the park. Not really. I wouldn't put myself through that. No goodbyes. Doors wide open, floating in space.

The Everest pano is glowing on my right side. It's silent now. No whooshing wind, no squawking crane. Just those scared men's bloated plastic faces.

I decide that after I hop over the back wall, I'm going to take the long way to the lot, find my car, drive home, walk through my door, and do whatever dishes are in the sink. I'm going to take a shower and get in bed and sleep, and Brendan can come over if he wants to discuss what's happened, what secrets he kept from me, why he kept them, what he knew, why he tried to keep me here, and what our lives might look like going forward. There will be consequences to this. Of course there will. But Towe was wrong to ask if I was done with him. Of course I'm not done with him. How can anyone be done, just *done*, with anyone? Without him I'd be left with too much choreography: The way I place the flat of my index finger in the dip where his nose meets his forehead. The way I'll reach for his hand, if I'm driving, at a red light. And I can't imagine what he'd do without our patterns, without the warmth of our inside jokes and fitful sleep habits. He's too soft to be let adrift like that. He looked so determined, but so pathetic, when he was throwing punches behind that glass.

The door appears just as I start to hear footsteps a long way behind my back. Towe had to wake up at some point. I pick up my pace. I don't bother with the card. The door is barely attached to its frame. Had I noticed that before?

The Cemetery's expanse is just as I left it. I'm not sure what I expected. For it to have been picked clean by scavengers? For all of the bits and bobs and beryllium frames and garbled control units to have mated and multiplied? A junkyard spilling out to the ends of the earth? All of it is virtually identical to the day before yesterday, down to the temperature. One in a string of hundreds of perfectly warm days.

I keep a straight path over tufts of dandelions, toward the concrete decoy wall. I'll set off security alerts by even touching it, but who's watching? A trap is only a trap with a trapper. When I find the crumbled spot, I start dragging over anything I can manage: concrete blocks, rusty feminine hygiene disposal boxes with lids limply flapping along the earth as I pull. The pile wobbles, but, climbing, I realize how light I've become. It's unstable, but doesn't collapse under my feet. I'm lighter than I thought. I notice that I'm starving.

It's so obvious to me now that this chunk of erosion is fake. The gap looks like the lava room in Caves, theatrical decay. I get traction from an elbow tuck and press my chest flat. The pressure cools my lungs. It crosses my mind to hang like that, dangling against the wall like some horrific scene from a gulag, but the muscles in my armpits start to throb.

Balancing myself in that blown apart bit of wall takes some time, too much time. The way I came, over the grass, there's a long gash where it looks like something different, something heavy has been dragged, but its path curves beyond my sight. There's a tear in my glove, just at the tip, on my index finger. I push my nail halfway through. It's long.

I perch a foot or two from where I hoisted myself, facing The Cemetery. I tie my boot. I look at the tops of the things I can see. I'll let the sounds of the city hit me first. It's so quiet out here. My back faces the real world, and it's nothing to be afraid of. But something is missing.

Its sounds don't come. Not the freeway, not the ambulances with sirens that our audio people have to plan for, draping the park with fabrics and insulations that mute and muffle. There's no city hum. Behind my back, Los Angeles is tapping me on the shoulder. Excuse me, miss.

I turn and look.

A dusty vista. The edge of C&C parking. A few strokes of green in the distance and a lot of dead grass in the distance. A clear view of the ridgeline that hugs the curves of the 5. That's all. The place where I always knew I was. A clear view. A *very* clear view.

There's really no smog at all. None.

There's a flicker, somewhere far, beyond the roads. I squint. Birds. Big ones, maybe herons. I've never seen herons anywhere near here before. What a peculiar habitat. My thigh is getting cold, but I'm breathing easily up here. Maybe I'll stay awhile, straddling concrete.

I'm readjusting myself when I hear footsteps. Towe. I take a breath and ready myself to jump. I won't let him talk me down. He sounded very kind last night, but he's an actor. I grip my perch. I let the soles of my boots angle down the outer wall. I look over my shoulder—one last look.

There are two women. They're walking side by side, steadily, nonchalant. Their heads are shaved, but differently: one clean, with a few weeks' growth; the other's scalp is dotted with a few slugs of scar tissue.

Whatever their differences, I see something in the way that they wave to me. Twins.

Sent from:
PO Box 538
4381 20th St W
Newberry Springs, CA 92365

I hope you don't get this letter. I hope you get the one I sent to the cabin. I've sent one to the house + one to the cabin. I hope you're in the cabin.

One of the guys here got his TV to work + we've been watching the news. Do you have water? Do you have a plan to get inland? Don't come here. I doubt it's still on your mind, after everything, but just don't. Avoid the main traffic arteries. In these situations, normal people can be the most dangerous factor. Remember that.

Did you manage to get gas masks? Are people really stockpiling those? Do you need them? What's the situation with the air quality? Everyone online is saying something different.

Christ. A helicopter crashing into a power station? Long Beach. Alamitos . . . There are like five different nuclear facilities crammed together in that inlet. Catherine, does that seem like a coincidence to you? Who was on the helicopter? Please understand what I'm trying to say.

I just saw about the blackouts. Is the mail still coming through? Will you get this?

There's been a change here. It's better now. Not better. But I have to stay. They're giving us work. They might let us back at the Ranch. It sounds like they need something from us now. I think they're bringing us a bot.

Don't write back. Just get somewhere safe. I'll be in touch soon.

CHAPTER NINE

The twins stop a few yards from the clumsy tower of trash I've assembled.

"It's a nice day out there!" the one who's built more square calls up to me. "What are you doing?"

"I'm trying to get out."

They look up and down the green wall. "Looks pretty tricky to me."

"I'll be fine."

They both nod. Their posture is the same. Strong shoulders underneath stained T-shirts. They watch with genuine curiosity.

Jump. Just jump. Do it. The muscles in my wrists and in my thighs tense once or twice. I flinch when my body comes close to hurling itself off the edge. I'm hissing inside: *Jump. Jump. Go.*

It's almost a relief when they speak again. A kind diversion in the face of humiliation, my failure. "Rumor has it you can get us underground."

Painful tears start to form. "Uh-huh." I laugh. "Sure."

"We'd love for you to help us out."

There's a moment where the laughter threatens to swell and swell until it's beyond my control, buoyed by all of the invisible parts of this mess, of these days, of the breathy whisper of secrets that I hear coming from underneath . . . underneath my . . .

I stop laughing. Somehow, I regain control. "Why don't I just give you my key? There's a card and a little needle thing. You need both."

"We know you also need your skin-print. For this door."

I swing one leg to their side of the wall. I can feel myself bristle, the notion that they're catching me in a lie. "That's just one door. There are tons of doors. I don't know where you're going"—a lie— "but I'm sure you'll figure it out with this."

I pull the key, attached to the needle, from my pocket. I throw it. It lands soundlessly at their feet, but they don't reach for it.

"This is the door we need, Delphi," the softer one says. "Let us in and you can leave."

"I can leave now."

They smile sadly at me. With pity. It reminds me of Towe, and I think, with sudden certainty, that he can't be far off. That, or he's left. I was what was keeping him in the park. And now I'm gone. If he has any sense, he'll be gone, with those letters.

Straddling concrete, like that, I find myself on the brink of laughter. I let mad smiles appear and disappear while I turn away from the women, back toward the horizon, to the too-clean vista and the birds I've never seen before.

After some time I look back, back at the unruly spread of The Cemetery. The women smile up at me, gently, patient and undeterred.

"I'm Rosie," says the softer one. "And this is my sister, Veta."

Veta waves. It's clear that Rosie is the talker.

"Hey, what happened to your hands?"

That exhausted laughter comes up my throat, and a tinny kind of whine from inside my own head. Sure. Why not.

"Oh." I examine the palms of my gloves. "I burned them."

They nod.

"My stepdad was a neon artist, and he taught me everything he knew, and his son was this loser dealer who sold some shitty synthetic LSD, we think, and he left it around and it got into our systems and I burned my hands in the shed where Whit—my stepdad, this cranky old Libertarian with some really bad mental illness—where Whit and I worked, and everyone assumed he did it to me, like, he hurt me, but nope. He didn't. I did it. But they locked him up anyway. Not in prison, but in a facility that's not great. I mean"—and here I do laugh a little—"not that I visited him. I never did. I don't know if my mom has. I don't know if Whit is alive or dead. I left as quick as I could. And now I wear these gloves all the time."

When I look up, Rosie and Veta are nodding softly, like this is the type of story they hear every day.

"That sounds hard," says Rosie. "I'm grateful that you shared that with us."

It makes me flinch. I start to say, "It's nothing," but a sharp sound interrupts me. Veta takes something from her hip: a walkie-talkie. One of ours.

She takes a few quick steps back toward the tunnel entry, where she's come from, and a flash of concern comes over Rosie's face. "Sorry about that," she says. "We had to take what we could find. I hope you understand."

"Did you get those from our lockers?"

She shrugs. "I'm not really sure."

Veta returns to us with a new look, a kind of pleading, something communicated to her sister wordlessly.

"Delphi, why don't you come down from there? We'll introduce you to everyone. We'll get through the door that we need to get through. And then you're absolutely free to go."

It's too convincing. It's too good. Someone else making a decision for me. I still want to laugh. I swing my other leg around to the twins' side.

I imagine falling backwards into the unknown, landing head or spine-first onto the ground out there. Maybe I'd knock myself uncon-scious, or break a rib, a vertebra, my coccyx, and I'd wander out into nowhere, in the direction of nothing, in pain. No, I wouldn't like that at all, I think to myself, although it's calling to me. It's telling me to get out.

I carefully lower myself onto the women's side. I let my feet touch the pile of parts. I land on solid ground, and I pick up my keys.

Before I come closer to them, though, I stand still, a hand shield-ing my eyes from the ferocious morning sun. "You're not gonna kill me in there, are you?"

They look hurt. "Of course not."

I nod. I can tell they're getting impatient. Veta, especially, who's looking over her shoulder now. How many are waiting for them back there? And if they are many, how do they intend to stay together, how do—

"Is there an old woman with you?" I ask, surprising myself. "A very, *very* old woman. Like, crazy old?"

Rosie looks perplexed; Veta, too. "No, hon. I'm sorry, there isn't."

I believe them. I don't know why I asked.

"All right," I say, a little shaky. "Let's get you underground."

———

Veta is the first to notice that I'm shaking.

"Nothing to be afraid of," says Rosie. "I mean it. I know that if you're afraid some strangers are going to hurt you, one of them tell-ing you they *won't* hurt you isn't gonna be much comfort. But really. None of us are bad guys, I promise."

I'm not shaking because I'm afraid. It's because I've never told anyone the Whit story. The shed. My hands. Saying it up on that wall left me exhilarated. Breathless. It's been decaying within me for so long I forgot how light I could feel. I never knew it was that simple: Speak it, and become light.

———

In Omaha, in the hospital, after it happened, they kept asking me what was in the shed. They assumed the worst: meth, explosives, unsavory memorabilia—all of which might make sense because of the drugs in our system and because of my hands. I didn't understand any of that at the time, what they wanted to hear from me. So when I was able to answer them, whenever a social worker would time their visit for when I was conscious, I asked them to be more specific. Finally, they told me they wanted an inventory. They really should have asked me that from the start.

Argon, helium, and neon. I thought those should be obvious. No mercury. Whit was scared of mercury, for reasons I never quite understood. Then the glass tubing, the electrodes, Lego pieces he had me practice with, but that felt like a lifetime ago. Valves, and what I described at the time as "fire equipment," because I'd lost the words for ribbon burner, that blue glowing scepter, and the water bottles, of course, the plastic-and-cardboard casing that the water bottles had come in, the blanket, and the CD player, and Whit's black zipped booklet of CDs. There were several sets of standard home carpentry tools, spare size 42 khaki pants, eczema cream, Aveeno Diabetics' Dry Skin Cream, 4% hydroquinone cream (prescription), two brooms, a waste box for broken glass, four spools of bubble wrap in various sizes, a plant, a kerosene lamp, neoprene, many, many lengths of rubber hose, swivels, Nutri-Grain bars.

Oh, and the gloves. Both our sets of gloves. Would mine be part of the inventory, though? By the time I was being asked for this list, they were still fused to my skin. They had to use local anesthetic to pick it all out. They couldn't use general until the tests came back, till they figured out what had been in the bottles.

That was another thing they were dying to know: what Whit's son had been storing on our property. They wanted to know so bad because they were looking for Daryl. They'd tried to interrogate Whit, of course, but he was still unresponsive. He'd stay that way, more or less, indefinitely.

We'd been working silently for a couple hours at that point. We

were making pineapples and hula girls. Whit had been in San Fran-
cisco in the eighties, and that kind of thing, the B-52s and the hilarious kitsch of a tiki bar, was really baked into him. If we ever went
out, he'd joke with some clueless teen waiter about ordering a Zom-
bie, and he'd laugh and laugh.

Over time the pieces of that day came back to me, so that I can
almost form a whole. I woke up whenever sixteen-year-old girls wake
up. I remember I had short hair then, that I'd cut it myself after being
sick of tying it back while working with Whit, and most of the time a
strand would make its way into my ear canal in the night, a horrible
insect feeling that made me wake in a panic. But that day I'd woken
softly because I heard music coming from the shed—John Denver,
Whit's favorite. It was a weekday, and I still don't know why no one
had made me go to school.

I put on an old pair of my mother's slippers for my walk to the
shower and kept them on after I'd dressed. I ate a packet of Cream of
Wheat, which Whit always called gruel and said he couldn't eat because
it would get caught in his beard, I think to gross me out, but it didn't
work, I liked it all the same. I wore the slippers across the wet grass,
trying not to trample any caterpillars, which were everywhere. It was
that time of year. If I thought about their numbers too hard, out there
on the grass, it would make me panicky. Whit was already in the shed,
setting up the thin rubber blow hose draped around his neck. John
Denver came from the CD player, something at once gleeful and sad:

Like the mountains in springtime, like a walk in the rain

When I was settled in and slid the bulky gloves over my hands, he
handed over golden angles of semi-molten glass, with the cones and
corks pre-attached. I realize now he did that in advance to make our
day smoother. Normally I'd attach the corks myself, but he wanted
to get on with it. He was making something wall-sized, designed to
look like stained glass.

We got thirsty. He kicked at the box under the blanket and said
"Bingo," and I was too busy getting my pliers to clamp a hex-nut to
pay attention when he kicked a water bottle over to me.

"Socket holes in that over there?"

"Yeah, brackets, too."

It was the prep that captivated me most. The process of heating glass, the even rotation needed, required patience and that made me antsy. I'd been trying to get better at it. But I loved this part. Fetching a stray bayonet nozzle that rolled off Whit's station. Checking that the extractor pads were clean.

We both drank from our bottles. Time passed. The prep came to an end, and I heard the click of burners. A little while later I started thinking about that shadow, the one racing around Wendy's room. Peter who was so violent with it, and also so desperate for its return. He didn't just want to gobble him up. The shadow was a duplication of Peter, so he wouldn't fit inside Peter himself. The shadow would have had to be half an inch smaller than Peter, and that simply wasn't the case. Wendy understood that, and so she got her needles and thread, and I guess once the shadow was caught, sewn on, it kind of went dead in the brain, stopped being so much a self as a thing, like in other stories and movies when a spell is broken and a singing plate goes back to being just a dead porcelain object.

Whit was holding up a rod of gentle pink, saying, "Did you know that inert gases can also be called 'noble gases'?" And I said that he'd told me that a million times before, but when I looked away the pink glow was still there. If anything, it was growing more vibrant at the corner of my vision, fizzing. I heard something roll and then crash, but Whit was still standing, if a little more still than normal. I didn't think he was anything but fine. Lost in thought. I know now that we were going through different things. The meds he was on. All that.

I asked Whit where the gas went when the glass shattered, and all I got back was "Uh . . ." So unlike Whit, who always had an answer at the ready, even if he hadn't listened to your question.

I was in a stargaze corridor of my own by then, the dark and the light sifting into smaller particles and settling somewhere far off, and over from Whit there was more *Uh*-ing, still trying to answer my question about gas. I wanted him not to worry about it anymore, my dumb question, but I couldn't find the words to tell him, and just then it occurred to me to get some air, to stick my head outside the shed and breathe, but I got stuck in the bog of an idea that the daylight would delete everything inside: Whit, the materials, the fire. It would be like when people develop their own photos, which of course I'd never done, but I knew about. Gotta keep the light out.

"Whit, why is it that you like to work in the dark?"

Like a storm in the desert, like a sleepy blue ocean

There was only a faint wheezing in response.

I switched on the ribbon burner. God, the blue. The blue had to be the source of something, something that people call God some-times, but I'd call it something else if I could find words. There was no blue like it in nature, the nature where I'd lived. This part of the world, this state, city, neighborhood, street. I didn't hate it, except that people were rude and careless and were obsessed with what's wrong with everybody else, even people who were just minding their own business, just doing things their own way, reading in cars or try-ing to get lost, and I wasn't mad about living in this place, exactly, but it seemed cruel that we'd get glimpses of things from another kind of place, things like the blue of the ribbon burner or the afterburn of a rock disintegrating in the atmosphere, a shooting star, but we still had to just keep on living here, in the absence of those more special things. Was Peter's shadow angry that he'd been taken to dreary Lon-don? Is London dreary? Did the shadow reject London, or reject his connection to an immortal beast like Peter, not aging and therefore not alive at all?

The idea made me feel awful. Just awful. The only solution was for the shadow to stay put, reattach and stay attached. That made me feel less awful. I know how to make things attach.

Blue hot. The fire made a whooshing sound like the sea. Whit sounded like he was getting sad.

"It's okay, Whit," I said. "I feel it, too."

He came close when my hands approached the flame. He looked at me peculiarly then, and once again I said, "It's okay," and it all made perfect sense. My heart raced, and shapes at the edges of my vision became the most beautiful, familiar faces, faces I'd never seen before, close-up. A goose, and a cat, and a prince—and more that didn't belong to any story I'd ever been told. Whit touched the tops of my hands as they came closer to the hot light.

Mom woke up and got help, after it happened. Whit had been burned, too, when they took us away, and so they decided it had been him, and only him, who'd done it. Of course it wasn't that simple, and I became less and less able to speak as the effects of whatever had been in those water bottles wore off. It didn't matter anyway. Whatever I managed to say, they didn't believe me, and he was in no state to defend himself. He didn't get straight for a few days. That's what Mom kept saying, in the hospital, just a few floors up from where she worked.

"He's not straight yet."

"He's not straightening out."

"Trash bitch Daryl. His dad won't ever be straight again."

Later, I watched the wall-mounted TV while I waited for my body to respond to grafts (never well), and for a social worker to ask in what ways Whit had been violent with me before. She mistook my confusion for a morphine high, and hospital security failed to keep my mom contained in a separate corridor. She shouted and shouted and then she went quiet abruptly and she got in her car and sped off and I know now that she was tearing down that shed just as fast as she could, with a blunt old axe that used to belong to my dad, and all the while I was trying to answer questions. Then I was trying to watch *Moesha*, *Step by Step*, *The Simpsons*. They played *The Simpsons* in a block of two back-to-back episodes, but one day I was thrilled to find that they played four in a row. When I said something about it to Tenitra, who had quietly appeared beside the window, she got a funny look on her face and told me that there hadn't been four in a row. Two days had passed. Then she went to talk to the doctor to tell her she was worried about me; they just asked her how she knew me, if she was next of kin. Some time after that, they asked her to leave.

The slippers I'd been wearing were waiting at the foot of my hospital bed when I was finally able to get up. My mother got an absolute fuck ton of money out of the company who manufactured the gloves. I guess they weren't supposed to melt like that. I don't see how they could have done anything but melt, in a ribbon burner. Some of it went to me, into a savings account, but not all that much. I don't think Mom knew I could access it. Most of what I took I took just before I left. Maybe that's why we haven't spoken since.

I would often remind myself that people stopped me from seeing Whit in his facility every time I tried, before California, but that's self-pitying drivel. I could have tried harder. I could have snapped out of the lethargy sooner. I could have mustered some adult sense of understanding, understanding what all those social workers and cops were getting at, and explained, with the eerie clarity of an adult voice coming from a child, that Whit didn't hurt me.

But by the time I slowly gathered gumption, other things had begun to take shape. Lose their shape. A laser focus on getting to the park. I remember taking a test that was a little bit like the GED, but a state-level one, that almost no college recognized, but it meant that I could stop going to high school so long as I attended community college classes each semester. I took speech and a class called Automotive Electrical Systems, and another one called Properties of Materials. I was at an advantage, having learned about wiring and gases in the shed, and no one spoke to me much, once they'd seen my hands.

The morning I left, about an hour before sunrise, I was surprised to see my mother in the living room, dozing in a chair upholstered in sandy gingham, which had been softened by years of Whit's weight. I couldn't tell if she heard me, until I reached the small table where we left our keys and loose change. I wanted to leave my keys there, as a signal that I was gone for good.

I heard her stir.

"Did you know," she grumbled, "when you were born you had the hiccups?"

I remember how the keys felt clenched in my still-bandaged hand then, hovering just above the table.

"You had them when you were in my belly, all the time. I couldn't figure how something so small could have hiccups that big. And then you had them when you came out. Your little chest pulling, all covered in my blood. The nurses got scared, but . . ."

I thought she'd fallen asleep then. The faintest feather of sunrise hit a bit of floor, and her ankle, and a plastic cap that belonged to a bottle of Advil. Still, I clung to those keys, and waited to see if she'd sleep. Her eyes had not opened.

". . . but it's how I knew that it was you."

For the life of me, I can't remember, now, if I left those keys on the table or not.

I thought about stopping by to see Whit. The bus, the one that took forty-five minutes to walk to and that took three and a half hours to get to the airport, went past his facility. I didn't do it. It's too sad to think about Whit now. I've never even told Brendan all that much about him. The shape of his belly and the growl of his voice. I hope that when Whit thinks of me, now, if he's still out there somewhere having thoughts, he doesn't get sad like he sounded in that shed. I'll stand in front of the black rumbling vortex in Caves of Chirakan, the warbling shadow on the rock wall, and pray to some pretend Mayan god that he doesn't feel anything like sadness ever again. Whenever I'm back on the ride, here or in Hong Kong or wherever the park reincarnates itself, I'll pray to the shadow and see what happens.

Sent from:
Catherine Moser-Towe
3848 S. Berry St.
Los Angeles, CA 91604

This is going to have to be quick I'm sorry.

There's no way out of the city right now, or that's what people were saying, but now there's all this conflicting information on the radio. I think I'll be able to mail this, because I went out for a bit, just because I felt trapped inside, and the roads were empty for about an hour, then jam-packed, then empty again, and I couldn't decide whether or not I was an idiot for using gas. They're saying that when the helicopter crashed into one of the nuclear plants it triggered the earthquake response in all the others nearby. So backup diesel generators kicked in, but then they didn't turn off, and they overheated and melted their cores—I don't know exactly how it works—but now there's poison in the water, fires approaching (I guess?? What kind of fucking world is it where no one knows for sure??), and blackouts. Maybe you know all this from the news. I don't know what you know.

You're right. I've seen people fighting on the streets. Not end-of-the-world shit, but agitation. There were two big families fighting in front of Erewhon, like, everyone fighting everyone. Thankfully I didn't see young kids involved, but then I wondered where the young kids were, you know, like, who was watching them if they did exist, and I started panicking again.

Even on our quiet street. Declan had to get in between these two PAs, working for two different families on the street, trying to get into the same Uber, and at one point one of the men from one of the families—this lawyer I was vaguely aware of—physically pulled one of the PAs in the house, by the hair. Declan didn't know what to do. He just stayed there holding a bunched up T-shirt to his mouth and walked back up the hill, kind of pale.

He said the best idea was to stay with the church. I didn't agree. We're with the church now.

Yule has made his house into this . . . I don't know how to describe it. Hazmat hotel infirmary yoga retreat. He's made it habitable for a lot of people. I'd never been inside all that much before. It never quite clicks that he doesn't live with anyone. He has photos everywhere, of him with Steven Seagal and Jon Voight and Josh Brolin and Dean Norris and someone from The Sopranos whose name I can't remember. He saw me looking in this den and he told me about his time getting work in the late 90s and what a big deal he was in a certain scene and it's nothing I haven't heard before, since moving here. People will talk to you about that kind of thing. What was. How close they were to becoming a big deal. It's a tic. Or an anthem. But it felt strange to be doing it there, while this one woman was borrowing my laptop to email her sister in Long Beach who we couldn't find, and we're all watching the abandoned cars on the 405, knowing that even if the fires make it here there might not be a way out. We'd all have to . . . what . . . get into the sea?

When we were talking, in the room, it seemed like he didn't want me to leave. I can't quite put a finger on it, but I don't feel safe around him. Not literally. He wouldn't hurt me. But he clearly gets something from being surrounded by bodies, and I don't want to contribute to that.

And his sermons feel different now. If any of his ideology stemmed from real like Judeo-Christian Christianity, it's become confused with everything else. He keeps asking Lander to balance shit on his face. He even got him to do it with a cheap-looking glass coffee table. This guy balancing shit on his face like a sea lion and this big older guy just seething with intensity, pointing to him, talking about how if we make it through this we'll know how different we are. And he's been talking about the park, too. He's been talking about Callie. None of it makes sense yet, but of course it made me think of you. How would he . . . Yule, or Lander, or any of them . . . how could they know about what you've been saying all this time?

I've told Declan I want to leave, go back to our perfectly good house with some distilled water and a flashlight or two. But he's in denial. He's still trying to arrange meetings for that film. He's still walking around outside, even in the smoke and horrible, off-color clouds, like a car will come pick him up, take him to lunch at fucking Pathé or whatever. He won't talk about Callie.

The helicopter crash happened on the morning of her funeral. Did you know that? Just a couple days after they opened the park to the public. That part I'm sure you knew.

They're sending you a bot? Good. Let me know what you find. Let me know what you think I should do.

Let me know if it's safe to come to where you are.

I'm going to try to get to the cabin, when it's safe.

You don't need to worry about me, though. Don't spend your time worrying. You have something important to do.

—C

CHAPTER TEN

The members of the church are mostly clustered underneath the belly of the Jaxartosaurus. Most of them are twins, their ages hard to pinpoint, but there are none younger than thirty. A few, both men and women, have the cherub cheeks of procedures undergone to conceal age, which always has the funny effect of making me assume they're the oldest people in the room. As a mass, they are of a range of heights and builds. They are mostly white, apart from Rosie and Veta, and the tall brothers have their backs to the far wall, the wall caked in sponge marks of flaking vermillion paint. There are maybe thirty, thirty-five total, all wearing different types of black: black lycra bicycle shorts, clinging to dimpled thighs, and black sweatshirts with the arms cut off, revealing pale arms goose-bumping underneath a ceiling fan. Black harem pants with low-hanging crotches, and black turtlenecks, giving off a feeling of corporate formality. As a whole, it reads beatnik, though I suppose it was meant to feel neutralizing, unifying, give a sense of community. I don't know how I could have missed them. They're giving off a smell. Some people are rolling up sleeping bags. I can't understand how long they might have been here: here in the dinosaur pano, or here in the park, undetected.

When they hear us approaching, a hush falls over the room. Their eyes go wide, and smiles spread across their faces. There's a chorus of "Oh!" and "We didn't think you were coming!"

A few of them run up to Rosie and Veta and clap them on the shoulders. Some of them well with emotion. Others make the strained expressions of holding back tears, though I can see their eyes are dry.

In the commotion, I see the door. It has a keypad, which looks fresh and un-harassed. I'm sure it has a near-invisible slot for the needle, and I'm sure it can read my skin. But the outline of the door itself is confusing to the eye. I peel off from the crowd that's formed around Rosie and Veta, and while I feel eyes on me, no one follows. I sit on a trellis that runs the perimeter of the room, threaded with imitation vines, with plastic seams running the lengths of their shoots. The door. The outline of the door.

It's skewed at an angle so slight it could easily go unnoticed; all it leaves is a whiff of ill-balance. Of the viewer being slightly off, not the door. But there it is. The slightest diagonal, with the very slightest curve, etched above the door frame.)).

"You see it," says a deep voice from behind me. He takes a seat on the trellis. His knees crack. "The marking that's everywhere in the park."

He has watery green eyes and broken capillaries across his skin. Ears that fold up along his head, unnaturally.

"Gwendolyn's lashes."

"No," he says. "That's not what they are."

"What are they then?"

He smiles what he must think is a placid smile. To me it seems smug. "All in due time, Delphi. I think you should join us."

"Join you in going down there?"

He nods.

"To find the bots?"

He nods.

"And watch them melt your brains."

"They won't hurt us."

"It seems like they hurt some people," I say. "Before."

The man puts a hand on my forearm, just above the glove. "We're not *some people*. We're different."

He keeps his hand where it is, and though the smile stays on his face, it's daring me to be the one who moves first. I notice the rest of the room become quiet—not silent, but a sudden change of volume that tells me eyes are on us. I slip away from his hand as gently as I can.

"You lead them?" I ask.

He nods. "You can say that. We've known each other for a long time. For a long time, we've known that this was our fate."

"Okay," I say. "Cool."

The man rests his elbows on his thighs and pivots so that he's facing me head-on. Before he speaks, I have a sense of what this will be. I've seen it before, in youth group leaders, and some of the social workers that came to the hospital. He's about to get real.

"My name is Yule," he says. "Jon Yule, but just Yule is all right with me."

I nod. "You guys seem to know my name."

"That's right. A question for you, Delphi." He lowers his voice. "Were you raised with religion?"

I fight the urge to roll my eyes. Quickly, I check the scene behind my back and let out a *hmm* like I'm thinking carefully about how to answer this. I don't have any thoughts: I miss Brendan. I shouldn't have left him. I should have asked where he was. Maybe he's looking for me now. I'm sure he is. He'd know exactly what to say to this guy. Something funny and disarming. No one would be mad. The conversation would simply change.

"No," I finally say. "Not really. My town was pretty Christian, I guess."

"Pretty Christian you guess," he says back. Resonant. Like he's just getting started.

I get to my feet. I consider unlocking the door right now, doing my part. The way that no one, aside from this man with all the bravado, has quite acknowledged me makes me think that the time is not yet right. Which is absurd. I tell myself I could just do it. Just open the door.

My back is to it, and I suddenly don't feel like even looking at it straight-on. Toward the glass and the train tracks, the members of the church are gathering things into bags. Black clothing and flashlights—C&C flashlights—and cans of macaroni, small bottles of barbecue sauce, and condensed milk, that I recognize from the kitchens in the Colonial Outpost. I can also see, atop their piles or in their hands or dangling around their necks, the same item: a mask. The kind for sleep.

"I thought the whole point was to see them," I say. "The bots. For transcendence, or to prove a point, or whatever. What's with the masks?"

He gets to his feet. He's towering, the posture of a dancer and the heft of a cage fighter. That face, still a mask of serenity. I can see why people listen to him. Some primate impulse within me wants to run from him. At the very least, keep him at arm's length.

"We don't pretend to know exactly what it will be like down there. Or *who* we'll find down there. Many of these people you see had characters modeled off of them, for the ride, you know. Myself included." He touches his chest with the tips of his fingers. It's effeminate in a way I didn't expect. Or maybe that's not it. Maybe it's just practiced. "But we didn't end up on that ride. After . . . well after the incident with Callie . . . I think they shuffled some things around."

"But you think that they put you guys in storage?"

"We know they did."

"How?"

"Someone explained it. In writing."

The messenger bag. The letters.

"Did you know Declan Towe's wife?"

His face changes. It makes me turn cold. "Yes," he says. "Yes, I did. May God rest her soul."

"Yule, we're almost ready." A woman with a shaggy pixie cut and an extremely strong jaw comes close. Her eyes sparkle wide, and she gives off a smell like a sink. Stale water. "Is she . . ."

Yule nods, but says no more, and after an uncomfortable moment, the woman retreats. There's a rip on the side of her fitted T-shirt, and I can see rib shadows, stark, underneath.

"Delphi, here's why I think you should come with us." He begins to walk in the direction of the crowd, slowly, so that it seems rude not to keep his pace. "You grew up godless. Without community. You came here searching for those things, but let me guess, it came up short. And now you're here, in the midst of a chaos that you don't understand, that makes no sense, and you've decided to retreat. To go home. To abandon the search for answers."

He's started speaking louder. Loud enough that the people closest to us—who are swinging their satchels onto their backs, who are taking swigs from canteens and double-checking their mask straps, striking the bases of their flashlights and dusting off twins' behinds—start to listen.

"But we're different. We aren't satisfied with a question mark. We aren't satisfied with nonsense, the kind of nonsense everyone else lapped up. When one of us, when our beloved colleague Callie, perished, unexplained, in a *nonsensical* way, did we accept what we were told?"

A few call out from the crowd. "Mm-mm, no sir!"

"When we were made to turn to each other, to like-minded community, in order to survive, did we follow the same mold as everyone else?"

More from the rest. No. No, they didn't.

"Delphi, tell me something . . ." A few of them gather close to us. One of them takes my hand, beaming. I notice the tall brothers hanging back. They aren't smiling. "If I gave you a list of songs, and asked you to choose one, and then asked you to tap out the rhythm of whichever one you chose, find a stranger on the street, and tap-tap-tap." He taps his temple, eyes wide, boring into my face. "'Turkey in the Straw,' *taptaptaptap-TAP*. 'Turkey in the Straw,' *taptaptaptap-TAP*. Would the stranger be able to guess the song? Yes or no."

I let a moment pass. "No?"

"That's right." He points at my face. "Only you have that knowledge. The knowledge of which song you chose. And it would be infuriating, standing there, tapping, trying to get this stranger to hear what you're hearing. You know you're doing it perfectly; you *would* be doing it perfectly, Delphi Baxter. Just perfect. I know you would."

The brothers in the back exchange a look.

Yule doesn't pause. "But it wouldn't work! They don't have your knowledge. Only you do. And here, now, all of us, all these men and women you see behind me . . . We all have the same knowledge." He smiles. Old veneers. Almost blue. "And we think we have the best chance of teaching the world our song. But to do that, we need the light. Too bad you're so afraid of it."

The woman who's taken hold of my arm—long skirt, tied into a knot between her thighs—rubs me a little bit. Encouraging.

I nod slowly. I can tell it's my turn to say something. "Why don't I unlock that door for you now?"

It lands like a rock. The woman drops my arm. There are one or two showy pouts from the crowd.

"Of course," says Yule. "It's entirely up to you."

A woman with a sharp jaw—the first woman's twin, I think— lets revulsion flicker across her face. Her sister, with her ribs visible, whispers something in her ear. The brothers in the back are watching me intently now.

"You heard the lady," Yule shouts. "Let's get a move on. What are we waiting for?"

They give me a wide berth. The door still feels like it doesn't want me coming near it. That angle seems more pronounced now. I can't shake the feeling that I should have known about this door. That by now, after all these years in the park, I would have known about it, at least. As I come close to the keypad, I can swear I hear something from the inside. A whine, distant. And an echo of voices. Something familiar.

"Delphi?"

I start.

"We lose you there?" Yule's voice still has that measured reso-nance, but I can tell he's getting impatient. Things have not gone the way he wanted them to go.

I slot in the needle. I press the card to the reader, I pull back a space of skin near my wrist, then press it to the pad. From the other side of the door, there's the clunk of metal loosening. I haven't heard a door make that sound before. A sound like a skeleton key would make. Something old. Ancient, even.

And then I step back. Yule pushes gently. Then harder. At the angle, the door doesn't swing open, but once it's been hefted into a certain position it comes away, and disappears into the dark.

"Lander," he says.

A man comes jogging forward. He's as tall as my shoulders and seemingly built entirely of muscle. Tan under a black sleeveless cotton shirt. Small eyes and a long scar across the bridge of his nose.

"The plan is Lander, our stunt man extraordinaire, will run up ahead and make sure there's nothing dangerous on the path. Down there there's not gonna be emergency exits!"

A few chuckles.

"Remember. If any of you want to turn back now, you're free to go. No one in this family is being forced at gunpoint to do anything."

The chuckles stop, and a peculiar energy passes through the mass. I notice the tall brothers have come close to me now. They're whispering to one another, and Yule is watching them closely.

In the blackness beyond the door, there's a strange heat coming through. If anyone else can hear the odd echo, no one is saying so.

Finally, Lander gives the crowd a nod, bleats out, "See you on the other side!" and gives a little bow before jogging into the dark. One of the older women gives a hoot of appreciation, and there's a sad smattering of applause, and then he's gone.

"Well." Yule lets his eyes drift from the brothers. "After you!"

He says this to no one in particular, and it takes a moment for anyone to move. But finally, Rosie steps to the front of the crowd. Veta follows close behind. I feel an instinctive pull to follow them, although I've already begun planning the drop pad I'll assemble at the far side of the wall in The Cemetery, anything soft or padded I can find to cushion my fall, how good it will feel to run, run, just run.

When about half of the crowd have passed through, my eye

catches something just beyond the slanted door. An open box. One of a tall stack that's been torn open inelegantly, the top shredded. Inside are packets of something, a powdered something. It could be anything, but what I guess, instinctively, is that it's Cream of Wheat. Something like it. It must belong to someone down here.

Something drains from me, and I'm back on the grass in Nebraska, in my mother's slippers, surrounded by caterpillars. There's a shed in front of me. Whit inside. The last time I'll ever see Whit.

Whit must be frail now. Very frail. I've left him inside a building to rot. I couldn't get him out, now, if I tried. I couldn't save him. I remember him moving through that one gallery, the neon exhibition, and holding my hand for only a few seconds at a time. I recall his side-to-side hobble as he approached each work, and how each one lit him up a little differently. Each one cast different shadows. We should have saved him. I should have tried harder.

I jump when I hear Yule's voice. "You're coming with us, then?"

I look around me. I'm inside the dark of the hall, on the other side of the door. Just barely, a few paces. I can't make out what's ahead. Black, and that strange heat, and the very faint echo.

Maybe it's because Whit came to mind so suddenly, but I see now that something underneath Yule's skin is incredibly feeble. He's being held together by very little, and he's expending his energy trying not to let it show. I can't help but feel a sympathy for it, for him. Maybe not sympathy. Pity. Something that would be pity if he weren't putting all these people in danger.

Has he put the old woman in danger? Part of me wants to think so; to understand that the reason I'm down here is that she's a guest. I have a responsibility to guests. Especially vulnerable ones like her. I can't not try to find her. I have an Action Plan. But that's not quite right either. There's a piece that I'm missing.

"Yeah," I say, not looking at the frightening man above me. "Yeah, I'm coming."

I got your letter. I'm glad you're safe. Go to the cabin. I wish you'd gone sooner. Make sure Declan goes with you. Seriously. I've been hearing about those militias that are forming in those commuter towns, around the reservoirs + gas stations + Costcos. Please don't go alone.

They took a few of us to this station they set up in the middle of the desert. About a mile from anything. When we're working with the bot, they don't want anything near us. Nothing we could hurt ourselves with, I think. It doesn't make sense. The bot doesn't look like any of us. But we've been running drills with it. Playing with its circuitry. Imagine: four engineers, sunburned, in the middle of the desert, with this merman attached to a generator wagging its tail + orating, totally silently, to emptiness. This goes on into the night. We've needed to set up these halogen work lights. It's the strangest scene I can imagine. A little beautiful. I don't know how to describe it.

We've spent days looking into his processor, the neural programming that lets him look guests in the eyes. It's creepy as shit, but I don't think that's what's causing the problems. We've looked at his guts, at his armatures, at the pneumatic nodes. I know nothing about how he was built, because I wasn't there, because they built him outside of the Ranch. So this is really useless. It doesn't seem to be about how he was built. There's an unknowable factor in all this + it's pointless to be working away these hours if we don't have his model, if we can't have a test subject to watch the bot in motion, but of course that wouldn't be safe for anyone. We can't do that.

I've been speaking to Oliver more. He told me about that one

party. About that Tomas guy who found Renata. He sounded
like a nightmare. One time he took his surprise-occult-party-
trick too far + there was some party with . . .
horses appearing, something really bad about horses +
Renata, <u>child</u> Renata Revere, having some dark shit happen to
her.

Oliver only heard about this in whispers during his heyday,
like a studio urban legend, but I guess the studio threw this
one enormous blowout after their first full-length feature
wrapped, at some countryside estate outside the city. I wonder
now where exactly it was. I wonder if it was around here. In the
desert. Oliver didn't know.

Tomas locked off this room that had special salt + some
animal blood + he made a mark, two marks actually, like
long scratches in the middle of the floor, like two wounds. It
got me wondering which came first, the party or the icon, the
Gwendolyn Goose lashes, everywhere, like everywhere in the
park?

But I guess as the night went on, people started to go in +
out of that room + according to different people Renata was
acting in different ways. Oliver said some people described her
as being quiet + still + creepy, others said she was laughing
+ sweet + more said she was sticking to Tomas's side like a
loyal pet. As the booze flowed, people tried their hands at bits
of ritualistic magic in that room + Tomas got more + more
agitated as the night went on. There were fifty rooms in that
place, but Tomas wanted to stay in the room where he'd set up
the salt + blood + marks on the floor + at some point he kicked
everyone out, everyone but Renata + the mood changed. I find
it hard to believe that people would let a little kid get locked
into a room with a crazy Satanist in the middle of the night,
but then it was a long time ago + you do hear fucked up things
about old-school Hollywood, right? Oliver didn't like talking
about this. + he said that this was the part of the story that

people wanted to talk about the least. This is where the story shifted the most, depending on who was telling it.

I'm skipping some parts, but cut to the next morning, when everyone starts waking up. Someone finds that the door is open. The blood + salt is gone. But there are two horses. One is alive + one has been slaughtered. Renata was there, quietly watching them. But Tomas was gone. + no one ever saw him again.

So I mean, I think maybe there were horses on the estate? Maybe they could have wandered in? That sounds ridiculous as I write it out. + whatever, this is all just an urban legend maybe, maybe absolutely none of it happened. But the way Oliver says it, everyone in that house was paralyzed with fear, even if they didn't see the horses, the one with its guts spilled out on the floor + everyone kind of knew that was the last crazy party. I don't know how Renata got home. What a strange fact to fixate on. But everyone assumed that the horse murder was Tomas's doing + that he fled in the middle of the night, that he knew he'd get totally fired from the studio, maybe he went back to his home country, Renata's home country, but I don't know. It just seems like a truly fucked up story, if it's in any way true. I guess I'm just getting to grips with the fact that secrets, huge secrets, secrets like the one that me +
these people have been sucked into, they're nothing new to the park. + people disappearing . . . that's nothing new either.

But like, remember, Oliver is old. I've seen him get confused a few times. Most often after sunset. Especially now.

Have you seen that drone footage of the park? Is that barbed wire out front? It can't be. But it looks like someone set up a barricade. I'd ask, but the only ones who will talk to us are Kendra + Nattson + they're not answering many of our questions. They look terrified, all the time.

Sorry, this went all over the place. Maybe it will distract

you in that weird fucking church. Go to the cabin. But don't go alone. I might not like Declan much, but I'm pretty sure that even he wouldn't let you do that.

—Bro

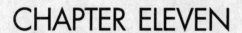

CHAPTER ELEVEN

This corridor is brick. There's no brick in California. Virtually none, and certainly not underground, anywhere that could buckle during an earthquake. It's the first thing that we notice.

The hall is narrow enough that the twins lose each other, and we become a sloppy stream of bodies. But when the light from this room strikes us, though, we breathe a collective sigh of relief. We even feel foolish for fearing the dark. This is a warehouse, taller than a school gymnasium and about as wide, lit with fluorescent bulbs, aseptic and familiar. Above us, starting halfway to the distant ceiling, is a criss-cross of grates and thin, steel-runged walkways, ones that don't look like they could support weight greater than a child or a large dog, and dangling cables. It's theater stuff. Soundstage stuff. Things were stored in this place—that's clear from the rows of black plastic boxes lining three of the four walls—but something was also captured here as well.

Yule is already heading to the farthest end of the room, the stage, to where Lander seems to have left the next door open. But no one else is in any rush. They mill around near the walls, and a few even pull out stray black boxes at the end of rows. I approach a woman who's arm-deep in one. She pulls out what looks like white table tennis balls.

"I did mo-cap a long time ago," the woman says. "You heard of *Pangolin*? It was the movie the *Nebuland* EP did before *Nebuland*. About pangolins."

She tucks some white hair behind her ear while looking dreamily into her handful of balls.

"Did you do your mo-cap stuff in a place like this?"

"Like this, sure. Not here, though. I thought the studio did all that out at the Imagination Ranch. Big facilities. Or in one of the Pasadena studios. Didn't even know they had an in-park soundstage."

I find myself peering behind stacks and looking for small footprints on the ground. I am, I realize, seeking any evidence of the old woman. I realize I have no idea what I'm looking for. The open box of food packets was an accident, surely. She won't leave me a trail of bread crumbs.

At the end of the room most darkened by shadow I make out a different type of equipment. Soldering tools and aluminum bars. Dead computers, but ones that I haven't seen since I was very, very young. It's a workshop. One that's not been used in decades.

I almost walk straight into one of the tall brothers, this one with some acne scarring in the middle of his cheeks. He's staring into a mirror.

"Does this look normal to you?" he asks.

It's hard to tell what he means. I'm watching the two of us. He has chipped indigo polish making continent shapes on his nails. I'm me. Just me. But it's not what's in the mirror that he's asking about.

"I think it's a little warped."

I take a step closer and see that the mirror has been laid into a cut-out section of the wall—set deeper than the wall itself. And there's something else. The mirror itself is curved, recessed inward. It's so subtle that you'd never normally notice. It makes the room we stand in look smaller.

The tall brother stoops and brings his face very close to the glass. He raises a hand and looks like he might tap it, but stops short.

"Have you ever done market testing?" he asks. "Or been caught shoplifting? Been in a room with a two-way mirror?"

"I don't think this is two-way. Aren't those usually kind of dull?"

In the reflection I see his brother pause in the middle of the room, looking our way. He waits, patiently, keeping an eye on us, and an eye on Yule, who's pacing by the second door.

"Do you really want to be down here with us?" the brother asks. "Pio and I . . . we have our doubts. We've come this far so it's hard to turn back. Like, it's hard. But I wouldn't be here if I didn't have to."

"I'm looking for someone," I say. "When I find her, I'm going to turn back."

"Yeah?" he says. "Someone who isn't with us, you mean?"

I shrug.

"You don't have much on you, do you? If you're gonna go searching for someone."

He's right. I'm traveling light. He looks over his shoulder and his brother, Pio, comes close. Pio doesn't have the scarring that his brother does, but I can tell by how he walks that he's a little clumsier. Longer feet, a little clownish. They exchange a few quick words that I don't catch, and then the one who isn't Pio is shoving something into my hand.

"Take it," he says. "But don't show it off." It's a walkie-talkie, exactly like the ones that C&C were issued, and a flashlight. "We're not gonna separate. We got more than enough stuff."

"Thanks," I say. He looks at the far wall, the door. "Would Yule mind?"

The brothers exchange a look. "You just never know," he says.

Before we leave, the tall brother touches the mirror once, just gently. He and his brother drift toward where the crowd is gathering, toward the back, but I squint at my reflection just a little longer. The fingerprint is duplicated again and again, trailing back into an illusory distance, and I feel certain that there's something behind the screen that I'm not seeing.

"Let's get a move on!" Yule shouts, and I can feel the shift already. He's anxious. He wants to get to the end.

He waits for us to gather in front of him, and though I place myself toward the back, I can see him scanning for me. Reflexively, I shove the walkie into my pocket, where it just about fits, but bulks out my thigh. I hold the flashlight behind my back.

When I pass through this new door, I notice that the frame, an aluminum lining, has come loose. You could almost yank the whole thing down. And underneath it is a type of polished stone. No, not polished—just stone. It's even sandy in sections, and where it's sandy, where it looks like it took the brunt of the bolts coming loose, it's an almost clay color, terra-cotta, something reddish and primeval, the vermillion of the skyline in the dinosaur room.

When flashlights dot the walls of the next hall, it's there all over. Sandy stone. Muddy, but red in spots. I notice that we're descending. Something catches in my throat, the idea that the lower we go, the farther we are from air. I remind myself that that's not how air works, and to keep moving. I can always come up the way I came.

The next room is more peculiar. It's smaller, with a lower ceiling. It has the smell of a family den. But like the last room, it's storing something. Screens.

Televisions are stacked on funny pilasters, odd protrusions coming from the wall, as well as glass cases, like you might find in antique shops. Most of the sets look old, but not *old* old: the kind of set that I grew up with. A box made mostly of gray plastic. But there are flat-screens, too, plasma ones, and stacks of tablets, which have collected cobwebs. The room's small, so we need to watch our feet as we weave through the maze of broken technology. There's carpet, in olive and avocado colors, with threads torn away in patches. The sisters with the strong jaws flank Yule in a corner while the crowd kneels in front of a mahogany cabinet containing a slate-gray screen no bigger than a loaf of bread, encased in thick glass like an astronaut's helmet. A model from the fifties, I'd guess.

On the wall nearest me hangs a painting of a window. It's not a very good painting. The sky is too yellow, like the artist was going for golden autumnal tones, but only had access to Crayola Dandelion and Goldenrod. But it gives that jarring half belief that the outdoors is just *there*. It makes me feel that my lungs are full of air.

There's something in the painting, though: white birds. Nothing in detail, only blurry and distant. But I'd swear they were the ones I saw from the top of the wall. The ones I don't know that I'd ever seen before.

"You see this?"

I make out Rosie's voice from the din of the room. Veta is squatting in front of a box like a toaster oven, one half made up of controls like a radio, like radar equipment, or something used for editing, maybe: dials and switches, some type of deck where physical film might be loaded. The other half is a screen showing blue static.

I see nothing built into the walls. No outlets, no plugs. I hover behind the twins. Gradually, I start to see what they see. Shapes. Shapes, and very faint sounds, that I recognize. It's the Land That Wasn't. That promo from long ago. The underwater vessel, made of huge glass orbs, and the enormous grimacing moon, carted out in some parade. A train locomotive, with some kooky conductor riding the top. A tower of electricity—something like a Tesla coil. I put my ear close to the machine, to some slits that look like a spot where sound could emerge. It's only a whisper. "And a beloved classic, reimagined . . . Peter and Wendy for the new millennium!"

Rosie doesn't protest when I push closer to the screen. Veta has gone around back, looking for where the thing is—must be— plugged in.

"The floor?" I hear her murmur.

The shapes on the screen are more indistinct now, but Veta finds a dial, in the back. I find myself almost telling her to stop. She touches something and I can't hear a sound anymore. But the next moment, there's a shift—the images come into focus. I can't make out any colors, but yes, there's an animated rendering of guests flying—suspended, individually, by some plastic harness—through a pirate ship, every inch of it twinkling in pixie dust, then soaring through a Skull Rock the size of a three-story building.

"They didn't build this, did they?" Rosie whispers.

I shake my head. "Scrapped it."

I think she asks another question, but I don't hear it: There's the guest, still suspended, but held upright, legs dangling, moving through a scene of enormity—a huge open flame, the inside of . . . a lantern?

". . . Shrink down to just a *Tink*, and see the world through the eyes of your favorite pixie friend!"

We're inside a lantern, Tinkerbell whirling around, gold light projected on the glass walls. Then an eye appears: huge and green. A wall comes away. And Wendy, ten times the height of the guest, brings her face up close, approaching the flame. It's animated. It's not real. It was never made. But the way the guest looks up at this girl the size of a—

"She's like a god," says Veta, from behind Rosie's shoulder.

The image of giant Wendy hovers there on screen, and then the scene changes: the park at night. Panning out from the castle. Fireworks in the sky. "Coming Christmas 1999!"

And then static.

I look away as quickly as I can, convinced I will see something terrible in the white grain on the screen. I remember the ad. I remember, in Nebraska, being entranced by it. Now I find myself shivering. Why would it play down here? Why would any of this be down here, half-rotting, half-preserved, in a purgatory.

A quiet has fallen over the room. Most bodies are sitting on the floor now. And one by one, they begin to look around, any smiles of exhilaration replaced by something vacant. It seems that they've each seen something that's left them shaken.

While they get to their feet, there's a chirrup from the static. A sound coming from the set. I put my ear close. It's a man's voice, and a strange assortment of words. ". . . fine . . . train . . . mountain lions . . ."

As we're collecting ourselves, wordlessly, to prepare for the next room, I look up. For some reason, it doesn't come as a surprise, but it makes me catch my breath in my chest, all the same. The ceiling is a mirror.

As we shuffle toward the door, Veta points up. The entryway to the next dim hallway is made of that terra-cotta stone, arching, and the double lines are carved above our heads:

))

It's clear now that they aren't, and perhaps have never been, Gwendolyn's lashes.

"It's okay," Yule says from some paces up. "Lander's tough."

One of the women, the one with her long skirt tied between her legs, is looking close at a patch of stone wall. She's touched something. On her fingertips there's a dark stain. Blood.

"He could have slipped in the dark," says Yule. "But he's a pro. He'll be fine. Up in Reno, you know, he used to train mountain lions."

Sent from:
CMT
2132 Lebec Rd.
Lebec, CA 93243

Your phone still doesn't work, or maybe you're still choosing
not to answer it, so I'm going to send this from the road, from
whatever post office I can find that's not crowded with riot
police. I'm about to get in my car. Everyone's leaving today.
From where we are, everything out there seems quieter than it's
been in weeks.

They started talking about Callie, and the news that one of
the victims of the helicopter crash had had their image used
for the revamped log ride. Nothing to do with Nebuland, as it
turns out. A new bot in an old section of the park.

Okay so it's like you've been saying. Someone saw
their bot, got in a helicopter, and crashed it—on purpose
or not—into a power station on the coast. A month ago
I would have—well, you know what I would have done.
You have my letters. You know what I believed then, what I
didn't believe. But that's not even the worst part. Here, the
people in the church are starting to talk about it, about their
Nebuland roles, and how a lot of them got told there'd be
bots modeled off them, but they never made it into the ride.
Some of them even had to send reference photos and videos
through. Close-up details of their skin and teeth and the way
they move. But the way they're talking about it, about the
possibility that there's a bot of them out there somewhere . . .
It's starting to mix with all the other God power uniqueness
cult-of-missed-opportunity stuff. It's really freaking me out.
They have a theory that the bots are stored <u>there</u>, too, in the
park. They think that's why the barricades have gone up. But
that can't be right. I know you said they didn't build these
bots on the Imagination Ranch, but I've never heard of like a

workshop or studio or anything underneath the park. I guess I wouldn't know.

And another thing. I brought your letters with me. I can't find them now. They were in a little suitcase I brought. Don't ask me why I brought them. I guess I just thought of the fires and . . . fuck, I don't know, I just wanted to keep them, and now they're gone. I think I'm getting paranoid but I feel like Yule, and that fucking Lander guy, are watching me more closely. They asked about you, once. They wanted to know about the brother who worked for the park. They're creeps, for sure, but they wouldn't have gone through my stuff. Actually . . . fuck. I really don't know.

I talked to Mom and Dad, who were pissed off about the church. You know them, they don't trust anyone, and they don't understand Declan's relationship with Yule. And I talked to Declan about it, and I think he saw how shaken I am, and he agreed to go back to the house. But not the cabin. I'll work on that more, try to convince him, but . . . I don't know. I think I'm going, with or without him. I'll be okay.

I'd been thinking this whole time that his problem was his laser focus on the movie. His movie. But I'm seeing now, it's not quite that. It's kind of the opposite. It's an evasiveness. Slipperiness. An inability to look at something straight-on. He'd rather let his wife go off into the mountains alone than face the end of something.

Can you come to the cabin? I know, probably not. I know not tomorrow or next week. But that's where I'll be, and I won't be leaving for a long time.

Can't wait to see you, whenever that is.

—C

CHAPTER TWELVE

We've been walking in the dark for ten minutes when there's a collision. People in front of me have stopped in their tracks. Murmurs, and a few of them press themselves to the damp wall, then recoil.

"Eugh!"

I reach out and touch it. The wall is caked in a kind of wet moss. Fuck it, I think. I'm allowed a flashlight. I click mine to life, and there's that red again, swirling up the wall, more like coral than any vegetation, any fungus I've seen. People are pushing past me now, crowding at the back. An elbow catches me at the hip. Something up ahead causes a scramble, but no one is yet returning to the television room.

I wend my way to the front. The walls have fallen away, and there's only Yule, and the twins with the sharp jaws, looking over a sheer drop, a cavern of wet black emptiness, the craggy contours of old, careless excavation deep beneath the earth. Yule stoops to look at the void below. Instinctively, he reaches behind him, looking for something to cling to. The other hand touches something tucked into his belt. I can't see what it is, but I've seen men do that before. I can guess what he has.

I take small steps toward him and feel a gust of algae air, made powerful from the bottlenecking of labyrinthine corridors. And below: what might be stalagmites. Caverns. At eye-level there are the hanging remains of concrete structures, slabs bisected and carved, large holes through their middle as though they were meant to fit tubing, a tunnel, maybe tracks. But now they have become home to plant life dangling like curvaceous tentacles, and a rot that, by now, must be deep in our lungs. Even farther below us, there's the sound of running water.

Voices pile onto one another behind me.

"There's only one path. We don't need the key to get back, do we?"

"Are you fucking joking, we've come this far."

"I don't want to go back there."

"This isn't what we planned for."

"I get claustrophobic."

"A little fucking late for that one, Janet!"

"This isn't what we prepped for."

"What are we waiting for?"

"I don't—I don't think I can breathe down here."

"This isn't what you told us."

"This isn't what was in the letters."

Yule tenses at that. "Oh!" he shouts, and it echoes, making our pathetic bodies feel even smaller in the enormity of the cave.

The rest go silent. Yule is no longer hiding the gun at his waist.

"It's like I've always said. You can go back." He fingers the grip, something compact, a 9mm, maybe. "But that will be that. You'll never know. You'll never know how you're different. You will have wasted your time."

A low murmur spreads. I find myself backed onto the mossy wall, and feel it seeping into my shirt. I take a few steps beyond where

Yule stands, where the pathway that we're on thins and descends into the space below. At a certain point down, the path gets obscured by debris, and some ooze I can't place, that terra-cotta color. I find myself blinking—something's caught my eye. A spot. A spot of light.

It careens around so fast, so small, I can't keep track of it. First it jumps to the far end of the cave, just a speck, then it hits what lies above our heads, some hundred and fifty feet up. It's the blinding blotch of a CD in the sun. And while my gaze flits to the distance above us, I think, for just one moment, that I can see what it's made of. The cover, the stony canopy, it isn't stone at all. It's plastic.

Could we be under the lake?

"The letters!" Yule booms, deeper. "Don't! Lie!"

"We don't even know who Oliver was."

"We know who he was." Veta steps to the center of the crowd. Behind her, Rosie's arms are crossed. "*We* know. He died knowing every secret of this place. He didn't die insane."

"Oliver could have been senile. He was old as hell, even then. And we've taken him at his word this whole time." Those of us piled onto the pathway turn back to find the voice. Bodies part. It's Pio. His brother stands by his side.

Yule is shaking. I fight an instinct to pull him back from the ledge. Pio is watching where Yule's hand is hovering, at what's tucked into the fabric of his waist, and Pio's brother is surveying the crowd. Looking for backup.

"You are free to go," says Yule. "But there will be nothing for you. You will be whoever you were before you came to be. Unspent potential. You'll never . . . know . . . whether you're *different*."

Pio and his brother exchange uneasy words. The murmur returns. One of the young women puts a hand on Yule's shoulder, and after a moment he becomes less red. Some people turn back; I'm not sure who leads the charge, or how reliable the pathway back is. I miss the details. I miss anything else that's said. Once again, I find myself crouching on the ground. Flashlight on. I'm staring at footprints, ahead of us on the path. Very small ones. Belonging to a child.

Or perhaps, a very old, very small woman.

I take the lead, keeping the footprints to myself, but not letting them get trampled over unseen. Our descent is slow, and our numbers have thinned. The tall brothers are gone, along with the woman with the knotted skirt and a handful of the older church members. Still, I find it hard to determine any ages here. They walk with the trepidation of someone very fragile. I'm tempted to run down the path, which is less marked now, as we approach the water, but something tells me that Yule doesn't want me out of his line of sight.

I reach the flow of water before the rest, though. The footprints have taken me to its edge, less a subterranean river than a ferocious trickle, bringing with it an unmistakable chlorine smell from the park above. While I wait, I realize the fact that I can see at all seems odd. There's no light source above us. That light-flicker appears at funny intervals, but there's something else. A larger offering of silver light, coming from somewhere impossible to pinpoint. I lean back onto my heels, and wonder how I could have come down here so unprepared. The water is almost certainly undrinkable, but I'm going to be out of options soon. And suddenly, that roving sense of light, almost a cloud of silver, appears just before me. I follow it.

There's another room. I can't see within it, but I get the sense from the sound of shallow dripping that it's smaller than the rest. I doubt very much that it will have carpets or equipment or electric lighting. This is a cave within a cave, pitch-black, with only the familiar markings at the top of its mouth to signal that someone has been here before.

The rest of them are still making their way down the path. I'm stepping into the dark before I decide that it's the right thing to do. My flashlight lets out a beam that shows me nothing more than formations emerging from the ground. It's colder in here than elsewhere, and I stick to the walls, flashing my light around the perimeter. No bigger than my bedroom. No sign of boxes or an old woman. Just those formations, stalagmites, and a very large hole.

Instinctively I press my back to the damp wall, although the hole is some three, four meters from me. My light reveals nothing more than slick contours leading to a gaping nothing. I continue to move in a semicircle, keeping my back close to the wall. I trip—my heart jumps to my mouth while I right myself and the flashlight slips from my hand. It rolls back, toward the far end of the cave, and I feel suddenly frantic, walking crazed, and I use my foot to feel for gaps, hands everywhere, touching everything, gloves wet. When I reach the flashlight, I see a foot. No, not a foot. Only a rock in the shape of a foot. An animal's foot.

A hoof.

I set the beam along it, up. It's still that dripping mineral and craggy erosion, but it's something large, like a horse. I survey the rest of the room as best I can. There's a shelf. There's a bottle. Yes, a coarse kind of carving, in the shape of a champagne bottle. I come close. I reach out. It's attached to the smooth surface on which it sits. It hasn't been built by any hands, any artist. Veins of sediment and mud, maybe peat, run through it. It was formed this way. I step over a shallow ledge (the shape, I see now, of a woman's legs, a woman who's sat on the ground), and find myself at the horse-shape. Yes, it's unmistakable. There's the curve of its thigh, the peculiar angle above its hoof, even a mane. There, sediment has shed away to form the oval of an eye. It becomes harder to make out more details; the light is unsteady. My hand shakes.

A scream.

I leap from where I stand and almost crash into the table rock. At the mouth of this room, three women are shining lights at the hole. More screaming.

I see it now. Someone sits at the edge of the abyss. I freeze. I shut my light off, while the women are illuminating the man—it is a man, a muscular, small man covered in filth. Lander. The women must be seeing him in profile. I can see his face. He's bleeding from a gash across the bridge of his nose.

The women are shouting incoherently, but a few words stand out: "Get up! Get away from there!"

"I came up this way," he says. "I got lost and walked up here."

His eyes are fixed on nothing. The blood on his face is fresh. It's still coming.

More people gather at the mouth of the cave. Yule appears, hobbling, exhausted, breaking through the flimsy barricade of howling women.

"What happened?!"

"I ran ahead and didn't come to any more rooms, boss," Lander says, flat. "Just a dark path that curved up, and my scar opened up, and it wanted me to keep walking up. Up and up. Then I came out of here."

"You walked *up*?" Yule cries. "How—"

"No rooms," says Lander. "Just up. Up and up. It wants me to go again."

Lander's form becomes hazy, from where I'm standing, obscured behind the back of the horse-shaped rock.

"Come over here!" It's one of the jaw sisters, trying to sound fierce. "Get over here now!"

Rosie and Veta are huddled to the side of the crowd, hands over mouths.

"Again," Lander groans. "Again. It needs me to do it again."

Yule starts to say something, but Lander slides himself away from his ledge and drops into the void before anyone can make another sound. There are yelps from the bystanders, but no one steps toward the hole.

More people disappear, back up the path the way they came, confident that they can find their way back. There's some effort to hold them back, I think. A scrambling of feet and the silent huffing of bodies straining to pull from one another's grasp. I can't seem to force myself to move, or make a sound. The old woman, the idea of her, made me certain it was my duty to make this descent with the others. Now I can't conjure her at all.

It wouldn't have saved Whit anyway, some voice seems to say. You failed to save him a long time ago.

Yule scans the cave, out of breath. I try to crush my body against the base of the horse. I can't see him, but there's something desperate in his wet gasping. It occurs to me that, for all his pomposity, he might not be used to losing people. He might not have foreseen the church falling apart this quickly. He might have counted me among them in some way that I can't and wouldn't want to understand. I almost feel pity. Almost. I stay put for nearly twenty minutes after he's left. Can't take any chances. I'm better off alone.

After the footsteps of the group have become faint, I stay where I am until my thighs go numb. My eyes have adjusted to the dark, just a little. The scene starts to come into focus: shapes among the blackness, the damp and the alien growth all around. There's that rock formation shaped perfectly, like a horse. Thick vine, like sinew, that looks like limbs and torsos, a few bodies packed into a small space. There's the hole, into nothing, in the ground. And there's another shape on the ground a meter or two from my feet. It also has four legs, could be an animal, but there's something strange about its middle. I approach cool, wet stone like the roots of a tree, spilling out two hooves, three, and then a great spread of wet matter, not quite moss, not quite silt; mineral, but loose. I touch it, and my fingers come back smelling metallic. Almost like blood.

The path up, back the way we came, is different now. Blocked by large husks of that coral moss. Maybe I didn't notice its thickness before, but I suspect that it's grown, while I was hiding. The path I take diverges from the footsteps of the remaining church members. They've taken a path along the far side of the streaming water. Above my head, where a faint cave ceiling might normally loom, I make out a bulge. It doesn't look like rock. It's the lake. The bottom of the lake. It drops chlorine water in fat *plunks*.

I wince, suddenly. The flicker of silvery light has made it directly into my eyes. When I look again, I can see it moving farther along my path, this side of the stream, keeping aligned with the dainty set of footprints. The old woman's.

After some time, the path begins to narrow, and it comes up against two rock walls, sandwiching an even smaller path. The moss is thick here, and as I wade in I find myself having to bat it out of my face. It's softer than I would have thought, like nothing I've encountered in the wilderness, though I am no outdoorsman. I keep in that awkward dance, heel-toe-ing my boots and using an arm to bat my path clear. The rock under my feet has turned muddy, and I imagine sinking into a bog, penned in. I hold both palms out to the stone surfaces and push, desperate for any suspension. I can no longer see the prints at all, but the light still flutters just ahead, just out of reach. When the walls become so close that I need to turn my body sideways, I consider turning back. It's not too late. My breaths come shallow and fast; but there—a gap? Yes, I can just make out where the walls end. I compress my chest, half-hold my breath, and push ahead.

The walls end. A few maneuvers and I'm out, on the other side. I bend, fill my lungs, and let the silver light—now drifting slowly around, emanating, rather than hiccupping, in an almost circular pattern—illuminate the space. All around are squat, smooth rocks, almost like an orchard of lumpy, massacred trees, like perhaps they had been support beams, eroded to irregular stubs over time. My eyes follow the light; I think I can just find where it's coming from. There's a patch of shadow, a gap in the nearest cave wall, on my left-hand side. As I approach, I see that it's a corridor, and the light roves from within it. I'm trying to make sense of the pattern, and then I notice the sign.

A torn patch of cardboard sits beside the gap. It's so damp it's almost mulch. Someone has drawn a large star, attached to a section of inner wall as though it was a Broadway dressing room. There's a name inside the star: *Rumjana Rakauskaitė*.

When I look up, I see her standing at the end of the dark corridor. Unmistakable now. Wendy. Renata Revere.

———————

I already know that later, if I get out of these caves, I will not be able to describe it right.

She leads me down a brief tunnel to a room big enough to fit an enormous turbine. I say that because she lives inside an enormous turbine, a hollow tunnel structure that's lined with reflective tiles. It's a stargaze corridor. A giant, mirrored, stationary kaleidoscope. There's also a floodlight, somewhere. There must be a power source. That's where the light has come from. It's bouncing around the tops of our heads. The turbine was, I must assume, reclaimed from the Land That Wasn't. Nothing else would explain how big it is. It must be from the new Peter and Wendy ride, where guests are made to be so small. Like in the commercial.

Renata Revere is in dark layers, though they look distinct from the uniform of the church members. An oversized T-shirt reaches her wrists. She's wearing paper slippers that I recognize from housekeeping's inventory. They go in the room inside the castle that can be won for a night or two. Renata hasn't said a word, but she must know that I'm following.

She carries on up some small steps so that we're in the belly of the cylinder. She reaches behind her and takes my hand. Hers is a shrunken thing, like dried fruit. But amid the endless blinkering reflections, I'm unsure what is up and what is down, and if the coin-sized shape of dark somewhere far in the distance is the end to this tunnel. I'm glad to have a guide.

This place is both wide and tall. You could drive two semitrucks through easily. Two trains. I see belongings, scattered. They seem to be spaced out in piles, pushed up against the curve of wall. We pass a mound of clothes, and a tower of cardboard boxes splattered with bits of black mold, and a file cabinet. On the far side, I notice a stack of paintings. No. Murals. Long planks, some wooden, some very long ones, in the style of Fairytale Grove. We're moving too fast for me to get a good look, but I can make out the topmost one. There are figures painted there, a story, surely. But something cold runs through me. I don't recognize any of the characters.

Up ahead, there's a glass sphere with an open top, like a huge fishbowl, rolled onto its side, filled with linens. Was Renata Revere sleeping in there? Beyond, there's that silent film moon, Méliès's *Lune*, its grimace carved into its surface. I can't imagine what she uses it for. Maybe company. She's built a home from the discarded props of a world that never made it to the surface, a world that was never born.

I spot boxes and boxes of canned food, taken from different dining areas around the park. We walk for another minute or two, and that coin shape does indeed begin to stretch into the end of this enormous barrel. There's the floodlight, a short drop from the ledge. Yellow base, the size of a dishwasher. Beyond that, back in the cool, rotten air of the damp, lifeless cave, there's no sense of dimension. Renata has stopped. I meet her at her side, my toes just inches from where the platform stops. I can't look at the light source for long before my eyes start to water. But I feel something out there. An unmistakable presence of mass. Of something towering above our heads.

"You have come to rescue me?" she croaks, still looking out into the dark.

Before I can answer, before I can think, she's toddling toward a row of plastic cups kept along an edge, and I watch as she pours from a mostly empty water cooler jug.

"I thought so," I say.

"Well," she says, handling two plastic cups, coming my way without seeming to move her hips or bend her knees. "There is no need. Look at my home. You are in my home."

The water tastes like rubber, but it's down me in an instant. I can't place her accent (the word *Slavic* comes to mind, though I'm not sure what all the Slavic languages actually are), and it cushions her voice so that it takes me a moment to understand what she's said. How on earth could this be a home?

She hovers beside me, smiling. Her teeth are so yellow it's like a skin has formed over them. There are no whites to her eyes. Blue-gray and bloodshot.

"How long have you been down here?"

Her cup has a kitten on it, batting at a ball of saffron yarn. She holds it up close to her eyes. She seems to deliver her answer to it. "Oh, since I was very young. And now I am ancient, as you can see."

There's a rattle when she talks, very soft, coming from deep inside some organ. I feel myself slide to the floor, take a seat on the wooden plank that runs across the tunnel, unable to remain on my feet. Past where she stands above me, perhaps all of five feet tall, I make out my own reflection, again and again, an infinitude, diminishing into slivers along the arch of this place.

"Will you tell me?" I ask, suddenly desperate. "Will you just . . . tell me anything? What this place is? How you got here? What the rest of them are doing?" It's flooding out of me, a little bit painful. "It's just been a long time since I understood anything."

She takes the cup back from me and doesn't refill it. Instead she examines me, and leaves me where I sit. Her shoulders are as far back as she can manage to get them, the practiced posture of a dancer. Then, she bends, moves away from me, somewhere back the way she came. After a moment she returns, large slabs in her hands, knuckles white. She joins me on the ground with surprising ease and starts to sift through the paintings. Those murals.

I want to ask what she's looking for, but she seems so hard at work. I stay quiet. She mutters something in a language I can't guess at and discards bits from her haul, tossing them into a little pile by her slippered foot. While she does this, I take a closer look at the large glass orb, a short distance behind us. Its mouth is detailed with a green plating that must have been gold, once. Squinting, fighting against the dancing of the stargaze dazzle, I recognize some of the items within it: a lace tablecloth from the Michaelmas feast scene in the Haunted House, Cornelius Claw's trowel, an overpriced orange boiler suit that sold in the main gift shop during the Halloween season. But there are other items, too, now that I shift forward and let my eyes adjust: a T-shirt from the bar Kenji used to drag us to. A yarmulke. Two loose tampons, lying beside their cardboard applicators. A photograph of a box turtle being held by young, chubby hands. Personal things. Our things. Things we kept in our lockers.

When I look back at Renata, she's holding a chunk of wall in front of my face.

"Do you see?" She pulses it at me once, twice. "It is how I knew that you were coming to visit."

I see lovely hand-painted swatches of pastel, with clear, careful attention to the scale of each character, each strange dangling vine and broken tower of rock in the background. But again, that chill: There's not a character here from a ride, or a film. All of the men and women are dressed in black.

"Oh," I whisper, something thickening in the pit of my stomach. The figures are marching, steadily, unsmiling, toward a door—a single paint stroke of green-black. Some of the people have little brushstrokes indicating hair that's come loose from where it was secured. Some have patches, surely painted with a smaller brush, of flesh showing along the bottoms of their bodies, a torn garment showing ankles. In the foreground, one is missing a shoe, and this illustration shows the careful detail of red dots along her toes. At the end of the procession, there's a woman dressed in lighter colors. Tans. Some lank hair is hanging past her shoulders. She's wearing gloves.

My hand covers my mouth.

"How . . ."

"It shows me what I need to know," says Renata, patting my arm. "It always has."

I bring the slab closer to my face. The woman with the gloves is, without a doubt, me, only something's different. She looks tired. And her face is lined deeply. On closer examination, everyone's is.

"Why do we look like that?" I ask, something electric fighting the exhaustion in my veins. A painting, who knows how old, depicting my journey which began mere hours ago. Why would I care about the details?

"There is more over there," she says. "If you'd like to see how it ends."

"No, I . . ." I shake my head, gently, back and forth, till the buzzing inside me stills. Till I can find words. "Please, I want to know how you ended up down here. And what all of this is."

Renata looks a little sad, like I've put the kibosh on some type of game. But she carefully lowers herself to the ground. I would have said that she was barefoot, but I can now see that she wears pink socks that are mostly holes, a few strands of fabric encasing her arches, and flaps, loose, at her heels.

"I was taken from my home. From across the ocean."

I nod, and wait for more. She takes her time. She searches my face for something, I'm not sure what, before she continues.

"I was born at the start of the war. My family survived it. I am an only child. No sons lost to fighting. We did not lose each other. But then a man from my town made it to California, with this art. And later, he came back for me. That is how my family lost me. Not through war. Through promises."

"I've heard that story before," I say, a little breathless. "I didn't know if it was true."

"Why would it matter to you if it was true?"

I'm too tired to laugh, to shrug, but I try. "I . . . I only want to know things that are true. Real. Please."

"Okay," she says. "Then I tell you everything."

Catherine, I've tried calling you. I've called maybe 200 times. It was going to voicemail at first + now it doesn't. ~~I can't fathom it seems perverse~~ I can't believe I wasn't calling you before. I'm hoping beyond hope that it's just a case of you not getting a signal in the mountains. I hope you weren't serious about driving alone. But I also know you weren't kidding. What kind of sick joke would that be.

There's no point in writing more until I know you're okay. But what else can I do? This is habit now. More than habit. Writing you is something I do. I think it might always be something I do, regardless of who's there to read it.

I'm going straight to the cabin after this. I've just left Oliver at a hospital near Bear Valley. I'm at a diner. Everyone here seemed nervous when I came in, but I haven't seen any violence. I don't think many people flee to the desert. Most people are going north from LA, I guess. Like you.

+ sorry but if those crunchy fucking psychopaths in Declan's church touched my letters . . . I don't know. Of course they went through your things. Of course they did.

But I guess I have them to thank for something. You said they'd developed a theory that the new bots were built in the park. Building things within itself. That phrase has been stuck in my head for a little while now. Earworm. Building things within itself. Building things within itself.

Oliver said something about the Land That Wasn't. He said they tried to build it from the ground up. Then he started talking about that horse again. The one from the party + Tomas. + his nieces. He's been in pretty sharp decline these last two days + there hasn't been anyone to turn to for help. I'll get to that later. But I didn't have any proof of there being any kind of facilities in the park. So I decided to go to the Imagination Ranch, one last time.

Kendra + Nattson stopped showing up to get our reports, or give us supplies. The last time they'd come, they looked

terrible. Both of them are always polished, you know, not a
hair out of place. This time they both looked like they hadn't
slept in a week + they were sweating through their clothes. So
we had to leave the merman in the middle of the desert, every
limb cut open, his torso cut open, on his side, still attached to
the platform that holds his circuitry. It looked like a murder,
except he had this serene look on his face. We'd paused him
there, at first. We didn't want to leave him. It felt gruesome +
cruel. Before we left, one of us turned him back on. That felt
better. The last we saw of him, he still had a smile on his face,
even with his insides spilled out + his tail + what remained of
his skin still very . . .what's the word? Resplendent. That's it.
Resplendent.

Even the handful of other engineers, the only company I've
had this whole time, aside from Oliver, have packed up +
left these last couple of days. We're not worried about
anyone stopping us anymore. There's no sign of anyone. A
desert compound, deserted. I figured the Ranch was clear
east, about 25 miles, based on visibility, how I couldn't see
any of it, but I knew we were within striking distance of a
couple of those little towns. It was closer than that, in the
end. About ten miles. The campus was the same as ever.
Palm trees + smooth paved pathways behind layers of huge
gates, painted in desert colors, you know, kind of cowboy
colors. Except that the gates were wide open. The security
stands were empty.

Everything there was empty. There was litter piled up on +
around the trash cans. About half of the buildings had their
doors wide open. There were a few wild turkeys roving across
the lawns, which had started to sprout dandelions + chunks
of weeds. Everyone's gone. Based on a few files that I found,
a few emails on monitors that didn't seem to be password
protected anymore, they'd gone to Hong Kong. New park. No
need to comment on what had transpired in the park. There

was the LA disaster + that was that. Time to start again on new shores.

I won't get into how long I searched, through how many empty buildings. I saw a turkey in one of the archives, in this stack of shelves holding plaster molds, the lights flickering. It was pecking at a model of Cornelius. I searched every building + basement + locked cabinet that I could get into, for close to ten hours. I forgot to eat until I found a cabinet full of Luna Bars that expired five years ago. I ate about five. Then I found a custodial shed with some hammers + I found a locked archive, in a section of the Ranch I didn't know existed. The doors that had been padlocked. I spent another hour smashing. It's harder than it looks. But when I got inside, I started in the back. Gut instinct. + then I found the Land That Wasn't.

They'd gotten so far with it. They had built full-sized zeppelins + bought some rights to The Little Prince + there were even correspondences to the Jules Verne estate. Everything they'd planned was huge. The Peter + Wendy ride they had planned looked nuts. The riders are made to feel tiny. But the thing is, they'd built it all in this space underneath the park. There was a map of the area in there, just drawn by hand, which was weird. It showed only one entrance, behind one of the panoramas where the train drives past. The least showy thing in the whole park + one of the few attractions that no one can get that physically close to.

There were records of the artists, engineers, everyone on each iteration of each project I could find—each blueprint + laminated document. But as I went further into the files, as time progressed, the names started to drop off. People seemed to disappear from the project. + then the land was canceled + no one ever mentioned the studio under the park. Not to me. Not to anyone I've worked with.

I didn't get answers bundled up neatly, but I had proof, like <u>actual documents</u>, that an underground studio existed.

+ when I drove back to the hotel, just after midnight, I started
to feel a little weird about those documents. When I showed
them to Oliver, who had been in his bed for about a week at
that point, he nodded like it made perfect sense + then he said
something about making sure his nieces weren't in that park
+ then he started shouting about getting the documents out
of his room. So . . . I don't know how to explain why I decided
to do it . . . but I grabbed a barbecue lighter from where the
hotel's kitchen used to be, walked out into the desert with
them, all those blueprints, all those papers, to where the body
of that merman was + I piled it up on top of him + I set fire to
the whole thing.

I considered sleeping, but when I got back, Oliver was in
bad shape. He was talking about echoes. Duplication. He
would whistle + then he'd stop + then he'd ask me where
he was + if we could stop + get Jamba Juice + then he'd
get serious again. At one point, clear as day, he said there's
always been something under the park. That nothing should
be made there.

I've decided to leave it there, Catherine. I don't think it's
about the bots being hyperreal. I think it's something to do with
where they were made. What happens when you see yourself
duplicated in the face of something made in the wrong spot
under the earth. We're never going to understand.

I can't put into words how badly I want you to be in the cabin
when I get there. I have so much more I want to say. There's so
much I want to listen to, from you, even if it's about the things I
give you shit about, childhood stuff, Declan stuff, I don't care, I
just want to listen to whatever you have to say. I think about all
the time I let pass + . . . please, please just be there.

+ if you're not, I'll sit in that wicker chair Mom got at that
garage sale a million years ago, the one she had to strap to the
roof because it wouldn't fit into the Stratus + I'm going to wait
for you to walk through the door. I'll wait for your footsteps.

I'm going to hold this letter in my hand + give it to you myself. I'm going to tell myself the story, over + over again, of how you walk through the door. I'll tell it to myself till I'm Oliver's age, if I have to.

I'll be here.
—Bro

CHAPTER THIRTEEN

Vines hang from this end of the turbine, swinging in some gentle gust. Out there, beyond, still, there's that looming presence that I can't name. She has decided that she wants our feet to dangle from the edge of the platform. I do what she says. She tells me to look down.

I see only earth, the dusty rock floor. Now she points. As I struggle to see more, she tuts, and begins the task of lowering herself to the ground. It's a distance of roughly her height, and her limbs shake while she does it. Feeling useless, I follow. I'm relieved to be out of the kaleidoscope chamber, here where things are still and steady. Renata is pointing at something, at ground level, just underneath her home. I lower myself onto my knees.

I hear it before I see it. A warm tone. A frequency. It's both stirring and tranquilizing, like a bellow of a dangerous beast, but from a very safe distance. Something familiar; inside out. Renata doesn't take her small eyes from me, relieved—surprised?—that I can hear it at all.

Then, I see it, faintly, deep underneath the cylinder. A little fissure, and a glow. It's not a color I can name. Burnt light behind the eyelids.

"This . . . ," I murmur. "This is consuming the park?"

"*Consuming*," she considers. "No. This is tricky." While she collects her thoughts, or simply rests her eyes for a moment, I notice the dim pulsing of the light in the fissure. Barely there at all. But I'm certain it's matching my own pulse.

"This has always been the park," she begins. "A place ready to receive all things wonderful. A place that tells its lovely little stories, and is also soft, rich ground for new ones. It was a special place before me. Before you. The very idea of a place like this is very magical. Of course."

I hear her voice, and I hear the hum from the darkness, but I find that I can't quite tell which is coming from where.

"The man who took me from my home took advantage of how fertile the park is. He tried to achieve something to do with gods and ghosts and America. He was obsessed with this idea, with this idea of him as leader of the magic men of California, I think. Pig shit in the brain. What he tried to do, with blood that he bought from butchers and stones that he bought in shops on the boulevards . . . those were child things. Daydreams of men in funny hats, throwing parties, hoping the parties turn to religions. To churches. New world nonsense."

I think, for a brief moment, that nothing can be nonsense down here. How could she say that?

And I think she sees that flinch. Her words become sharper.

"But when Tomas—the man—when he brought me here," she continues. "I think something came with me. And he could not have known this."

"What?" I ask. "*What* came with you?"

She shrugs. "There had been war. I was born in a place by a sea that was many places at once. And soon after the bloodshed stopped, there was a great confusing dance of liberators and *okupantai*—the ones who occupy, quickly, big dash to occupy, big dash over bloated corpses, you know. New men and new statues and new weapons and new enemies. My mother had some family in the defeated country. My father's father was from one of the nations to the east, but he spoke the language of the new regime. His name was one of their names. But he didn't think like them. If I had not gone with Tomas, I would have followed my family to the place west, to the defeated place, and who knows what would have become of us? So much confusion, like I say. When I flew away from all that, I think the spirits of my home place must have gotten confused."

Renata strokes a patch of her knee with a very long, chipped fingernail.

"By *spirit* . . . Do you mean real, or, um . . . symbolic?" I almost feel silly asking.

I can see her try not to laugh. "This is not a ghost that is unheard of, where I'm from. Sometimes this ghost, this *echo*, this warm voice, would get attached to a girl and her life would become slow and sad and then she would die."

I blink. My hand is sliding along the ground, in the direction of the fissure. If she notices, she doesn't say.

"But the day I felt it on my shoulder, a day in August when new wire fences went up in my town, I knew it would treat me differently. I still don't think it wanted me to leave. But when the man, the men, took me to America . . ."

She smiles again and despite everything, I light up, a little. I see Wendy in her. I can imagine her flying with bird-Peter across the night sky.

". . . I could tell it was happy to come, too. America and this place, the studio, then the park, and the tricks and the beautiful music . . . I think it made the spirit very big and very strong. It wanted to get bigger and stronger inside this place. And when those silly men went scratching at the door of the unknown, when Tomas tried to be a little wizard, the spirit beside me decided to show him how strong it was. There was a night. A party. There were horses outside."

Horses. The cave. The hole.

"Tomas hadn't been treating me well. Everyone knew it. No one minded very much. So when the spirit broke the floor . . ."

Lander, down into the dark.

". . . I did not say goodbye to Tomas. I did not feel sorry for him. He went inside, and some things came out. Inside out. The poor horse, inside out."

"Tomas fell into . . ."

She nods.

"One of the horses . . ."

"My ghost, this place, the hybrid they became . . . it has a *complicated* relationship with duplicates. With echoes."

Echoes. The rides on their tracks, looping, thousands of times per day. The sign, two identical marks, Gwendolyn's lashes, hidden everywhere throughout the park. The *bots.*

This place is made of echoes.

"They tried to build shallow things down here . . . Studio things, storage things, filming places. *Teatras* things. There was a new world they tried building. They built a new kind of *robotai* for it."

"The Land That Wasn't?"

She nods. "It went wrong. Many people became sick in the mind, you know . . . Some people, people who designed the place, they became lost down here. And this space began to grow. My powerful friend, the voice, the spirit, kept growing."

"I . . . Does it . . . does it feed off of . . . hurting people?"

She rocks a little bit, on her heels, where she's crouched. "No. Not quite."

"Is it that . . . ," I start, "we feed it?"

"And it feeds us." She smiles. "The park brings so much joy. You know this. But the new *robotai* . . . and when they tried again, in the alien land. That was something new."

"So your spirit, *ghost*, from your country . . . it's doing that to the robots? Making them deadly? Making the people who see themselves in the animatronic do awful things?"

She leaves me hovering in quiet, for a moment, only the hum marking a sort of harmony between us. "I don't think so," she says. "I don't know. I think people, *all* people . . . I think that they don't like automation, or duplication very much either. I think they cannot see themselves made double, so perfect. I do not know if my ghost has anything to do with that."

How can you not know? How?

"When did you come down here?" I manage to ask, suddenly realizing how badly I need her to keep talking.

"I crept down here into the earth, where they were building, whenever I could, in the beginning. You can find photographs, I think. The man, the men, breaking ground, wandering this site." I watch her drift. Her eyes, what I can see of them, lose some of their focus. "I had been a fearless child. I may have turned into a fearless grown person. And because of those men, I will never know."

There's more silence, and I wonder if there's something I should say. I'm too tired. I let her regain the strength to continue, though I can see now that her breathing is a little bit labored, and there is a new heaviness to the countless folds of her skin.

"But one day, after I had some photographs taken in front of my ride, I found my way to the lower levels. Not far, just a little ditch where something large was being built. As they built deeper into the earth, I found reasons to return to the park, to slip away, and to get close. I spent time in the trenches, here. And the lower I got, the more corridors I found my way into, the safer I felt from the rot above. The rot of men like Tomas. The rot of the city. It felt more like home, down here, until something down here began to grow. My spirit, my ghost, began to take root."

She presses a shaky hand to her heart.

"I discovered that I could stay. With the right planning, I could stay, and this thing that I planted, this voice would be with me always. It would be a little bit like being home again."

The heat from the fissure begins to stretch toward me, warm every inch of me. It starts to feel like a cradle, like a sturdy hand at the back of the neck. Renata sees me staring into those depths. She nods toward it.

"When I hear it, it is my mother's whistle," Renata finally says. "But the whistle she saved for vermin being swept from our home. A whistle to say: *Leave our family be.* I loved that whistle very much. What is it that you hear?"

Though I imagine myself waiting patiently to recognize the tune, as composed as I can be in a cave in the dirt, I feel tears start to form. My throat gets tight.

I know it. It's something triumphant. From the old Kingdom of the Future. The pomp, and the horns, except sung from the depths of the earth.

"It's from something long gone," I say.

She places a hand on my back.

"You wondered how you might have lived if you never came to the park. But I only started living when I came here," I say.

"How can that be? I'm sure you were someone when you arrived."

"I don't think so. Have you been watching me? When you come up to the surface?"

"Oh," she says. "Now and then."

"Then you know. You know how I am. I don't know who I was before I got here, but it was better when I was here. It's better when I stay here."

I don't try to hold back tears now. And finally, I think I understand why I came down here. I think I understand what I came here to ask. "Renata, when did I arrive at the park?"

She takes my hands between hers, pressing on the satin with extraordinary care.

"Look for yourself."

I take off one glove, and then the other. I let them fall to the floor.

"Ah," I say.

We look at my hands like that, together, for some time. The topography of scars. And the rest of it. The other thing. I look up past my hands, along my forearms. I flip my arms so that my bare palms are facing up, and I can see my skin, up to the elbow and just beyond. The limbs are lined and withered, like old fruit. On my hands, there are a few brown-gray spots. If you were to squint, my skin wouldn't look very different from Renata's.

A kaleidoscope requires constant twisting to keep its magic in motion. This one has finally come to a stop.

"I'd like to show you how this ends," she says. "I think it will bring you some comfort."

We return to the stack of broken murals, where the frontmost image has taken on new shapes. The little procession of men and women wearing black has come to a standstill before several looming figures of different sizes and colors, standing on plinths of some sort. Their paint strokes are thick. One figure is a man dressed for war, two are mermaids with blackened eyes who rest on their sides, fins dangling almost to the floor. There are two different children, both covered in layers of pelts, with ice picks and ropes attached to their middles. There's also a young man in a top hat. I recognize him from the haunted house.

When I blink, the paint changes. The shapes are in a new configuration, like they've snuck across the slab. No slow unfolding. It's imperceptible; something new takes shape the moment my focus drifts from it, to one corner of the canvas or the next, even for the most fleeting fraction of a second. Each hairline rivulet of the brush is new, but dried out, the way very old paint is dry. I wouldn't have believed it a day ago. I'd believe anything now.

The larger figures on the plinths stand overlooking the smaller figures in black, almost enveloping them. I blink, and there's a little eruption of yellow light at the base of each plinth. I blink again and the looming figures seem to be in motion, limbs caught in the movements of dance. When I look again, the image stays nearly the same. The people below don't move. Transfixed.

Then a few of the procession bring their hands to their faces. Some cover their eyes. All figures in black begin to move across the canvas. Many now have down-turned mouths, and large, sad eyes. They collide, and fall. When they do, those unhappy faces turn to toothy grimaces. Another blink and one face is enormous, coming straight at where I might be standing, viewing this as I am now, through the safety of the mural. In the next instant, the face is gone.

Some stand and begin to move toward one another, more steadily than before, no longer frantic. More join, in the center of the room. Before long, it's become a black mass, like a terrible rain cloud. Particles of that mass begin to fall from it, small pieces drifting to the ground.

There is an echo of wailing, coming from very far off. It starts faint, and grows in intensity. I couldn't have said where it was coming from. It seems to seep through every stone. I feel Renata watching alongside me. Her face is calm. I look back—I begin to blink fast, eager, and terrified, to see what unfolds.

The large figures on the plinths are still moving, swaying in place, the same pattern, over and over again. And underneath them, underneath the black mass, a pool of vermillion forms. One body breaks away from the rest and reaches the edge of the board. It disappears, then reappears, carrying something large and nondescript. Debris. A stone. It flies across the painting and lands in the black mass. We hear more animal screams.

I blink and a few of the figures in black have crawled from the center, and their bodies have been drawn, now, at frightening angles that don't make sense. Their faces are expressionless, dots and lines. Soon they become still, no matter how many times I blink.

Blink. Blink. One of them has a red vine now. He wraps it around the neck of another. Blink. The largest of the figures in black has moved to the back of a plinth, stationary in this chaos. He seems to struggle with a cord. He struggles more, then stands upright, hands on his head. He bends back down, more toil, hands on his head once more. The large bodies on the plinths don't stop moving.

Then, the large man below takes something small from what looks like a pocket near his hip.

A loud crack like thunder. Breathless, I reach for Renata. She hasn't moved an inch, watching the story unfold, unfazed.

On the mural, Yule has disappeared.

All black seems to dissolve from the painting. All that remains is that brick-red layer beneath the bodies, that's grown to a certain thickness. It's become a kind of serpent. The red and the figures on the plinths. That's all that's left.

I blink maybe fifty times, waiting for a change. It doesn't come. My hand is covering my mouth. I can't catch my breath.

"You thought this would bring me comfort?"

She finally looks away from the canvas. "Not this part."

She toddles behind the piles and pulls out a new square section. My heart is still racing. Renata, still smiling serenely, places the new slab in front of me. It's entirely blue. A cool and lovely blue.

"What is it?" I ask.

As if in response, there's a vibration under our feet, and a roar, from beyond this chamber. It's the rushing of water.

"This is what comes next," she says. "You'll need to leave."

I recall each rocky outcrop and downslide along the path, the descent, the loose chunks of concrete and sharp crag. Out beyond the mouth of the turbine, from the narrow passage that Renata led me through, there's a blast of fluid low to the earth. I grip her arm, nod, dumb. I try to retrace my path.

"Grab what you need," I say, breathless. "Do you have shoes? You'll need shoes."

"No. Not me."

I loosen my grip, and face her, this small creature, ancient, anchored to her spot. "I'm not leaving without you. Get your things. Get—"

"Delphi. You know now." She looks at my hands. My throat

tightens. "By my count, I am over one hundred years old. I have been blessed to live this long, in a place that cared for me."

"Cared for you?" I cry.

"Yes," she says, serene. "In its way."

She moves from me with impressive speed, toward the back of the tunnel, stopping at the floodlight. The roaring gets louder. I can feel it under our feet. For a moment I panic, animal rage, thinking about the fissure. Our fissure. It . . .

No. It's not mine to protect. I run to Renata's side. She's using all her strength to reposition the floodlight, gripping the rubber handles, until its thick beam hits the chamber's shadowy end.

"I only need one thing from you before you go," she says. "You've worked machines before, yes?"

And I see it. My limbs go cold.

Wendy is two things at once: so huge it makes you feel like you're falling, simply to behold her, just as the new Peter and Wendy ride wanted from its guests. And hyperreal. I'm looking into pores, pores in her near-teenage skin, made giant, and down where her hairline reaches her ear there's a bare patch of pale skin. Then an ear which is glossy on the inside. She's only shoulders, neck, and face, more than a story tall, and she's anchored to a slab of concrete, which rests on the cave wall. There, a boom bursts from her back, a battering ram. A thruster.

The whole thing is situated on an elevated platform, and as the blue-dyed water—the lake water—begins to pool on the floor of the chamber it avoids any of Wendy's machinery, the circuitry connecting that thruster to the generator, which powers the floodlight. All it will take is making sure she's attached. That's all it will take.

Side by side, Renata and I examine her. Her lashes, thick as oak leaf veins, and the dimple under her bottom lip. The ridge of her shoulder blade where it meets with her pale rose nightgown, streaks of black mildew melting up into it from the ground. Her scalp, where her part sits, is red in a patch, the faint irritation of a comb, and on the ear there's a flap, a tragus, a sand dollar in size. It's nestled just where it starts to get glossy. Her lips are parted in a soft smile. Her eyes are half-closed. Her nostrils are narrowed; she'd been taking a breath, the last time she was shut off.

My body feels uncertain standing beside this enormous thing. Like nothing inside of me knows its own scale.

"It . . . it was built down here?" I manage.

"Yes."

"And you want me to . . ." It can't be. Not after the bloodshed that we've just seen. I don't believe she could ask that of me.

"I want to know, my dear. The last thing I want to know, is what it's like."

I break my gaze from the giant and try to say anything to Renata. "You know what it does. It won't be . . . You've lived this long without—"

"I have faith that this place will protect me."

"It won't, Renata. Nothing can protect you from . . ." I look back at the first mural, lying where it was left. It's now entirely crimson.

"I don't mean that I'll survive. I mean that this is what was always to come. This is how it was always meant to end, for me. Please." She takes both my hands in hers. "This one thing. And then you run. And then this will all be done."

I search Renata's face for anything to help me make sense of this. I feel my tears coming thick now. I hear the music from Whit's CD player. I see the light from the shed, those flames. The beeps from my hospital bed, as some signal, as a code that I couldn't possibly read.

"You are not here to save me, Delphi," Renata says with extreme kindness. "You never were."

———

At Wendy's back, the topmost notches of her spine, the few visible before her body ends, contain ports. And below, the workings of her machinery. Water pools thick underneath the turbine now. I left

Renata there. It looks like she should be waving farewell to me, as if from a dock as I pull out to sea.

There's a large central control cable, sheathed in a polymer, there's a junction cabinet a little . . . frame . . . something to do with tensile . . . stability . . . something . . .

What is it? What is any of it? The words escape me, like something here under the earth has taken them from me.

In the end, Wendy is ready to go. All I need to do is hit the switch.

I look to Renata one more time. She sits on the mirrored floor on which she's lived for such a very long time. She is smiling for what's to come. The smile is still as I flip the switch and bring Wendy to life.

It didn't want me to leave. The underground. It didn't let me go back the way I'd come.

I twisted my ankle in the rock corridor where I'd followed Renata's mirror-light to find her. I hobbled, gasping, till I reached the base of the path where I'd followed the small footprints. I kept a wide berth from the cave with the horse and the hole.

Water was at my waist when I began to climb. And then the path was gone. It simply evaporated. What sat before me was broken lumps of concrete and shattered glass. I can't be sure, but I think it was from the television screens.

In the end, I descended back into the waters and swam till I reached the far side. The relentless push of the water had ceased; wherever it was bleeding in from must have run dry. The whole of the lake was under the earth now, there, with me. Pulling a thick rope of vine, I hoisted myself onto a fragile rock shelf. It spiraled partway up the vast wall of this place, and then thinned to where I could no longer go. Above my head, I saw that an ancient, industrial ladder had been embedded in some concrete. I stretched the entire length of my body—flung myself up toward it with a pathetic assault of little jumps. My fingertips grasped at empty space. I stopped jumping. I couldn't even shout, in anguish, or anything else. I didn't have it in me.

Now I sit, legs dangling off a ledge, overlooking daylight spilling into this void. I've been here a long time. Maybe an hour. At first, a hunger was scraping at my insides, and the sickly ache of dehydration, or infection, or disgusting wastewater having made its way into my body through my pores and my small wounds. But now, just now, something has dulled all that pain. Something has been humming in me, around me, for a few moments. I'm breathing easier.

Under my feet, the waters and the blood of the church sift through one another, and eventually become one. Deeper in there, Renata's floodlight has been drowned out. No light on those mirrors. I wonder what remains.

Yes, the humming has become warm. A familiar warmth. It's started to spread to my limbs. It takes me a moment to recognize it, a kind of déjà vu, a memory of something that can't be remembered. It's the warmth that comes at the end of every day.

A few images come: a sky with unusual soot clouds, building in thickness overhead, on the midway to the park gates. But my feet don't move. There's a stillness that is bigger than my body. There's a voice, I think Brendan's, a man's, pleading. This memory, if you can call it a memory, takes on the feeling of a cube, something with dimension to it; not one memory, but many, maybe hundreds just like it, stacked on top of one another over time.

I welcome that stillness now—the warmth—knowing, somehow, that I don't always welcome it. I let it grow under my skin. I feel it in the spaces between my ribs and the arches of my feet. It seeps into the strongest muscle of my jaw, and from there, the length of my spine where it meets my skull. I feel that it wants to talk.

Stay, says the warmth, which I know is also the voice from that fissure, the one that kept Renata company here for so long. *You won't like what's outside.*

It's right, I breathe into myself. I won't like what's outside.

My grip on the ledge loosens. I lift both hands away and place them onto my legs. My feet softly, slowly kick at the empty space below.

The voice from the fissure is a little louder this time, and the warmth in my skull has turned into a true heat, one that another person, another me, perhaps me of only an hour ago, might find worrying.

She brought me here, from another place. But she's not here anymore. It could be you. We could stay, together.

My own voice sighs in return, a breath that's a twin to the voice. It could be me. That's true.

Then: *I'm not a god. But this place is a god. Live inside the god. It's what you always wanted.*

Every gasp I've made inside these gates, every wide-eyed spark of fascination, every moment of wonder I've preserved by refusing to turn the lights on . . . it's been me, living inside the god, wanting to bore deeper. Yes. That's an excellent point.

And then it's everywhere around me, and it doesn't matter if I'm on the ledge or falling onto the shard-sharp slimy rocks below: Something molten and intricate is circling my body. A glow, ribbons of light that have leaked out from the most hidden room of the cosmos. It's the heat from inside me, twinned, dancing across my vision. I know that no one else could see it, if anyone else was near. I know I'd follow it to the bottom of this ravine.

It's the blazing glow that I built in the shed, with glass and noble gases, and with Whit. It's the afterburn of a shooting star, seen from the bottom of an empty pool. It's ten thousand shards of mirrors spinning, reflecting light across four walls, darkened by men with fabrics and magic tricks. It's every play of lights that's brought me to this place, and every light that's kept me here, all this time.

The voice begins to speak in a language that I don't know, but I take another breath, to answer it in return. I move my weight toward the edge of the rock. The cool rush of void beneath me begs for the heat of what's in my body, soon to be out—

"DELPHI!"

It's hoarse. I rupture.

I open my eyes. The warmth bleeds out. Pinpricks all over.

"DELPHI, can you hear me?!"

I can't make sense of it for a moment. My name. For a moment I sit there, and let Brendan shout and shout. For a moment I want him to shout so much his throat bleeds.

Then I look up. I see his face. Just the twinkle of him. Dark eyes under a cloud of hair. Then he slips away, and there's only the scrap of sky far above me. Then something else: a long line. Brendan is lowering something. It looks like a serpent, a bleached and deadened eel.

"Delphi, is that you?!"

I stand. He makes a cry like I've never heard him make. I get on tiptoe, to try to see him more clearly. He replaces whatever was in my blood. My lips were ready to speak ancient words to the voice under the earth, moments ago. Now I speak new words:

"Is that a hose?"

There are his teeth, his smile. The thing is knotted in sections. I wrap my arms around it, and position the knot underneath my thighs. I hang on tight, because he is yelling as loud as he can: "DELPHI, HANG ON TIGHT, I MEAN AS TIGHT AS YOU CAN, HANG ON LIKE FUCK! TIGHT! YOU UNDERSTAND?"

While I ascend, I feel one last grasp of the fissure under the earth. It's weaker now, wet and maybe dying, but still, I know that it's reaching for me.

And then it slips away.

I roll onto my back and gasp, painfully. There's sunlight on my face.

"Is she okay?"

"Delphi?"

"Pull her over here."

"Delphi!"

I'm in and out, desperate to be unconscious, despite all the noise. Then there are hands on me, and someone lifts me up. I force one eye open.

I'm back to that day, speaking to Old Sam Ybarra, who startled me while I noticed something funny about one of the turrets. A lifetime ago. Now, there's a quick back-and-forth in a language that I don't understand, and some water on my face. More voices and soft hands wiping at my forehead and my cheeks. I let my eyes open again. I get to my feet. I look at the castle. I see what was wrong with the turret. It's gone. Collapsed. It's dangling in space, midair, connected only with cable and some feathery strands of insulation. Deeper, there's a bomb smash of struts, fractured beams, and dead leaves.

It was there, like that, staring me in the face. I just couldn't see it.

There's a faint chorus behind me: "We gotta go if we're going to catch up," one of them is saying. "He can't be past the 101."

"Fuck that. I'm not going. He's gone."

"Nah, man. He has to know."

"He doesn't want to know. Just let him be."

"Are you hurt?" a voice I know is saying.

I can't look at him. Not yet.

Behind us, Rosie and Veta are arguing with Pio and his brother. A few other members of the church, who must have turned back, have scattered themselves, dazed and perhaps concussed, on stretches of grass. Someone has given them bottles of water.

When Veta spots me, she runs to me, throws her arms around me. "Fuck," she whispers.

Rosie's there, suddenly. "Where did you go?"

I laugh. What a question. What does it matter? "I needed to find someone," I say. "I'm glad you're here."

Rosie and Veta have deep lines on their faces. They're old. I couldn't see it before.

"How did you get out?" I ask, hoarse.

"We split when we got to the room with the bots. It sort of crept up on us, after all the hiking through the caves, after we left you at the horse . . . thing. Yule was right. There was as big storage room. And it was just bad in there. And Yule had started swinging that gun around. He wasn't letting people leave."

"But we slipped out when we saw ourselves. The kids. *Us* as kids. Before they got turned on."

I can feel in their pause, and in the way that they don't look at one another, that it wasn't that simple. That there was something more complex in what they saw in that room, and in their decision to leave. I know now, more than ever, that it would be agony to abandon a perfectly preserved version of yourself, even if you knew that clinging to it would kill you.

"How did you make it back?"

"Just the way we came," says Rosie. "The same path."

The tall brothers approach now. They've both got silver hair down to their shoulders. They explain what they're fighting about. Whether to follow Towe. What, of what just transpired, he'd like to know. He headed for the mountains. There still aren't many cars out there, they explain. They say that decades later, LA will still be figuring things out. I ask if there was something about the mountains in his letters. They nod.

"He thinks it's where his friend is. His friend, his wife's brother. He's hoping he's still there. That's all he said. He left as soon as they pulled you out."

I still feel Brendan at my back. The others drift away, in time. I feel him take my hand in his, and when I turn, there's horror in his eyes.

"Where are your gloves?"

I touch his face. I try my hardest not to shake. There's so much I couldn't see before.

Age looks sweet on him. His eyes have become darker and his ears have grown large. I hope he doesn't try to count out the days and years to me. I don't need it. It wouldn't do either of us any good. I see that we've been here for a very long time.

"You asked me what we do at the end of the day, every day," I say. "Tell me what we do."

He speaks so that only I can hear. He touches my neck. He looks me in the eyes. "We go to the gates. You stop. You look at the spot where Callie was, and everything beyond. And you say, 'I don't want to go out there.' And so we don't."

"Every day?"

"Every day."

"Sometimes if you tried too hard to leave, you'd get sick."

"What do you mean?"

"You'd disappear inside yourself for a long time. I'd lose you."

"But I'd come back, right?"

"Yeah," he says. "You'd come back. But it scared me."

There again, the faintest memory of his pleading, underneath a sky darkened by something.

"Every day . . . ," I whisper to myself. I look, once more, at my hands.

He continues. "I hated to see you in pain. And you'd be in pain when we got too close. When these people showed up, and I didn't know what they wanted. I just thought it was best to avoid them. I thought we might find a way to leave, in time. But then they stayed. I guess they were planning. They stayed for weeks, I think. Sometimes it got hard to keep track."

Something quiets. Rosie and Veta, the brothers, have come to some resolution.

"Those two are going to stay awhile," Rosie calls. "If that's okay." It takes me a moment to understand that she's asking me. She's asking like this is my home.

"Of course," I say.

"What about you two?" calls Brendan. He's still holding on to me.

"Me and Veta are going to follow after him. Towe. We knew him, a little, way back when. He's a good guy. He deserves to have help getting wherever he's going."

There's more arguing, then a renewed fire in the debate. If the church is gone, then there's work that needs to be done here. They lost decades—they say decades—trying to prove how special they were. They should prove it, in the city, by rebuilding.

We let them argue, and at some point we've drifted so far that we can no longer hear them. I think that it can't be that easy. How can people be devoted to someone, a mission, an idea, and then switch like that? Change plan. But I let the feeling go. As it turns out, they didn't want to die. It's as simple as that. Good for them.

We're some ways off, toward the castle, and Brendan is helping me walk. My ankle hurts electric, but I shake him off me, gently. I stop and lean my head on his chest, my arms dangling free. He inhales the top of my head. We're not so different from how we were, really. This isn't something that time can take from us.

I can see the ruins of the lake. The rubbery sheets that have collapsed into the earth, the debris that's clouding above the pit. There's the fire hose that they lifted me with, fraying. And there's an industrial digger, some of the equipment that I saw in the barricades outside the gates. Parked at the lip of destruction.

"You did that?"

Brendan nods. "We did. Towe told me that he'd seen you go underground. We couldn't find a way in. So we . . . you know . . ." He looks a little bit sheepish. "We destroyed the lake."

"You weren't worried about drowning me?" He can't see that I'm smiling.

"Of course I was," he says. "But we didn't know what else to do."

"It worked," I said.

"You must think I'm a monster," he says. "But I didn't get comfortable with . . . things like that . . . overnight. Keeping people away. Keeping people out."

The piles upon piles of fire cannons, from storage, from The Cemetery. The barricade, outside. The marks in the grass: drag marks, the long scars in the dirt.

"You did that?" I ask. "The pile of everything outside the gates?"

He nods.

"There's no way. . . . That was massive, it looked military. There's no way you could have done it. . . ."

Of course. He did it slowly. Over years. It must have been how he filled his days.

"It took a long time, and I was a mess the first time I had to . . . protect us. Everyone wanted in, after the city—" He hesitates. "There was a time when everyone wanted in."

We walk farther, and the state of the park unfolds. It's revealing itself to me in sections, in the beastly swatches of black that scar the landscapes, the mold and debris, in the spiderwebs interlacing the machine parts of the river animals beyond the fencing that flanks the castle. There's something in the distance, past that dry river, almost as far off as the Rainbow Calistoga Geysers. Old Sam Ybarra, so much older than I can fathom, almost like Renata, pushing his mop and bucket.

"You weren't the only one," says Brendan when he sees him, too. "The only one who couldn't leave."

"How did he act?"

"I never quite figured it out," he says. "I assumed he was like you, that the way things seemed really bad outside made his mind . . ."

He pauses to choose his words carefully here. I wish he wouldn't.

". . . that something happened and he couldn't understand exactly what was going on. But other times, when I'd get close enough, I'd think he had so much clarity behind his eyes. Like he was just getting on with his job, knowing where he was and when he was and what was happening. That he just preferred it in here. Even if the terrible thing outside hadn't happened, he would always prefer it in here."

Sam stops and picks at something on the pavement. Whatever it is, he holds it up to his face, close, and then slips it into his pocket.

I want to ask about the terrible thing, but I don't. Outside the park seems so big I'd lose my way, and nothing would make sense to me. I try to think back to what I do know about what happened, here, inside the gates.

I recall my daily routine. My duties. My Action Plan. Brendan

was there for it, every day. The rituals. The walking and the maintenance, tending long-dead rides.

"Where did we sleep?" Of all the things I could ask, I'm not sure
why I've landed on this one.

"There's no home furnishing floor in the gift shop, Delphi. It's a
gift shop. That's where we sleep."

He explains that up there, we'd made a nest of anything soft, and
he kept food stored in the inventory lockers.

"When was it really bad?" I ask. "Out there."

"After Callie, they still went ahead with the launch of Nebuland and the new bots. All the performers, all the press. Within a
few weeks of that, it got terrible." He says that last word unsteadily.
"There was an accident at a power plant on the bay. And the fires.
Blackouts. It seemed to be connected to someone who might have
been . . . affected by the bots. There was no water; the only safe places
were where there were huge stores of it."

"Like here."

"Like here. LA, all the way up the coast, down past some parts of
San Diego even—it had to be evacuated, and it's never really recov-
ered. Based on what I know."

What he knows. Because he never left. He was here, with me.

"So no one's come looking for us? For the people left . . ." I stop
myself. Who would be like us? Who would have stayed, and stayed,
and stayed, this long.

I choke that back. I rub my face, and feel the texture of my skin,
which is softer, looser, than perhaps I'd noticed before. I don't dislike
it. But I can hear my pulse in my ears. I must look upset; Brendan
looks worried. I try to focus.

"It . . . It must have destroyed the studio. If they couldn't roll out
to Asia."

He barks a bitter laugh. "Delphi, they *did*. They rolled it out."

"Not with the new bots?"

"With the new bots. They didn't have the same problems." He
looks to the sky. "It's anyone's guess as to why."

I know we'll share our ideas about the bots. I know we'll have time for that. To wonder, and guess, to compose elaborate theories about mankind and neural pathways and whether ghosts can occupy machines and electricity and twin-ness, and never quite know anything for sure. We wasted time, yes, but I know that there's more to come.

"Did Brooke make it home?"

"Home? I don't know," says Brendan. "She tried to get in touch with you a few times, but you weren't making a ton of sense by then. I tried to talk to her, but she never really liked me."

There's grief clattering within me, threatening to settle. I'll feel it, eventually. But—a clear vision: The Christmas DVD. The ones I found in The Cemetery.

"She landed a role?" I ask.

It takes him a second to follow my train of thought. But he figures it out eventually. "Yeah. Yeah, she did. Mrs. Claus's Australian cousin."

I laugh. It was a strained bark, and I cover my mouth with both hands. She would have been overjoyed.

We're almost at the castle now. We're almost face to face with the wreckage of its one half. I stop in my tracks. Not yet.

I see that Brendan's face is a mess. I trace my fingers around a fresh wound on his jaw, which is already starting to harden. It wouldn't have been easy work, breaking through the lake. That equipment isn't easy to maneuver. But then, he's had a long time to learn how to use everything in the park. All its parts.

He understands. "I finally found something I'm really good at." He smiles wide, even though I can tell that it hurts. "Building barricades? Keeping a crazy woman alive?"

He shrugs and I think that now isn't the time to make him think about all of that. All the time we lost. There will come a time. Now's the time to let him feel the way he looks: Content. Accomplished. Maybe even gifted.

The turret hangs above us. The sun has sapped almost all color from the façade, but plant life has grown wild and lush everywhere. Bulbs of flora spill onto footpaths. From this height, I see the Colonial Outpost, in its perpetual palette of antiquity, which looks the same as ever. Close by, there's a burnt patch of earth. It's a sick little crater, but I also kind of like it. It tells a story, even if it's not one that I can recall.

I reach for his hand. He wants to ask me questions, just as I want to ask him many more. But not everything has to come to the surface. That and the rooms down below. Those things will invite you to dwell on them for all of your days. I tell him I want to keep going.

While we walk, while the wear and rot of the park makes itself more apparent to me, I start to wonder. If we'd left when everyone else did. If I was able to. I start to see what our lives might have been. Sad at first, with both of us jobless in a city where it's so easy to feel lonely, even when you're a pair. We would have spent more time in his home, with his little projects, the things he built and mended, mounting. I might not have liked it. Maybe we'd have fought. But we'd both have found purposes. We'd have shaken ourselves out of it. We'd have found a rhythm, a way out of our own lifelong habits, worked in different places, doing different things, that would have made coming home to one another more of a reward. I wonder if I would have gotten stuck in time less, if I'd have found some inner rhythm that would have kept me awake and able to look the present in the eye. To be more courageous about the unknown. I wonder if my hands would have healed differently if I hadn't kept them hidden. I might even have taken pride in my scars, and let people see them without shame. I wonder if I'd have ever donned a costume again.

I wonder if we'd have gotten married: something small, something that wasn't where he was from, that wasn't where I was from. Maybe somewhere in between, in the part of the country that's mostly mountains, where our handful of guests would have needed to arrive a few days early to adjust to the elevation. I'd have wrapped myself in layers while we said vows, because we'd have done it in the fall or winter, to save money and because we'd have been so, so tired of the heat.

Maybe we'd have had children. Just one. A girl, maybe, who would have been peculiar or ordinary, as she saw fit. Brendan would have taught her to hammer nails into wood, and I'd have taught her how to take it apart.

But something comes into sharper focus when I remove Brendan and this maybe-child from this vision. Something becomes more pure and electric when I let them go. Maybe I'd have traveled. Traveled to places I'd barely heard of, with money I barely had. Maybe I'd have found myself in difficult situations, stranded, defeated, but I'd have used every ounce of resourcefulness I had to find a way out: to barter and hike and improvise with wild gestures when I didn't speak the language, and no one spoke mine. Maybe I'd have proven to myself that I was hard to defeat. Maybe I'd have traveled to the place that Renata was from. I'd have taken trains through rolling European hillsides, far from the tourists, to little villages where I'd have taken part in moments of stillness and boredom, with no dazzle, no illusions, no tricks of perspective or darkened rooms. I'd have quietly eaten dumplings alone. Maybe I'd have met someone, someone who wasn't Brendan and who wasn't very concerned with the wellness of my mind, who cared about me but not *for* me, whose clothes-smell would have been nice but would also have been a smell I could live without. I think I'd probably have spent most of my time alone, in all those new places. Would I have been afraid? Maybe if I'd found myself on enough trains, moving through boundless, un-gated landscape for long enough, I would have felt fear less and less until it became an occasional bodily nuisance, like hiccups.

Maybe I wouldn't have needed a place like the park anymore, because I'd have found the real peaks and mesas and dungeons and moonlit veldts on which the park was modeled. The sources. Maybe I'd even find wherever it was that the voice in the fissure came from. Maybe there were more voices, in more fissures, in many beautiful, secret corners of the world, and some of them would have liked to hitch a ride on me, although I doubt very much that I'd have been able to hear what they had to say anymore. By that time, I'd have seen too much to be willing to listen.

Off to the side of our path, there's a small animal skeleton lodged into some underbrush. A raccoon or the torso of a duck. There's the wide lens of a light tucked in there, too, shattered. My feet feel steadier. I will always need a place like the park. There are many places I could have found myself, in the course of my life; I feel happy to have been here.

While we approach the castle, Brendan starts to ramble. He's talking to himself, mainly. He has ideas about why I was the way I was. The shed, some lasting damage. But that wouldn't explain the rest of them, the mother and son, and Sam. While he's talking, I think about what I've said to him at the end of every day, each time we reached the gates, and I understand why he wanted to tell me all about his teen years, all about the girl, Thea, the one he loved once, who wanted to stay inside his car that one night because she knew something bad would happen if they left it. He was trying to tell me something. He was trying to wake me up, gently, I think. I wonder when he gave up doing that. How old we were then.

On the drawbridge, frayed banners shiver, limp in the wind. When we reach the vaulted arch, Brendan's still talking about his own fear, his fear of harming me, his fear of what would be outside, his fear of finding out what happened to his family. I want to listen, but I'm looking for a way in. There's a section of plywood that's been bashed in, and it's big enough for me to slither through, and with a little bit of effort we tear enough of it away that Brendan can follow.

Inside, it's an outcrop of compressed dirt, construction parts, and a couple of small mammal skeletons. We kick up residue and I feel the faintest light on my scalp, coming from the absence of the enormous turret. When did it collapse? Everything here looks like it's been undisturbed for decades. From all around us, slats bisect our path. Dowels and splints. But a little stairway brings us to some flooring above our heads. I give it a go. The first step creaks, but holds steady under my weight. Brendan has stopped talking. He's looking up, straight up. I'm happy beyond words to find that he's not ready to catch me if I fall. It's a nice change.

On this level there's a long stretch of wood, and a very small walkway leading to the barbican between castle halves, a footpath to allow cast members to pop up on special occasions. More dead animals: cats and ducks and something bigger that I decide not to look at. There are sheets of plastic and cannisters with long, thin pipes. Insecticide.

A stile leads to a ladder, which doesn't wobble when I pull on it, but I feel more anxious now that we're this high up. Brendan goes first. He tells me not to look down,

At the top I'm startled by pristine white and a soap smell. It's a hotel room. The one room that was occasionally occupied by a VIP family, or a lucky contest winner, and the two double beds are still perfectly made. Why didn't we think to come in here? Brendan's eyes are wide. He'd forgotten about it entirely. I almost laugh, and so does he.

It's in perfect order, a bedchamber straight out of a Bavarian palace, except for the enormous section of wall missing, halfway up where the turret once began. It's a gory mess of foams and bare wood, torn vents, and thick layers of bird's nests. He crouches down and invites one of my boots into his interwoven hands. A boost. Hot tentacles of pain whip through me as I lift myself onto a flat section of metal plating, where the crenellations of the remaining castle are almost within reach. With a thud Brendan lands beside me. It shakes a little, but I think we'll be okay.

Through our violent window, across each section of park, a thousand illusions show us their insides, uncanny and bare, none meant to be seen like this, from this angle, but no longer bringing up that sickness inside me that they might have, once. We watch our park, side by side, with pure love. I can feel the warmth of it coming off of

Brendan's tired skin. And beyond, the world starts to become fiery with the rising sun.

"I think I want to find Whit," I say. "And your mom. Just . . . family."

He strokes my hand. "You know so many of them will be gone."

"I know. But I want to find them, all the same."

A single airplane, a speck across the golden morning, catches our eye. The trail that it leaves is flimsy, but there. Not an illusion at all. There are people, not that far off. They've forgotten us, and let this place rot, but they're there. Out there.

"When do you want to start looking?" he asks.

I shift onto my knees. I grab the rough fibers of torn plaster and look back, back to the Fairytale Grove, to the stand-alone marquee with the wood carvings and the elaborate queue. Peter and Wendy. The stargaze corridor that lies just behind its walls. My favorite.

"One more ride," I say. "Just one more ride, and then we'll go."

ACKNOWLEDGMENTS

First and foremost, thank you to Lyle, whose capacity for support, love, and patience should be studied by a team of large-animal veterinarians. I'm so unbelievably lucky to have you around.

To May-Lan Tan, my parents, Francis Spufford, and the broader, emergent cascade of creatives who have come into my life and taught me how to tell stories.

Thank you to the vast online community of park-eeriness enthusiasts who supplied me with endless inspiration for the world of Delphi's park, and who reignited a long-dormant childhood obsession. A special thank you to *MAZE* author Christopher Manson who shaped the earliest contours of my mind, and got me thinking about long strings of spooky rooms.

Anna Russell, Laura Williams, Michael Curran, Claire Stancliffe, Lucas Mathis, Andrea Holck, Stephanie Yang, Jenny Baldwin, Jessica Griggs, Helen Mercer, Brendan Deneen, Rebecca Rehfeld, Marisa Tom, Seth Fried, Luke Dumas, Krystal Sutherland, Zachary Mack, Cristina Martin, Ona Adhiambo, Kristina Koppesser, Aniela Murphy,

Tim Fox, Irene Yu, Arnell Thompson, Traci Kim, and all those who sent weird YouTube videos, architectural texts, stray memories, and general good vibes. And specifically to Ben Fergusson and all those involved with The Reader Berlin, who looked over pieces of this story in its early stages.

Dave Eggers for the life-altering internship and consistent support. The Edinburgh University, City University, and British libraries for the access. Allpress Coffee for the Allpress coffee.

I still can't believe that the universe provided me with an agent like Liz Parker, who remained committed to my work even when it was barely coherent. Also to Haley Haltom, Noah Ballard, and the whole books team at Verve.

Loan Le for being an editor of extraordinary kindess and clarity of vision, for helping this story truly take shape, and for guiding me through every step with care and enthusiasm. To the rest of the team at Atria and Simon & Schuster: Holly Rice, Rick Willett, Erika Genova, Liz Byer, Shelby Pumphrey, Dayna Johnson, Paige Lytle, and Elizabeth Hitti. Chelsea McGuckin and Jacob Iacobelli for the stunning cover, and Alexis Seabrook for the exquisite map.

Olin for being born. I love, love, love you. To Lyle, again, just because.

And finally, to my grandmother, Georgiann Feltz, who left Nebraska for California in the 1950s, and who passed away while I was writing this book. Her fascination with the West Coast, and the greater unknown, blazed the trail for the rest of us. I hope that wherever you are there's wine, butter, and dazzling lights.

ABOUT THE AUTHOR

Arianna Reiche is a Bay Area–born writer living in east London. Her award-winning fiction has appeared in *Glimmer Train*, *Ambit*, the *Mechanics' Institute Review*, *Joyland*, and *Popshot*, and her features have been published by *New Scientist*, *USA Today*, *Vice*, the *Wall Street Journal*, and *Vogue*. She currently researches metafiction and lectures at City, University of London.